I0544829

Evernight Teen ®

www.evernightteen.com

Copyright© 2024

Constance Kersaint

ISBN: 978-0-3695-0990-1

Cover Artist: Jay Aheer

Editor: Jessica Ruth

ALL RIGHTS RESERVED

WARNING: The unauthorized reproduction or distribution of this copyrighted work is illegal. No part of this book may be used or reproduced electronically or in print without written permission, except in the case of brief quotations embodied in reviews.

This is a work of fiction. All names, characters, and places are fictitious. Any resemblance to actual events, locales, organizations, or persons, living or dead, is entirely coincidental.

CONSTANCE KERSAINT

DEDICATION

To TRB, for your wonderfully grumpy and unwavering support.

CONSTANCE KERSAINT

Constance Kersaint

Copyright © 2024

Copyright © 2024

The gods are alive, and they're in Michigan.

Chapter One
Hello Again

"Just as it was before ... so shall it also be now."
—Merseburg Incantations

Can I share a secret? Something between friends, of course.

The Irish can't brew beer worth a damn.

There, I said it. I'm allowed to say this. Mom and Grandpa have to call Ireland to talk to our cousins. You can disagree with me, go ahead.

Why did this come to mind? I watched my grandfather pour an Irish dry stout into today's chili and I can tell you, with absolute certainty, that it's going to taste like the bitter tears of our people. Oh, the regulars will eat it and say good things, but that's because Doug Redmond was the fire chief of Bellhaven for twenty years before he gave it all up to retire, or in my mom's view, to be the short order cook at the family diner.

"Could you at least use a lager?" I complained as I lifted baskets of cheese curds and jalapeno poppers from the fryer.

"Did you forget we're an Irish pub?" Grandpa grunted.

"We are a café, and no," I answered. "A lager would make that chili taste so much better."

Grandpa grunted noncommittally and went to the butcher's block. I took the opportunity to add some cocoa powder and apple cider vinegar to the chili.

I stared Grandpa straight in his bushy-bearded face while I did it. I refuse to be cowed by a man who won't wear a shirt unless it's plaid.

"Sweet pea, this is important. The ale adds depth and flavor. You would know this if you had my refined palate," Grandpa Doug lectured, lumbering over to the oven with a pan of what would soon be his famous corn bread, which is more like pudding and better than dessert. The heat from the oven blasted him, but the black knit cap stayed on his bald head no matter what. I was pretty sure he slept with the cap on.

"You eat ravioli out of a tin can last night. I don't trust your 'palate'. And don't underestimate me. I know plenty about beer." I hefted the tray onto one hand and headed toward the pass-through.

"How?" Grandpa asked, his eyes still as sharp as they were when he was the fire chief. "You're not old enough to drink."

"Oh please, we live in Michigan." I winked at him and opened the pass-through with my back.

Mom deftly set a cherry limeade and Arnold Palmer on my tray as I passed by. She worked the bar and register today, her curls pulled back from her heart-shaped face. I had her green eyes, but I will always regret that I didn't get her blonde hair. I got my mahogany curls and café au lait skin from my father, whom I have never met.

She gave a pointed look at my yawn, and I batted my eyelashes at her. I had that dream last night again, the one with the stormy beach and me screaming my head off on a cliff. It was a glorious way to start a Saturday, let me tell you.

I doled out the orders as I made my way clockwise about the diner. I didn't need their order sheets to remember who got what. There were perhaps thirty customers for lunch, and I had known most of them my entire eighteen years of breathing.

Dani was the only other server working because Agnes was late, as usual. It was fine. I could use the tips. I handed Dani the chicken-fried steak, and she gave me a squeeze on the shoulder before waddling over to her section. I bore down on my set of regulars.

"Really?" I asked Sheriff Lou Loggins, holding up his cherry limeade. "Do you know how cold it is outside? How about what month it is?" I set down the limeade and served Deputy Sheriff Marty his sandwich and poppers.

"Judge not lest ye be judged." Lou rolled up his newspaper. He was probably one of the last people in town who still read the news on paper.

I noticed some white in his beard now. I remember when his hair was as dark as his cheeks, but those dark brown eyes were still as warm as ever.

"I think it's a soup and sandwich day," he decided.

"I'm shocked, I tell you, shocked," I teased. Lou had ordered a soup and sandwich every day for lunch for the last decade. "Grandpa made chili. We have clam chowder, too."

"Let's do a pastrami on rye and a cup of chowder. I have to watch my girlish figure." Lou patted his belly. I snorted and set some napkins by Marty, who gazed at his pulled pork sandwich like he had just fallen in love.

It was September, and it was lunchtime, so we had the college season opener on the two flat screens Mom had let me buy second-hand. I had spent an all-nighter watching how-to videos and wired up the antennae myself.

As I had predicted, the big-screens had been a good investment. I am sometimes magic like that. Our profits bumped up by a third, though Mom was still very anti-screen during mealtimes.

None of the Michigan teams played until later, but naturally we had America's most Irish college football team on. Our diner was called Bridget's Cross, after all.

"You should be at that game," Mom said in passing as I bussed a table. She was not taking my gap year well. In fact, she was the only one calling this my gap year. I called it being an eighteen-year-old high school graduate who didn't know what I wanted to do with my life so I'm stalling.

To make her happy and have something, anything, on my resume, I was volunteering at the hospital. Not interning, as Mom would have liked, but I was a productive member of society. One battle at a time.

I didn't intend to work at my mother's diner for the rest of my life. Well, the thought had crossed my mind, but not seriously.

"How many times do we have to go over this? I don't know if college is for me. I can't see how it makes sense to go into debt for a degree I'm not sure I even want?" I hefted up the loaded tray and wiped the table.

"That piece of paper opens up so many doors. Get the easiest and fastest degree, anything at all. Look how well Trish and Marley are doing," Mom pointed out.

"They've been at college three weeks, Mom," I said, ignoring the twinge in my heart. My best friends have not moved on without me. Just because someone is in a different city and on a different path does not mean they are not still your best friend.

"And you have been moping for three weeks. You could go with them. You know they miss you," Mom said.

"Appealing to my sympathy is not going to work. What is the point of those four years then if I have a degree I don't care about?" I said. We had gone over this so many times. I was frustrated, but I knew she was doing it out of a place of love and not trying to rectify her past mistakes through me.

"I don't want you to wake up down the road and have regrets," Mom said for the umpteenth time as she poured coffee into a truck-driver's ginormous travel mug.

"I don't know how a person can go through life without regrets, not unless you can see the future," I said, for the umpteenth time also.

Then I turned and almost upended a tray of dirty dishes on the walking epitome of all my wildest fantasies.

He caught the tip of my tray before all was truly lost and then I was lost anyway. He was here. Why was he here? I hadn't been this close to him in years.

The person I knew to be one Erik Vanner gazed at me with pale hazel eyes and there was a flutter in my stomach. We had managed to avoid speaking to each other for the last four years, the entirety of high school. I felt good about my winning streak.

The boy, now almost a man, whom I had grown up with and had abruptly stopped speaking to me at the end of junior high, set the tray on the counter since I was still hunched over like I was having a stroke.

Erik was still so beautiful, with his tawny skin and silky black hair. He always made me feel like a dwarf. I swear his dad made him drink a gallon of milk a day when he was growing up because his wrists and ankles were always sticking out of the hand-me-downs he got from his brother.

And he still moved with the easy lope of an athlete. I had loved watching him on the football field. When he started dating Helena, I wept into my pillow for a week before I decided that I was being too pathetic.

Oh. I think he was waiting for me to say something. Well, that certainly wasn't going to happen.

"Erik." Mom's voice was weird. She was always so warm and welcoming, but right now she sounded like a frigid breeze off an iceberg. "I thought you were at Western Michigan now?"

"Mrs. Redmond," Erik greeted her. She wasn't married, but Erik was polite like that. "I will be. I'm at a community college in Muskegon right now. I'll probably transfer in two years to Western."

"Your dad must be happy that you're so close. Listen, your brother's order will be ready in five minutes," Mom said. Erik nodded and asked for a pop while he waited. It wasn't until the god of my high school fantasies sat down at the counter that I snapped to. Agnes chose that moment to breeze in like a petite tornado.

"Oh my land, that traffic." Agnes waved her hand dramatically, bracelets and earrings jangling. She noisily made her way behind the counter to stow her bag and grab her apron. Dani rolled her blue-eyeshadowed eyes. I almost smiled but was distracted by the only person in the diner my own age.

"No open tickets," I told Mom as I picked the tray back up. Was he looking at me? No, I'm delusional. *Don't look.* I snuck a look. Wow, Erik's shoulders had gotten broader.

"Okay, cash out," Mom said. I escaped into the kitchen without looking back and went upstairs to change. In my head, I walked at a dignified pace. In reality, I'm pretty certain I scampered like I was being chased.

When I was dressed in khakis and the world's most unflattering hospital polo, I took a moment to lean against my door and collect myself. It was difficult because my composure was scattered to the winds, but I was legally an adult. I had to act like it.

Erik and I had gone to school together all our lives because Bellhaven had exactly one school. We were in the same class for years, but once puberty had hit, I don't know why, we diverged. Playground to parking lot, we had found ourselves in different places and never spoke to each other again.

None of that was by my choice.

It was rather uncanny how complete our division was. The problem with the gulf between us was that my hormonal brain had latched on to him as the object of my fantasies and lust at the exact same time he stopped speaking to me. Most boys my own age I had known since they were in diapers so the mystery was gone, but Erik, perhaps by fact of separation, became unknowable and fascinating to me.

The fact that the skinny quiet kid who read fantasy novels had somehow morphed into a varsity running back who worked at his dad's garage on the weekends meant that he was the closest thing to a stranger I had in my life. And we didn't speak to each other, not through four long years of high school, even though we lived blocks apart. I could see the back of his dad's garage from my bedroom window, but that was as close as we got. He seemed to have outgrown me.

After graduation, Erik had planned on going to college somewhere, so I had heard from other people. During the summer, I hadn't seen him around town often and I was busy sorting my own life out. I thought I had a good ten years until the high school reunion to amaze him with my aspirational sophistication. Him walking into my mom's diner was not in the plan.

Shake it off, I thought loudly at my work clothes on the floor. *High school is over. And you're going to be late for the hospital.* I placed my dirty laundry in the hamper because I'm not an animal and skipped down the stairs with my backpack. Grandpa got a kiss on the cheek as I breezed past him, because he is exactly that wonderful, and I burst out the back door of the diner only to pull up short.

There he was again, like a bad penny. A very shiny, pretty, bad penny. That metaphor got away from me. My god, he was looking at me, actually looking at me.

"Hey, where are you headed?" Erik asked, stowing the takeaway in the backseat of a dark blue fastback coupe that belonged in a museum. Erik and his older brother, Duston, always drove classic muscle cars. It helped that their dad was the best mechanic west of Detroit.

And he was speaking directly to me for the first time in years.

"I volunteer at Trinity. Sometimes." I may have mumbled. I may have had a stroke and this was all a dream. It was still quite difficult to concentrate around him.

"Want a ride?" Erik asked, resting a forearm on the hood. I wished he was wearing a jacket. I could see the outlines of his biceps through his thermal. *This is ridiculous. I should be over this by now.* And it was bad form to objectify a person in this way.

"I've got my bike." I hooked a thumb at the green touring bike I've had since Grandpa had upgraded me when I was sixteen. I gave a little scream and jerked back at the werewolf in the backseat of his car.

The enormous dog barked fiercely then panted, his tongue lolling out to the side of his mouth. I gave a hesitant wave and looked at Erik. Only Erik had picked up my bike and stowed it in his trunk, which I didn't think was dimensionally possible.

I could either make this worse by blathering an excuse or do what I'd always wanted to do and get in Erik's car.

"Trinity is out of your way," I pointed out, stepping closer.

"Callie," Erik said, and I stopped breathing. I couldn't remember the last time he had said my name. "Let me give you a ride to the hospital."

I frowned, thought about it, then gave in very quickly. A beautiful young man was asking to take me to work. Let fate take me on its broad wings into the unknown.

For the length of a car-ride, I could forget that we had not spoken in four years.

"Okay, okay," I said, looking up at him as he opened the door for me. "Don't let that wolf eat me." Mom had come out of the back, and I waved as I got in the car.

"Nothing is going to hurt you," Erik promised. He didn't say it casually, I noted as he shut the door after me. He said it like he was taking an oath.

Erik gave Mom an oddly formal bow before he got in the car, and I glanced back.

Mom looked scared. I gripped the seat as I stared out the back window. The powerful V8 engine roared to life, and we pulled out of the back parking lot.

Why did Mom look scared? We're in Bellhaven. Nothing ever happens in Bellhaven.

****

"You got a new car," I said as I sat back, breathing in the scent of old leather and chrome. "What happened to the gray one?"

"The Chevelle? I sold it to some hipster in Grand Rapids. It paid for this Javelin," Erik said, taking a right. I just looked at him.

"You say that like I should know what you're talking about," I hinted.

"This is a 1972 AMX Javelin, one of the last independent muscle cars out of Kenosha. How do you not know this?" Erik stopped at a light and looked at me. God those eyes. Pale hazel and almond-shaped, those eyes had haunted my dreams.

"I didn't fix cars growing up," I said, focusing on the road. "And Kenosha is in Wisconsin, a state which I have never been to. You want a Detroit pizza? I'm your girl. Cars have never been my thing."

"That's why you're not driving to the hospital?"

"I'm not driving because cars cost money," I pointed out gently.

"Is that why you're not going to school, too?"

"How did we go from not talking for four years to sharing our deepest, darkest secrets?" I asked daringly.

"Ah, point taken. What do you do at the hospital?" Erik asked. I guess we weren't sharing secrets today.

"I'm an inpatient therapy assistant. I work with the physical therapist. Erik, do you realize this is the first time we've spoken to each other since middle school?" I asked stubbornly. He kept his eyes on the road.

"Well then, I'd say we're overdue."

"I say this is weird and I'm wondering what's going on."

"We can have a conversation without an agenda."

"I see, so after ignoring me all through high school, today you picked up lunch at my mom's diner, which you have never done in your entire life, and we're friends again?" I said. I heard the emotion in my voice and could not help it.

Erik was quiet. *Well, this has been an entertaining episode of A Day In The Life of Me.* I could not wait to relive this mortifying moment over and over again ad nauseum.

"I wanted a pretzel sandwich and you have the best in town, the only pretzel sandwiches in town, in fact. And when I saw you again, I wanted to know how you've been, what you're doing. We used to be friends, right?" Erik said quietly, in his thoughtful way.

"We used to be friends," I said tonelessly, "when we were seven."

"You always saved me a cookie from your lunch," Erik said. I frowned and turned to him. He glanced at me and looked away quickly. *Still shy*, I noted.

"You always walked with me to make sure I stayed with the group," I remembered in kind. I was spacey as a kid. Truthfully, I'm spacey now.

I had tried to forget that we were ever friends. The absence hurts less when you don't remember what you used to have.

"What are you doing next weekend? Have dinner with me," Erik suggested.

I stared at the side of his face stupidly. Had he asked me that two years ago, maybe even one year ago, I would have screamed and melted into a breathless puddle on the floor. High school was over, though, and I was almost late for my shift at the physical therapy unit.

"Erik, we've been in the same class since second grade. We have eaten together for almost a decade." I was working toward a point. I'm never articulate under stress.

"I'm not thinking of a cafeteria, and we've been in the same school since kindergarten. Maybe Little Bavaria? You still like those paczkis?" Erik said. I blinked at him owlishly.

"Yes," I said slowly. *Was he asking me out? Was college so disappointing that he had been driven back to Bellhaven for company?* "This is very bizarre."

"That's not a no." Erik grinned, showing his dimple, and I was toast. No one can resist the dimple. "Pick you up on Saturday?"

"I have a shift on Saturday. Are you in town Thursday?"

"Muskegon is fifteen minutes away, Callie. I still live with my dad and Duston. You want me to pick you up from the hospital or the diner?"

"I'm done at the hospital at five," I said shyly. "What's your number? I'll text you." My phone blipped in my hand. I looked down at a new text from an unknown number.

"I've always had your number." Erik held up his cell, then dropped it into his lap to pull up to the hospital. He got out and took my bike from the trunk, me following jerkily. "I'll see you here Thursday?"

I took my bike and stared at Erik there in front of the hospital, stunned silent. Clearly, my wit had done its work. I had charmed him into turning my high school fantasies into reality.

Erik stared back patiently, knowing that I would answer eventually.

"Yes," I said, happier than I'd been in a long time. "See you Thursday."

Chapter Two
The Nerve

Mom was waiting up for me when I came home, sprawled on the couch with a paperback. Saturdays at the hospital were always booked with wall-to-wall appointments, and my feet hurt.

Mr. Johnson had taken a few steps without his walker today. He didn't believe he was going to walk again after the car accident, so today was a very good day. I had helped work with him for weeks, and I was there today when he walked by himself. Then I had spent ten minutes desperately attempting to not weep all over him because I was so proud.

Afterward, Dr. Wyndham had scheduled me to shadow Nurse Angie to the pediatric side. I had no idea why. She worked with special needs kids, which I had no experience with, but I watched a session with the permission of the mom and even helped out a bit. It was hard but a lot more satisfying than I thought it would be. I planned on completely ignoring the fact that Nurse Angie seemed to hate me beyond reason, for no reason.

I was exhausted from it all. Battling someone's dislike can leave you beat. By the time I had finished up the admin work and inventoried the equipment, six full hours had gone by. This was after my morning shift at the diner.

I enjoyed it, though. I was nearly, almost sure that this was what I wanted to do. Just a bit longer and I would be certain. I really liked physical therapy, but now I wondered if I should look into occupational therapy?

"Good shift?" Mom asked.

"Mr. Johnson walked without his walker, my youngest played catch with me, and Dr. Wyndham had me shadowing a therapist to the pediatric unit today and I really loved it. He wants me to check out the kinesiology program at Muskegon Community College. It's some sort of exercise science pathway so I can transfer to a university if I keep with it to finish the degree." I lifted her legs to plop down on the couch and set her feet on my lap.

I started kneading her foot sole and she groaned appreciatively. Mom used to do ballet until she had me, and she still had all the foot pain that went with it.

The hospital usually kept my brain busy so now that I had a moment, I remembered that oh yeah, my wildest dreams had come true.

"It's very interesting that Erik took you to work today," Mom said. I heard a warning in her voice and looked up in surprise.

"You're the one who's been telling me to expand my horizons," I said, rolling my knuckles into her arch.

"I meant go to Notre Dame or visit your friends, not jump into the dating pool feet first," Mom said drily, her book open on her chest.

"I'm going to Muskegon, not running away with him," I said. The look on her face stopped me cold. "What is it? Mom, he's not a serial killer."

"I don't want you to get too attached," she said, sitting up to take my hands in hers. "You don't have a lot of experience with boys, and I need you to be careful."

Mom had me young. She didn't finish college because she was raising me. I understood completely where she was coming from.

"I promise, Mom, everything is going to be okay. I will die a virgin," I joked, trying to assure her, and that was exactly the wrong thing to say. She still looked at me like I was about to dive off a gang plank into a horde of piranhas. "It will be better than okay, if there's food. I'm famished."

"I could use a bite, too," Mom said, swinging her lithe legs down. She was so graceful and petite. I sometimes compare us and wonder what kind of a big, clumsy oaf my birth father must have been that I was the product.

"Do you want a tuna melt? Because I'm making tuna melts," I said, pulling out plain yogurt, cheddar, tomatoes, and butter out of the fridge.

"*We* are going to make tuna melts." Mom set the panini press on the counter. Ten minutes later we had toasty tuna melts with sharp cheddar oozing out of the sides that we stabbed at with multigrain chips. I had told my mom all about my future dinner with my childhood friend.

"I'm glad you're having fun, but be careful," Mom said, munching on a slice of pear.

"It's dinner." I stole a slice of pear from her. "We're not eloping. And I'm certainly not going to sleep with him." I said it as a joke, because the very thought was outlandish to me, but the look on her face stopped me from laughing. "Seriously, I'm not. Not in the cards at all."

"This is only the second time you've said it," Mom said seriously. "Okay, I trust you. I trust your judgment."

"You know, just because I'm not in college doesn't mean I'm lost, Mom," I said lightly. "I will go when I'm ready. My plan is different from your plan."

"I know that. I know you'll make good choices. I don't want you to make the same mistakes I made," Mom said, her eyes a little misty. Oh, that hurt.

"I don't think I was a mistake," I said. Growing up, I'd always wanted to know why I didn't look like my mom. I'd always felt like a cuckoo hiding in someone else's nest. I was loved, always loved—that was never in doubt—but it didn't change the fact that one of these things was not like the other.

"You were an accident, but you were never and will never be a mistake. Your father and I made you in love," Mom said fiercely. "We were just young and unprepared. I have always loved you, and I love being your mother, but I know you want to do things with your life—and those things don't involve children yet."

"Okay, okay, okay, those are some wild jumps there, Mom," I said tremulously and jumped up to hug her. She was shaking a bit so I hugged her harder, totally ignoring the lump in my throat. "It's not going to come to that, really. I want paczkis, not promises."

We pretended that I was telling the truth.

****

At six in the evening on Thursday, I came to terms with the fact that I had been stood up. In the rain.

I had texted him twice and there was no way on God's green earth I was going to call. I don't mind being hopeless, but I draw the line at desperate. Thank heavens I hadn't gone with the dress and the pumps, but I was wearing my good jeans and my nice boots with the heel. All for nothing.

Standing under the overhang, the neon lights of the hospital sign illuminating my disappointment, I stared out at the circle and wondered who I was going to call. Mom had dropped me off because we thought I was going to have a ride. Trish was in Grand Rapids and Marley was in Muskegon.

This was my worst nightmare. I should have known. Girls who look like me don't get dates with guys that cool. What was I thinking? This was a cruel trick he had played. He probably knew I was half in love with him. What better way to spend an afternoon than teasing the dog that sniffed at your heels?

My senses prickled and I turned, searching the shadows. Was someone there? Was I being watched? It was early in the evening, but I was alone at the hospital pickup.

Then I saw them. In the parking garage across the street, there were two figures. I couldn't make out their faces, but they were stunningly large, even from a distance, and they were definitely, definitely staring at me. Cold washed down my spine, and I wished I had remembered a jacket.

"Callie?"

I gave a little scream and jerked up, then saw it was Dr. Wyndham, the director of physical medicine and rehabilitation. He pushed his glasses up his nose and peered at me.

"Is your ride late?" Dr. Wyndham asked.

"I … no?" I said, whipping back around to search the parking garage entrance. Empty. I still felt like I was being watched. I turned back to Dr. Wyndham, trying to think of something to say. I was saved by the screech of tires against pavement.

A dark car careened into the drop off and banged to a stop in front of us, rainwater flinging itself from the dark finish of its hood. Dr. Wyndham and I stared as the passenger window rolled down.

"Duston?" I blinked. Erik's older brother waved.

"Calliope." Duston dragged out my name, making it sound like he was falling off a cliff, kull-aaaiiiiyyyyeeeeee-oh-pee. "Yo, Erik got held up. He sent me here to pick you up. Ready?"

Dr. Wyndham and I looked at each other. He was clearly doubtful about whatever he was seeing. I attempted a reassuring smile and knew it looked sickly.

"Erik was going to give me a ride to Muskegon,"

I said vaguely.

"Oh good, so you're looking into the pathway program I spoke to you about. Not tonight, surely?" Dr. Wyndham pushed his glasses up his nose.

"No, no, we were going to discuss the … route," I improvised lamely. I don't improvise well.

"I see," Dr. Wyndham said slowly. "Well, do tell me when you plan on being there and I'll have one of my colleagues show you around." Dr. Wyndham handed me his card, still eyeing Duston. Duston was staring out the windshield, absently gnawing on a hangnail.

"Thank you," I said brightly and gave him a little wave. After an unproductive tug, I managed to yank the door open on the second try and got in. I kept my keys in one hand, teeth sticking out from my fist, and my phone in the other hand.

I gave Dr. Wyndham another little wave before Duston screeched out of the hospital pickup lane like we were being chased. I stared out at the dark, wet shadows.

"Erik didn't send you, did he?" I asked after a long, very long, moment of silence.

"Not so much," Duston said, taking a turn much faster than necessary. "He texted me, asking what I wanted for dinner."

I slumped down in the seat, the rain turning Bellhaven into a blur of light and darkness.

"Why are you here?" I asked bluntly. I turned to him, not hiding my displeasure.

"This is my car," Duston pointed out.

"Duston!" I snapped. All things considered, Duston was handsome bordering on beautiful, with a face that belonged in a Korean drama series. He was much better looking than Erik, and he knew it. The arrogance he radiated allowed me to be blunt with him because no matter how much I tried, I would never be able to chip that massive ego.

"Okay, okay. Can you at least put your keys and phone away? Yes, I see how you're holding them and no, I'm not going to torture and kill you. The sheriff eats at your diner every day," Duston said reasonably. Not at all mollified, I stared at him flatly, my keys and my phone still firmly in hand.

Duston sighed.

"I know you guys were supposed to go to Little Bavaria today, which, if you ask me, is the wrong venue for a first date. You want to be comfortable and chat, not debate the finer points of geopolitics or whatever, but what do I know. Anyway, he didn't show, and no, I haven't the faintest idea why. I got his text, and I saw you waiting in the rain. I thought to myself, I'm going to rescue her," Duston said grandly.

I fought the urge to cover my face. Duston used to play with my hair at carpool pickup when we were kids. He would eat whatever snacks I left unattended.

And in high school, Duston had beat the crap out of some older boys bothering me. It happened more than once. Duston never said a word to me afterward, just walked me to my friends. We had always pretended that it never happened. The guys Duston beat the crap out of never forgot, though, and I was always that much safer.

"Thank you for getting me," I said grudgingly. I looked around the dark gray interior that matched the paint job I'm certain the Vanners did themselves. "You upgraded your car, too?"

"Yessiree, I had the Camaro in school. This is the Eliminator. So much better than that Javelin Erik has," Duston said with conviction. None of that made sense to me. A car gets you from Point A to Point B. Everything else is details.

"Oh brother." I propped an elbow on the car door

and rested my forehead against the back of a hand.

"Ah, she's getting it now. Consider yourself blessed that you're an only child. No competition."

"I'm a bastard, Duston."

"That means nothing in this day and age."

"Whatever. You missed a turn."

"I did not. You're coming over for dinner."

It took a moment for Duston's words to penetrate my brain. Then I exploded in panic.

"No! Absolutely not! Duston Vanner, you take me home this instant!" I shouted, getting ready to grab the wheel.

"Calm down. It's okay. You know, if you had been half as vocal with Erik as you are with me, you wouldn't be in this situation. You would have found out that he is the much less interesting and charming brother, and that you had wasted all those years pining after an import," Duston said calmly. I stared at him as he watched the road, oblivious to my distress.

"I don't know what that means," I said, my heart racing.

"You never buy foreign. Don't betray your roots that way. Domestic, baby, that's the way to go. Nothing feels better than all-American steel under you," Duston explained with passion.

"Duston!" I hollered.

"Not a euphemism!" he shouted back. "And stop yelling. We're home."

I stared at the love child of a warehouse and a log cabin. The Vanner men lived in a wood-paneled house attached to an auto shop, similar to how my mom and I lived over the diner. On quiet nights, you could hear the Bellhaven river from both the diner and the auto shop. The garage was three times the size of their house, but it really was their actual garage.

The chain-link gate was open and the parking area in front of the garage was filled with cars, some double-parked. Duston pulled into the lot and got out, trotting to open my door with his jacket yanked up over his head against the drizzle.

I was torn, undecided, and just short of wringing my hands with indecision. Duston's foot tapped in a puddle next to the car.

"Go inside," Duston ordered. "Call your mom. Have a sub, and then I'll take you home."

I glared at him and was immensely displeased when he wasn't incinerated by the fire of my indignance. I got out with as much dignity as I could and Duston tossed his jacket over my head, because of course he didn't have an umbrella.

"You look nice," Duston offered belatedly.

"Shove it," I said grimly and headed toward the house.

I was almost to the door when Garth trotted out to meet me in the rain. He wasn't a big dog, but he was sturdy under the thick grey and white coat. His dark brown eyes narrowed, and he angled his wedge-shaped head down like he was going to head-butt me. He started to growl, but I stared him down.

"Not now, dog," I said in a low, firm voice.

Garth stopped growling and we were friends again. He tilted his head quizzically to the side and barked once, loud and sharp, his pink tongue lolling out. Then he turned and trotted to the house, his plume of a tail lolling back and forth across his rump.

The dog pulled the storm door open by a rope tied to the handle, probably there expressly for his use, and held it for me. Bemused, I entered. Garth darted around me and gave a cheerful bark before leading me into the living room.

Erik was sitting on the couch, a book in one hand and a mug in the other. He looked up and dropped his paperback when he saw me. I hung Duston's jacket on a hook but had no idea what to do with my hands.

"Hey, Erik, you lost your date," Duston said, toeing off his wet shoes and strolling past me.

"Where are you going?" I hissed.

"Discretion is the better part of valor," Duston said. "And I'm hungry."

"Subs are on the way," Erik called out, standing up.

All my previous righteous indignation had fled. Now I was in a strange house, about to confront a guy who had been negligent with my feelings. I should have just sent him a very emotional text message but screw it.

What the heck. What was I going to do, let him get away with it? That didn't work for me. Mom was always telling me to rise above. Sometimes I just can't.

I walked into the family room. Erik stared at me, as awkward as I felt.

There was a moment, just a short one, in which all the words ran dry on my tongue. I shoved that all aside.

"Your brother brought me here," I said, with more bravado than I felt.

Erik muttered something that sounded like "I'm going to kill him" and came forward. Suddenly, the room was much smaller than before in context with Erik's size. Garth bumped his head against Erik's thigh, and he absently ruffled the dog's ear as he stared at me.

I could practically see the wheels churning in his head. It would be interesting to see if he had any sort of justifiable defense.

"I can explain," Erik started diffidently but stopped when he saw my disbelief and heard the lameness of his excuse. That certainly didn't pass the sniff test. "I can't explain. I chickened out."

"Then you text me. You have my phone number, for occasions like this, and you tell me so that I'm not waiting for an hour in the rain." I found myself emphasizing the verbs to keep calm.

"I'm sorry I ghosted you," Erik said quietly. "I got nervous."

"I've seen you run down a football field against a whole team trying to take you down. I'm not buying that excuse," I said just as quietly. "Listen, it's okay that you didn't want to have dinner, but then you shouldn't have asked me in the first place."

The doorbell rang and Duston came barreling down the hallway, a bag of chips falling from his grip to Garth's immense delight.

"Damn it, boys, can't you run less loudly?" Norm Vanner groused as he trudged into the living room, rubbing the sleep from his face. He must have taken a nap after work. He stopped when he saw me. He looked like a grayer, thinner version of his sons, but still tall and handsome. His pale hazel eyes were more worn out than his sons' eyes. "Callie? Did your mom's car break down?"

"Ah, no," I stuttered as I attempted to take the potato chips away from Garth.

"Callie and Erik were supposed to go on a date, but Erik backed out and didn't tell her, so I picked Callie up and brought her here," Duston said as he brought the takeaway bags to the kitchen. "Callie, can you get the paper plates? They're in the hallway closet." Of course, because it makes sense to put something meant for the kitchen in the linen closet.

I stared at the Vanner men wildly. Their dog took the opportunity to lick my cheek and get chips in my hair. Norm seemed sympathetic to my plight.

"I'll get the plates." Norm patted me on the shoulder. "Callie, why don't you stay for dinner? Pop is in the fridge. Help yourself."

Chapter Three
Ice Cream Penance

Thursday sub night at the Vanner house was surprisingly nice. Erik and I silently agreed to temporarily forget our awkwardness. I was happy to play pretend for Erik's dad. Norm was always the lone dad at school pick-up, but he never failed to have me wait with him until Mom or Grandpa showed up.

I had never had dinner with a family of bachelors before, and it fascinated me how they talked. I was completely unfamiliar with cars, but I recognized the rhythm of a parent owning a business and the children also being part-time employees. Given an hour with the books, I could probably figure out what the overhead was, labor costs, suppliers, and such.

What I was not prepared for was the amount of shit-talking that happened between brothers, primarily about Erik's adamant refusal to put a Hellcat engine in his Javelin, or at least I think that's what they were talking about. I was so nervous to start, but then I couldn't stop chuckling. I got a hold of myself after I laughed some root beer up my nose.

After dinner, Erik asked if he could drive me home. I was stuffed with meatball sub and chicken Parmesan, so I said yes.

"Hey, I parked behind you," Duston said. "Take the Eliminator." Erik caught the car keys before they smashed into his nose.

"Thanks," Erik said drily.

"Not a scratch on her or there will be blood," Duston said absently, tying up the trash bag.

"What? Should I be scared?" I asked, alarmed. Duston paused and looked at me pointedly. "Oh," I realized, "you meant the car."

"It's not just *any* car, Calliope. That is a 1969 Mercury Cougar Eliminator. That's my girl," Duston said with conviction. I wondered if I would ever love anyone as much as Duston loved his car.

"Is it GM?" I asked with a straight face. I wondered if I could make him cry. The horror on Duston's face was amazing to see. "Or Pontiac?"

Erik ushered me out of the house as Duston roared behind us.

"Vanners don't drive Pontiacs!" Duston's bellow followed us.

"Are you trying to give him a heart attack?" Erik said, amused.

"As if I could," I replied.

When I was outside standing next to the Eliminator, I paused. I had to remind myself that not three hours ago, the guy about to take me home had stood me up.

The rain had stopped during dinner. The Vanners didn't live far from my house. I could walk it in a brisk fifteen minutes.

"Would it make you feel better if Garth went with us?" Erik asked, completely misreading my hesitation.

"To what end? Your dog is a wuss."

"Garth is mostly Norwegian elkhound and isn't afraid of anything but vacuum cleaners." Erik slapped his thigh, and Garth hopped into the backseat of the Eliminator. There was a blanket covered in dog hair for Garth's muddy paws.

"None of this would be necessary if you had just been there," I muttered to Erik as I got into the seat. He was quiet for longer than was comfortable for me as he pulled out of the parking lot.

I remember this from when we were younger. He

chose his words carefully, always had.

"I made a mistake." Erik took us onto the main road.

I was just getting more relaxed when I realized where we were not going: to my house. I tensed up like a spring and wondered how I could surreptitiously ease my keys out of my bag. This seemed to be the day for getting kidnapped.

Erik pulled into a parking space off Main Street and jogged over to get my door. He stepped out of the way and stood expectantly.

"This is not where I live," I pointed out. Getting kidnapped twice in one night was a record for me.

"We'll get there. This is an apology," Erik said, closing the door after Garth, who was busy sniffing every inch of the sidewalk.

"What's going to make this all better, may I ask?"

"The Creamery," Erik said gravely. Oh, he was good. The evil genius had guessed my weakness.

The Creamery was the best ice cream parlor in Michigan. I can't really qualify that statement because I haven't been all over Michigan, but they made the best ice cream I've ever tasted. They churned a handful of flavors every morning, all of them heavenly. I walked from a damp Michigan evening into a waffle-cone-scented nirvana, and all my cares floated away.

It was Erik's turn to wait as I perused the candy-colored selection. I take ice cream very seriously. I can cook or bake almost anything, but ice cream I have never mastered.

"There is a flavor of ice cream for everything. An apology, a thank you, a question, anything," Erik said, handing me a waffle cone of black cherry vanilla and Mackinac Island fudge. "This is my apology. I'm sorry I didn't show up today. I'll make it up to you." We sat down at a sidewalk table, still dry under an awning. Garth sat patiently in front of us, his attention on our ice cream.

"I didn't hear a word you just said," I said, very involved with my ice cream.

"I said I'm sorry for being a jerk and are you free tomorrow?" Erik wrapped a napkin around his double scoop of peanut butter honey and mint brownie chunk. I got my ice cream to a point that it wouldn't melt over the sides and sat back to look him in the eye.

"*Now* you decide to not be a jerk to me?" I asked pointedly. He had the grace to look ashamed.

"I have no good excuse. It's been a rough week, a rough year really. I'm sorry I was an ass."

"Is that really why you bailed on me?"

"Yes. I've been distracted. I really meant to come, but I started second-guessing myself and let myself get busy. This isn't normal for me," Erik swore.

"Not normal for you to forget you left someone waiting in the rain?" I was beating a dead horse, but he was squirming. I kind of enjoyed that. Me, Calliope Redmond, can make a guy squirm.

"I meant being a jerk to you."

"I know what you meant." I forgave him. "Just teasing. How have you had a bad year? High school is over and you're in college. You are technically an adult."

"That's a terrifying thought."

"The truth is terrifying. There's no way that's good for him," I said. Erik continued to discreetly feed his dog pieces of his waffle cone. We talked about nothing and everything, sometimes didn't say anything at all. We started walking to the car when it got unforgivably late when Garth growled.

"What's up? What's got you worked up, buddy?" I asked the dog.

Erik tensed and moved in front of me. I frowned

at the dog and poked my head around Erik's broad back. Two older guys had stepped out in front of us, forcing us to stop.

Two giants, I corrected myself. They looked like guys who were not unfamiliar with factory work or logging. You could have dropped them in the middle of a professional football game and they would have fit in. And they seemed familiar.

"Hey, Erik, won't you introduce us?" one of the giants said.

"No," Erik said, staying in front of me.

I didn't say anything. Something dark and not altogether safe was simmering, and I didn't want to set it off.

"Yo!" The blond giant waved. "I'm George, Erik's cousin." He smiled at me in a way he probably thought was affable. It showed off far too many yellow teeth and I was not impressed.

"Oh," I said. "Pleased to meet you." The words came out automatically since Mom had drilled manners into me from birth. These guys were Erik's family? What on earth was going on? Families did not act like this. At least they should not be borderline combative.

"And I'm Freddy. Freddy Janssen," the dark one said in a voice like velvet, coming forward. His eyes widened as he reached out, I think for me. Erik snatched Freddy's wrist and gripped it hard. Erik glared at Freddy, who smirked back.

I didn't want this to escalate, even though I had no idea what was going on.

"Hi, Freddy," I said. I stayed behind Erik and extended a hand to his cousin.

Freddy Janssen's hand was cold. He held it longer than I thought appropriate. When Freddy showed no signs of letting go, I tugged—then tugged again. I yanked my hand back with as much dignity as I could.

"Miss Redmond, so lovely to meet you," Freddy said.

"Yes," I said slowly. "Well, if you'll excuse us." I gave Erik a discreet shove toward the car. He grudgingly moved with me. "Garth, come."

The elkhound finally stopped growling and loped after me, staying always between me and the Janssen cousins. For that, I will love the dog forever.

George moved toward us, but Freddy held him back. Erik glared at them hard, but I ushered him on.

"What was that?" I hissed the moment we were out of the Janssens' earshot. "Your cousins are creepy."

"My cousins," Erik said, "are psychotic. You have to stay away from them."

"Not an issue," I said. "Thank god they don't live here." Erik gave me a look. "Did they move here?" As a person born and raised in Bellhaven, I have a good handle on most of the residents.

"I don't know, but they've been around," Erik said.

"Okay, I'm completely confused. What are they doing here? Don't they have a life somewhere? Where are they from?"

"They're from Duluth, and they're delinquents. I'd be surprised if they even had jobs right now." Erik checked over his shoulder and ushered me into the car.

"So, your cousins are here now, being vagrants, fine. Erik, it was like they wanted to hurt me." I frowned.

"They're bad news," Erik warned.

"I don't need convincing," I said. "But they're your cousins, right? Family?"

"Nope," Erik said definitively. "Just because we're family doesn't mean we're friends. Their mom left when they were kids. Their dad never made sure they stayed in school," Erik said. "Some people try to rise above their circumstances. Those two would rather slash and burn everything. Listen, they just don't know how to act around a pretty girl. Probably be best if you stayed away from them."

"I'm not trying to get close. Wait, what did you say?" I turned to him. Had I heard right? I tried not to smile. "Is the pretty girl you're referring to me or you?"

"Smart ass," Erik said, pulling up to the back of my condo. He got out and opened my door, which allowed the Norwegian elkhound to get out before me. "Garth, come! He probably saw a squirrel or something," Erik muttered.

I stood there awkwardly, trying to figure out how to say goodbye on my own back porch.

"Well," I said. "See you around." I didn't move

"Can I see you again?" Erik asked. I blinked.

"Yeah, because that worked so well the first time," I scoffed.

"I will follow through this time. One more chance," Erik said quietly. This is not the kind of guy who begs. I remembered that, and I remembered that we were once friends.

"You know, you have not said a word to me in four years. I can't imagine that was not on purpose, so I find this complete change quite suspicious," I said lightly. Erik glanced at me, and my heart stuttered. The look in those hazel eyes was not casual, not in the least. "I need to go to Muskegon to check out the college," I offered. I wanted to spend time with him. What could it hurt.

"Well, I have a morning class. Pick you up at nine?"

"Yes," I said, peering at him in the yard light from the diner kitchen. Then Garth bumped his enormous head against my hip. I stepped toward the dog before I could stop myself, and he darted away. Garth dropped down into a playful crouch, his tail wagging madly.

"Now is not the time to play, Garth," I said, stepping toward him. He darted away, then ran in a tight, mad circle around me. I made for him again and he bounced back again. I didn't even know what I'd do if I caught him.

I heard the back door swing open and my mom appeared. We lived above the diner, and there were stairs going from the diner kitchen door to the door of our apartment. Mom stood on the upstairs landing and stared at us.

"Garth," Mom said. Garth stopped instantly and looked up at her, his tongue lolling out adoringly. "Car." Garth obeyed immediately and Erik shut the door.

"Ma'am," Erik said respectfully.

"Hello, Erik," Mom said, not smiling. I still didn't understand that. Mom likes everyone.

"See you tomorrow." I waved. Erik waved back and I went into the diner kitchen. A few steps in, I stopped dead at a disturbing thought.

How did the Janssens know my name?

****

Muskegon was a completely different world. I had grown up in a seaside town, so it wasn't the waterfront that impressed me, but the bustle. I've never thought of myself as a small-town girl, but everything enchanted me, from a center devoted to performing arts to the museum we passed to all the different restaurants. It was different from home and completely fabulous. Sitting in Erik's car, it all passed too quickly. I wanted to go back and explore.

The college itself was an adventure. I really liked the campus. While Erik was in class, I chatted with Dr. Wyndham's associate, who happened to be free that morning. I took that as a good sign.

To be frank, I had been intimidated by the whole idea of college. I had lived in Bellhaven my whole life. Venturing away, even fifteen minutes, was a step, and it would lead to many more steps, and who knew where I would end up?

Now, I was excited. I could do this. It was frightening. It was an adventure.

There was so much to see and talk about that I lost track of time. I got all the paperwork I needed, gave a promise to apply for the pathway program, and dashed outside to meet Erik by the creek that ran through the campus.

I talked non-stop about the therapy program, and Erik interrupted long enough to suggest grabbing tacos from a food truck. I was a bit confused until he got me back in the car and we drove toward the marina to a street lined with food trucks.

I wanted to look at each one of them but followed willingly to the taco truck Erik seemed to know well. I grabbed a few menus from the other trucks to peruse later. There were a few things I could adopt for the diner. Italian beef, why had I never thought of that?

It was a beautiful day, probably one of the last sunny and somewhat warm days we had left before winter. I was wearing my favorite eggplant sweater and a jean skirt. My tights kept my legs warm to my boots, and because it was September in Michigan, I had on a battered leather jacket I had found in Mom's closet. We went to the marina and sat on a bench to watch the boats as we ate.

"A bit of a change from high school," I said, thinking about the college. *I think I might be ready.*

"I hated high school." Erik tucked in to a fish taco.

"What?" I stopped with my bottle of guava pop

halfway to my mouth. "Really? But you did so well."

"I hate to break it to you, but doing well is not the same thing as being happy." Erik chomped on a taco. I had al pastor, but he was willing to trade one so I could try the fish taco. The al pastor was better.

"Well, Mr. Varsity Football, honor roll student, founder of the robotics team, why was high school so terrible?" I asked. He chewed thoughtfully.

"I couldn't be me. I couldn't do what I wanted to do." Erik chose his words carefully.

"I'm not sure I understand?"

"I did football, but I didn't love it. It was something I did. School was fine. I didn't mind it, but what I really wanted to focus on was robotics. I couldn't, because there's only so many hours in a day. I wanted to give up football, but I knew I needed it to round out my college application, and I had student council on top of that. It was busy and hectic and I still worked after school. If I had a do-over, it would be different," Erik said. On any other person, I would call this sulkiness, but not on Erik.

"I'm sorry it wasn't a better experience," I said lamely. I had Trish and Marley, always. I'd had marching band and there was a volunteer club I belonged to, but I wasn't passionate about it. I'd worked after school, too. "I had no idea."

"How could you?" he asked. "We didn't talk. That was something else I regretted."

"It happens, though, all the time. People grow up and grow apart," I rationalized.

"Not you. You, Marley, Trish, you've been best friends since we were seven," Erik said.

"I can't believe you remember that," I said. Erik magically produced a sleeve of churros and I laughed, taking one.

"Where are they?" Erik asked, crunching away.

"Trish is at Hope College and Marley is at Grand Valley," I said, ignoring the twinge in my heart. We had been together, all the time, almost our entire lives, and now they were in different cities. One hour of distance was apparently an ocean of difference. They felt so far away.

"You could have gone with them," Erik said.

"No, I'm not like them. I'm good here, you know?" I said. Everyone else had left. I wasn't ready to leave yet."

"Yeah," he said. "Yeah, I get that."

Then I realized how close we were. My left leg was flush against his right leg. I couldn't be any closer to him without sitting on his lap. Anyone passing by would think we were a couple having an intimate moment. I didn't move away, though.

This felt right. This felt good. This felt dangerous.

I blinked suddenly, focusing down the marina. A familiar helmet of blonde hair on the docks, but it couldn't be.

"That's weird," I muttered.

"What?" Erik threw away our trash.

"I thought I saw Nurse Angie. She heads up the rehabilitative therapy program at Trinity. She should be at the hospital right now," I said. I looked at him and frowned. Erik's face had gone completely flat and expressionless.

"Come on, let's head back," Erik said.

CONSTANCE KERSAINT

Chapter Four
Reinforcements

Erik pulled up in front of Bridget's Cross and shut off the Javelin. The lunch rush was over, but Friday nights were pretty lively. Trish and Marley came back tonight, and I wanted to see them. I wasn't certain I was going to have the wherewithal to, though. It had already been quite a day.

"Want to see a movie tomorrow?" Erik asked. I stopped in the middle of gathering my things. He'd asked me out twice already and one time had completely bailed on me.

I stared at him. I knew it was awkward, that I was awkward, and I also knew he didn't care. What I could not comprehend was why this was happening now.

"What are we doing?" I asked quietly.

"Hopefully go on a date," Erik said. I raised an eyebrow and he smiled back, guileless.

"Why? Why now? What's going on?" I asked.

"That's a lot. Can we start with: we used to be close, we lost touch, and now I want to take you to a movie?" he asked. I gnawed on my lip.

Why the hell not?

"Trish and Marley come back tonight. We have plans tomorrow. What about Sunday?" I suggested. He whooped playfully and I swear, my heart grew three sizes. He got out to get my door and helped me out of the Javelin.

"I promise I will be here. I won't let you down," Erik said, walking me up the stairs to my back door. I stepped into my kitchen and turned to him. I smiled because he made me happy.

Erik paused in the doorway, one hand on the door.

He looked down at me and I stared into depthless hazel eyes. He could touch me. Without much effort, he could reach out and touch me.

"You always had the best smile," Erik murmured. I shook a little, my smile shook a little, and I gripped the door handle tightly.

I wanted to lean in. I wanted to say something sexy or clever.

Instead, I was me.

"Thank you," I said breathlessly. "Rest hard." I hurriedly shut the door and locked it, ignoring his laughter. I waved through the glass as he drove away. Then I collapsed into a chair, my heart beating like a drum.

****

For some reason, this Saturday was kicking my butt.

The brunch rush was an actual rush and today, I felt a bit off. Usually, I could handle a shift in my sleep, but alas, I had not slept last night. These stupid nightmares. The girls had vegged at home the night before, but they were coming over today. I hadn't seen them in three weeks, and I felt like there was a huge gulf between us, but today was not cooperating with me.

I did what I always did when I'm not well: I baked. It probably wasn't the most practical thing to do during a Saturday lunch rush, but it's what I needed. Dani and Agnes understood, probably more than I deserved, and made space for my project.

I am a stress-baker. My frustration manifests itself in the form of baked goods. Someday, I may find a more productive way to channel my emotional distress, but this has worked for me so far. Anyway, cranberry chocolate chip muffins made the diner smell heavenly as I worked. The millionaire's shortbread was already cooling on the counter and spoken for by customers.

I swept up to two guests from out of town.

"Hi, welcome to Bridget's Cross. What can I get you to drink?" I asked.

"Well, don't see the likes of you around here much, do we?" one of the men said. I think they were truckers.

"Waitresses?" I said lightly. I knew where this was going. I don't get this a lot, but every now and then, someone pops up to irritate me. "I think you'll find waitresses everywhere, even in Michigan."

"What's your name? Sha-nay-nay? Taneesha? Go ahead, I've heard it all," the other trucker said. A few heads turn our way. Sid and Roman from the fire station frowned at the newcomers and set down their menus. I had to head this off now.

"We'll get some water out to start you off and come back for your order," I said hurriedly and stared down the firefighters. "I'm good. Sit down," I murmured as I passed by and patted them on the shoulders.

The truckers, I noticed, saw the very frightening expressions on the firefighters' faces and buried their noses in their menus. I looked at Dani, who patted me on the shoulder and went out with waters without me having to ask.

I went to the kitchen and took a deep breath. The guys would have tossed the newcomers out of the diner for me. In fact, they had in the past, but I didn't want to deal with that today. I would rise above.

Billy the fry looked at me and handed me a cup of iced water. Smiling, I gulped it down, thanked him, and grabbed the orders.

"Here are your champion's portions, gents," I said, serving the sheriff and the fire chief. Dani had taken the orders for my trouble table, bless her.

"So, you and the Vanner boy? How did that happen?" Lou asked as I topped off his coffee. I set his mug back down carefully, one of Bridget's Cross's good stoneware mugs that wouldn't break if I threw it against the wall. Which I had no intention of doing, surely.

Across from Lou, Scottie from the firehouse chuckled and dug into his Reuben. I pulled extra napkins from my apron and tucked them next to Scottie's plate. He got a little messy sometimes. Most of the time.

Scottie had been deputy fire chief in Bellhaven for two years now, working up the ladder from hose boy, and did a good job running things while Ted dealt with the big political issues of being fire chief. I think Ted lived in constant hope that Grandpa would come back and take over the firehouse.

"There is no 'me and the Vanner boy'. I have no car and I needed to see the college. His name is Erik, by the way," I pointed out, warming up Scottie's coffee, too. Sometimes I think the firemen should just IV the coffee straight into their veins rather than drinking it, they went through so much.

Lou chuckled and set his paper aside.

"I know Erik. The station uses his dad's shop for the fire trucks. Good kid, kind of quiet," Scottie said around a mouthful of corned beef. He had somehow gotten a splatter on his bald head. I wiped it for him. "I like the older boy, Duston, more."

"Duston, the one who won't stop talking. That's annoying, not likable," I said. "First of all, I'm not dating either of the Vanner boys. Secondly, why are we even talking about this?"

"Just wondering is all. Maybe you should wait a bit. I think there's someone else out there for you."

"What is that supposed to mean?" I asked. Lou squeezed my shoulder and popped a sweet potato tater tot into his mouth.

"You, princess, are smart and strong, the brightest young lady I know. You deserve someone who treats you like the treasure you are and don't you forget that," Lou said, with more ferocity than I'm used to hearing from him.

"Oh good lord, Lou, we're not getting married. I hitched a ride to Muskegon," I pointed out.

"He still got the Chevelle?" Scottie said around a mouthful.

"No, he traded it for a Javelin. AMX?" I said and rolled my eyes at the clamor that comment caused.

"What year?" Scottie asked intently.

"1972?" I guessed, praying I hadn't just lied.

"The boy has taste," Lou said reluctantly. He winked at me. "Goes to reason that's why he asked you out. You tell me if he steps out of line. I'll throw him in the drunk tank for a night."

"I think that's illegal, but thank you," I replied politely. I winked back at him and went to get a box of the bacon biscuits he enjoyed and honey butter, because I like Lou and my love language always involves food.

The two college coeds who were still my best friends breezed through the back door of the kitchen while I switched out muffin tins from the oven. Finally, reinforcements.

Oh, they were on a mission. I could see it. Excitement over seeing my best friends turned into wariness. Must defend myself.

They stared me down as I pretended to ignore them and plated food.

"Spill," Marley ordered, pulling down an order from the carousel. It had been the kind of morning where I had to write things down.

"I couldn't sleep last night and had peanut butter

toast for breakfast. It was delicious and I am tired," I responded, taking a moment to gulp down some water. "Let me get my tables settled."

Trish and Marley looked at each other, the kind of look you gave your partner to figure out who would play good cop/bad cop.

"Are you dating Erik Vanner?" Trish went in for the kill, picking up a tub for dirty dishes and throwing a towel over her shoulder.

"No," I replied evenly, piling four plates on my arms. Serving trays are for amateurs. I smothered a yawn. "What would make you think that?" I walked back into the dining room, the girls trailing after me. I served a table, then turned back to see all of my orders delivered and my tables bussed.

Marley hooked her arm through mine and led me back to the kitchen.

"Oh, maybe because you had dinner at his house with his family, then went for ice cream. And yesterday, he took you to Muskegon," Marley pointed out.

"Didn't you just get back last night? How do you know this?" I broke a muffin and gave half to Marley. Trish was nibbling the caramel off the shortbread, tossing her blonde hair back from her shoulders.

"We know all, see all," Trish said. "Really, we've been gone barely three weeks and come back to find that you've moved on from us already?"

"You guys are reading way too much into this," I said nonchalantly. My mom came back into the kitchen.

"Close up your tickets and go," Mom said. Marley and Trish squealed and squished Mom in a bear hug. "And don't forget you need to start thinking about a Halloween costume for the Fall Festival!" she called as we hustled out the door.

When I finally slid into the back of Marley's car,

Trish turned to face me while Marley chauffeured us to the discount store.

"Now do you want to hear about how Erik broke up with Helena or do you want to tell me?" Trish asked.

****

Few things are more awkward than shopping for clothes that you couldn't afford. Technically we were looking for clothes for Trish and Marley. Really, they were trying to find me an outfit for the homecoming game, which I had several opinions about.

"I love that skirt." Marley eyed Trish. "I want to twirl in it." The pleated skirt looked gorgeous on Trish, and her father was a dentist, so she was good for it. I never begrudged my friends their good fortune, but I had my pride.

"I want you to go back over what you were saying before," I said, pacing the tiny dressing room, my feet getting tangled among the stylish yet understated wardrobe staples for college freshmen, which I was not. "You *saw* Erik break up with Helena? Recently?"

"I'll talk about it after you try something on," Trish said, pouncing on me with a gold dolman sweater.

"That works." Marley eyed the outfit critically. "Maybe for the homecoming game but definitely not the dance."

"We're not going to the dance," I said in exasperation once I found a hole for my head to go through. "We graduated. We have moved on."

"*We* have moved on," Trish said, then bodily moved me in front of the mirror. "You are terrified and stagnating. This needs a belt."

"I have a belt that works," Marley volunteered. "Black jeans, boots, maybe a jacket."

I growled playfully and quickly changed into a fussy lavender blouse with tiny pearl buttons up to my chin, just to be contrary.

"I don't hate it," Marley said carefully. I sighed.

"Why are we putting in this much effort?" I asked. "It's a football game. They happen all the time." Trish shook her head and flipped through the hangers, wearing nothing but a pink bra and rainbow panties.

"I am worried that you're going to stay here because you're terrified of change and I'm going to find you here thirty years from now, growing barnacles or something," Trish said.

"I appreciate that. I do, but I need time, that's all. It's September. It's just September. I have to be sure before I drop that much money," I said.

"Absolutely, that's a valid point," Marley said, "but are you sure that's it?" We heard kids trample by like a heard of elephants and slam into the door of our dressing room. We ignored it.

"I volunteer at the hospital to research what I'm interested in. I went to Muskegon yesterday, and I really liked the college. There is a program I want to do. I'm not scared of change. I just change much slower than you guys," I protested. My reasoning sounded solid in my ears, but maybe, just maybe, they were a little right. They were concerned because they cared.

"Okay, all right, we get it. We will re-discuss at Christmas. Now, back to the stud," Trish said. I groaned. "They broke up after graduation. I'm talking right after graduation. I was at lunch with my family, and I could see them arguing in the parking lot and then poof! Done-zo."

"Oh, I see. So theoretically, if I were dating him, I would be the rebound girl," I said. I zipped myself up and turned to the mirror. "What about oh no."

"I don't love it," Marley said about the grey lacy number I was wearing. She was being kind.

"You look like you were heading to a funeral and got caught in a wood-chipper," Trish said bluntly. I nodded and changed again.

"You're over-thinking this," Marley asked. "You like him. End of story. Admit that you're dating, Calliope."

"Ugh, please don't call me that. I want to like him for the right reasons, not because of hormones or because I have a pulse. Like, I don't know if he volunteers on the weekends or is kind to children and small animals," I said, pulling something over my head. I turned to the girls and slumped again when I saw their faces.

"You may not want to look in the mirror. Just take it off," Marley urged.

I looked in the mirror anyway and winced. Someone somewhere had thought it was a good idea to put peplum on lime-green polyester. Someone somewhere was out of their mind.

"It's fugly," Trish said. "Anyway, you're not a saint and you wouldn't want him to be a saint anyway. It's just dating, Callie, not an epic romance or the end of the world. I would not be distressed if something normal started between you and Erik."

"Normal? I should be normal about this relationship?" I said with a Southern California vocal fry. "Like, should I go blonde? Should I get one of those bras that adds two cup sizes? Is that the type of normal we're talking about?"

"That's right, because the only way to get into a relationship is to talk stupid and wear something trashy." Trish looked at her outfit. "Trashier. Where are my pants?"

"No one is dressing trashy to get a boy's attention. Provocative, yes. Trashy is just crass. There is no excuse for looking like a skank, unless it was an accident."

Marley helped me into a yellow sundress, not listening to me when I pointed out that it was autumn.

"Helena's kind of a skank," Trish pointed out, digging through a pile of clothes for her pants. I wonder if they had forgotten their own shopping goals. "She doesn't dress like it normally, but all the hallmarks are there. That's a comparison we want to avoid."

"I know, I know, but she's a super-sexy skank and the skanks get the guys." I worried the hem with my fingers. Marley zipped up the yellow dress. I could already tell it wasn't going to work.

"Really? We really have to talk about this?" Marley eyed the dress critically. "We are better than this. Ow. Not yellow. My eyes."

"Okay, maybe not that one," Trish said, indicating the yellow nightmare I was wearing. She was already rifling through the hangers. I sighed and took it off. I was getting really good with the quick-change.

"I wonder if maybe I should go with something outside my comfort zone," I said.

"That's something I would usually advocate, but something sounds off." Marley frowned at me. "You do realize that we're going for guys who like us for who we are, not how easy our pants come off, right?"

"I think I know where this is coming from." Trish grabbed me by the shoulders. "What does your mom always say? Chin up, shoulders back, look me in the eye. We are not the type of girls who resort to skanky dresses or … whatever to get the guys. We are smart, strong, and resourceful."

"And we're hot," Marley pointed out, handing me a sweaterdress. I automatically changed into it.

"And we're hot," Trish added. "A nice boy asked you out. You don't need to be anything other than yourself. Leave the desperation to someone who isn't comfortable with who they are."

"Desperation is a stinky cologne," Marley added helpfully.

"Trish, I'm not uncomfortable with who I am. I don't know who I am," I pointed out. I felt that weird peppery feeling in the back of my throat that I associated with tears and distress. I didn't know if this was about the dress or my life in general. My friends are in a different place than me, and maybe I do need to do something drastic to get myself out of a rut.

"You are Calliope Redmond, one of the best people I've ever met. You're a great daughter, my best friend," Trish said.

"One of them," Marley corrected.

"One of my best friends, nothing but heart. You worry way too much about what other people think," Trish said. "This other person, you're not her."

I threw my arms around Trish and squeezed tight. She made a little gurgling noise and hugged me back. Oh, I needed that. I did that sometimes, stressed myself into a blathering mess. More than once, the girls brought me back to the ground. *I'm okay. We're all okay. I've got this.*

CONSTANCE KERSAINT

Chapter Five
The Ex

In the delightfully retro pizzeria bathroom, I surveyed my reflection critically. Trying on clothes played havoc with any sort of hairstyle, so I quickly wrestled my curls into a side-braid and called it good.

Marley and Trish were probably digging into the artichoke dip already. I started moving fast, not seeing Helena until my shoulder plowed into her boobs as she was coming out of a bathroom stall. Neither of us were happy about this.

"Watch where you're going, Redmond!" Helena snapped. Of course, I would see her today after months of complete absence, in this very place of all places. That's my luck for you.

"It was an accident. Are you okay?"

"Take your awkward self away. I'm just fine," she said. Well, that was quite a bit more vitriol than I had expected. "Are you stupid or deaf? Get out of my way."

"Okay, what is your problem?" I asked Helena.

"You," she snapped. "Always you."

"Yes, me, same as ever. Doesn't give you the excuse to be rude," I said, standing my ground between her and the door. She had a good couple of inches on me, but I was solid.

Anger fueled my courage. High school was over and this crap had to stop.

"I'm not going to apologize to you," Helena said.

"I'm not looking for an apology. You need to understand that you're behaving like a child," I pointed out.

"At least I'm not so desperate that I'm chasing after someone else's boyfriend," Helena said. Ah, now we were getting somewhere. "Don't take this personally, but I have no idea what Erik sees in you." One of the perks of living in Bellhaven seemed to be that my social life is a matter of public concern.

"Right, because there's no way I could take that personally," I said. "I'm getting really tired of saying this: I'm not dating Erik. Is this why you're acting like this, because you think I stole your ex?"

"Oh, like you ever could. Just forget it," Helena muttered, her face pinched. I was a hair's breadth away from physical violence. I couldn't fix the problem if I didn't know what it was, and Helena obviously didn't want to fix anything.

"Okay, fine, but let's get one thing straight. You can act like an adult and be civil to me," I said.

"Fuck you and your trashy family and the people you call friends," Helena sneered and tried to shoulder past me. I shifted and she ended up bouncing off me into the tampon machine. She looked stunned and I was, too.

I didn't know I had it in me. I'm not sure that was a good thing.

"Inappropriate," I said evenly. "That's not how this is going to work. High school is over, Helena. Time to grow up. Are we clear?" After a long moment, Helena nodded and I let her finally wash her hands.

When I realized it was weird to watch another girl in the bathroom, I left. This, I could tell the girls about.

"Where are her parents?" Trish wondered. "They raised a terrible child." She bit into her garlic knot with gusto. Our server did another drive-by to check on us, specifically Trish. She cheerfully sent him away.

"And it's such a one-eighty." Marley precisely spooned dip onto her chip. "She was fine during school. We did cheer together for years."

"Where is she now? I was surprised to see her

here." I shredded my garlic knot.

"Western Michigan," Trish said. "I see her around town sometimes."

"And?" Marley and I prompted in unison.

"And we don't talk. We don't even acknowledge each other," Trish said.

"Mean girl alert," Marley muttered. "Twelve o'clock and closing." I sat up a little straighter and briefly wondered if I was about to get into a slap fight in the middle of the pizzeria.

Helena walked past us without a word and exited. I was fairly certain she hadn't eaten anything. I wondered if she had followed us.

"Well, the drama thickens." Trish sipped her pop. "Someone is a little hurt her ex moved on. Did Mr. Perfect tell you anything about his ex-girlfriend?"

"I can't believe we're talking about this." I bit into my slice. "Why would we talk about our exes?" I said around a mouthful of sausage and mushroom. Yeah, I was still mad, but I wasn't going to let that interfere with girl-time.

"His ex," Marley corrected. "You don't have any exes. You've never dated anyone. Manuel doesn't count. You went bowling."

"Thank you for reminding me," I said drily. I frowned a bit, pondering Erik's ex. I could already feel the thought nagging me like a rock in my shoe. That just made me madder.

"Okay, so you may or may not be dating Erik Vanner," Trish said, wagging a finger. "Just be aware that his ex thinks you're dating, and she will probably egg the diner. Tell us everything as it happens or I will be so mad at you." I rolled my eyes.

"Fine, fine," I said "I will keep you updated with my terribly interesting life while you're both off on exciting college adventures." They snorted.

"Do you realize that we've known each other since kindergarten?" Marley said. "You wouldn't hold out on us, would you?" Her hazel eyes bore into me. I stared back serenely, shoving my emotions deep down inside.

"Never," I swore, and inside I let my anger go in a rush. Then we jumped at the sharp clap of thunder.

We stared out of the front windows of the diner at the dark gray clouds and pouring rain. I swear it had been clear and sunny the moment before.

Lightning streaked the stormy sky, and thunder shook the windows again. It had been like this in my nightmares. A storm so violent and turbulent that the very sky seemed angry.

The wind whipped the tree branches, and someone's bike tumbled over the sidewalk. Car alarms went off when the rain started blowing sideways. A rock slammed into the window of the pizzeria, cracking the glass.

Then it stopped. As suddenly as it had begun, the storm was done. The clouds started to dissipate, but the sun did not peek through. It was probably as shaken as we were.

I wasn't shaken. Weirdly, I felt much better.

****

After my volunteer shift on Monday, I was changing in the locker room when I found Mom's present in my bag. I usually wore my uniform home, but I wanted to stop by the library to do some research on the pathway program. I didn't want to look like, well, a hospital volunteer.

Mom must have sensed something was off with me after I got back from the theater. I had gotten into my room fast and barely left until it was time for the hospital.

I had been working in a daze all day, wondering what was going to go completely sideways next.

This pretty thing was something nice. I wished I had more nice surprises like this. I read the note, written in Mom's pretty cursive, and smiled as I opened the small green box.

Nestled in tissue paper was a small round pendant that was the size of a quarter and had three birds in a neat repeating pattern, maybe ravens. I quickly yanked on my corduroys so I could put on the necklace.

It seemed very old and had a nice weight to it. I liked the way it looked on me. I tied my hair back with a scarf to keep it off the chain.

I was about to shut my locker when I saw the surveys from the Osterhout family and cursed myself. I hurried to Dr. Wyndham's office, the lilting strains of a Puccini opera flowing out of the open door.

Dr. Wyndham's office seemed to be a workshop of random body parts, but they were actually used prosthetics. Prosthetics could not be reused in the United States, but Dr. Wyndham shipped them to other countries that could use them. People regularly turned in old prosthetics, and his office was the most convenient place to store them until he could ship them.

I gingerly navigated my way through a Puccini aria and a maze of assorted limbs while inside, I was screaming. Intellectually, I understood the noble purpose behind what I was seeing, but emotionally, I was looking at dismembered limbs.

I found Dr. Wyndham going over patient files at a table covered with assorted hand prosthetics. His tea had gone cold.

I cleared my throat to get his attention. He turned a page. I scuffed my boot and he looked up, blinking owlishly from behind his wire-rimmed glasses.

"Hi!" I said. "So sorry. I was going to leave these with Nurse Angie, but I didn't see her?"

"Yes, she left early today. Is that from the Osterhouts?" Dr. Wyndham asked.

"Yup!" I handed them over. "See you tomorrow, doc." I turned.

"Why don't you wait a moment, Callie, and I'll walk you out." Dr. Wyndham started to get up. I snorted.

"Oh come on, Dr. Wyndham, we're in Bellhaven," I said with emphasis. "Safe as houses. Goodnight!"

I hurried through the maze of halls, lost in thought, and didn't even feel the cool air as I exited the building. I was at the bike rack before I realized what was missing.

My bike was gone.

I stared at the empty rack. I was sure I had locked it here, like I always did, because this rack was closest to the rehabilitative medicine unit.

Had someone stolen my bike? That would just be the cherry on top of a really eventful week.

I headed for the parking garage to check the other bike rack. At worst, I would have the operator connect me to Dr. Wyndham's office. Maybe I could catch a ride.

The parking lot separating my building from the parking garage seemed bigger than usual. Every step let the cold seep deeper into my bones. I needed to do something about the transport situation because I didn't want to keep biking home after dark.

The mouth of the parking garage yawned before me. I never noticed before how badly lit the place was. I didn't let myself hesitate and plunged inside.

My bike was lying on its side by the parking garage bike rack. I was certain I had not left it that way. There was no sign of my bike chain.

This was all so weird, and I was in no mood to deal with it. I picked up my bike, my head snapping up at the sound of an engine revving.

I heard the truck before I saw it. I scrambled to get myself situated on the bike, then raced out of the garage just as the dark truck rounded the line of cars between it and me. My hair whipped in the wind, the scarf gone.

I knew it was the Janssens. They were after me. There was no one else. I pedaled as fast as I could, but I was a bike being followed by a truck. It had me in its headlights. The entire world was illuminated by the harsh glare.

Before me stretched a main thoroughfare that was straight as a pin. Usually it was teeming with vehicles, but it was empty tonight, a Monday evening during which people should have been heading home from work. I didn't bother sticking to the sidewalk and went into the road, crossing several lanes of traffic to the other side.

I glanced behind me and saw the truck jumping the median. I was never going to lose them on the thoroughfare.

I knew Bellhaven. I made a sharp turn onto a residential road. Biking as hard as I could, and now keenly aware how out of shape I was, I made several sharp turns and looped back. The truck was between the houses a few times, so I went deeper into the residential area.

Going across a grassy shortcut I knew, I burst out onto the other side of the area into another main road and went straight for the next block of houses. I was going to lose them. I had to.

****

About a heart-wrenching half an hour later, I raced up to Vanner Automotive and dropped the bike.

Garth trotted out like a good boy, bumping his blunt head against me. Hurrying to the door, I stopped short when Helena come out, perfectly pressed and coiffed.

She was still so gorgeous. It wasn't fair, it really wasn't, for so much beauty to be gifted to one person. The blonde hair, the perfect face—she looked more like my mother than I did.

And I was sweating and breathing hard, my kinky curls plastered to my head. I did not glow when I sweat.

The sight of Helena defeated me more than those asshole Vanners ever could. Why was I even here? I had walked away from Erik. What did I expect to find here?

Of course he would call his ex.

"Did you want something?" Helena asked.

I shook my head, breathless still, and I couldn't talk around the lump in my throat anyway.

"He's great, isn't he," Helena said, gracefully strolling toward me, a princess among mortals. For that alone, I kind of hated her.

Garth lifted his head like he was going to go greet Helena. I kept my fingers scratching his ears gently, and he stayed with me, gazing up adoringly. Dogs were easy. Girls were evil.

Helena was quiet for a moment. I'd always thought of her as one of those charmed creatures who flitted effortlessly through life. I made an effort not to envy her, but today, right now, I would have traded places with her in a heartbeat. I bet she had never run away from two psychotic weirdos.

"Let me do you a favor, Calliope," Helena said. I mentally crumpled a little more. Apparently, rising above the situation wasn't going to cut it today.

"Spare me." I finally found my voice. I had intended to talk to Erik about his cousins, but now I wanted nothing more than to flee.

"This is for your own good, little bird. He's too good for you. In what world did you think someone like you could be with him?" she said. Garth looked at the two of us, his usually friendly canine face seemingly concerned.

"What do you mean, someone like me?" I asked slowly.

"Come on, don't make me say it. You already know. I can see it in your face. Do you even know where your father is? How about his name?"

I wanted to reply with a biting remark, walk away with dignity, slap her across the face, anything other than rooting in place. I kept staring at her like the stupid girl she had just accused me of being. The problem was that I was fighting the tears pooling behind my eyes, and I couldn't believe someone would say these things out loud.

On top of everything else, this was just too much.

"What happened to you, Helena? What made you this way?" I said, truly curious as to why a person could be this awful. I was desperately grasping at anything to keep me together.

"You can talk all you want. I know I am loved. I wasn't abandoned like some puppy in a cardboard box. Tell yourself whatever you need to so you'll feel better, sugar. We both know who made out better in life."

Something sparked in me. *Oh, fury. That's good. I can use that.* I was so close to slapping her that I could already feel the stinging in my palm, but I used the anger to push myself into motion.

Rise above. I heard it as clearly as if Mom was standing right next to me. I stood up straight, slung my bag over my shoulder, and walked away with my head held high.

I don't have a dad. This is a fact. Well, I do have a

father, but I've never met him. He ditched my mom before I was born. Yeah, it hurts. It eats at me that someone didn't want me to such a degree. I think it's one of the reasons why Mom is always trying to empower me. And most days, it works.

I have a great life. Each day, I'm making my life better. There is nothing about my life that I am ashamed of.

Still, there are some dark moments when I know, deep down inside, that my father, a person who is supposed to love me unconditionally, didn't want me. I know what fathers are supposed to be like. Grandpa Doug has tried to fill that hole all my life.

That saved me from weeping all the way home.

Chapter Six
Fire Retardant

On Thursday, I shooed my mom out of the diner after the dinner rush. It had been slow and the last table had left an hour ago. Grandpa had left for his poker night, and Billy had shut down the fryer.

I could tell Mom's mind was completely elsewhere. I made her go upstairs for a bath while I finished closing. I kind of wanted to be alone anyway.

I turned up the surround sound and pushed the last table out of the way. I've been in charge of the music of Bridget's Cross since I turned ten. Mom insisted on sticking with a theme, but my interpretation of her theme was "remotely Celtic."

Tonight, I had the Irish and British punk bands of yore jangling over the speakers as I mopped. All thoughts drained from my mind as I let the music soak into me. Nothing was real besides the mop and the music. I listened to them sing about windows in the skies and being blinded by rainbows and was content. This was the best kind of therapy.

I finished by the wall, turned around, and muffled a terrified shriek.

"Hi," Erik said quietly, somehow standing in the middle of the diner. My heart was beating in my throat, and my nerves were jangling. He moved as quietly as a jungle cat. Someday, I wouldn't assume that every movement was someone trying to hurt me.

"Can you do that never?" I said, trying to catch my breath. I took stock of him, lean and tall in a red thermal shirt and worn jeans, and my breath went away again. His dark hair was still wet from his shower. The sight of his damp hair did evil things to my heart rate. It wasn't right that someone could look that good out of a shower. It just wasn't fair.

"I haven't seen you all week. You aren't taking my calls. If this is you ghosting me, then I just need you to tell me, but I don't think that's it. Are you okay?" Erik asked, picking up my mop. His eyes never left me, a clear hazel that cut through all my excuses.

"Yeah, sorry about that. I wasn't feeling well. You didn't need to come all the way here," I babbled. Erik took my hands in his. That was all. I looked down at his big strong hands holding mine and felt the pressure behind my eyeballs again.

"I just want to know if you're okay. Helena said she talked to you. What did she say? There's nothing truthful she could say to you that should upset you," Erik said quietly.

"Sticks and stones." I tried to smile and failed miserably. I felt my face crumple and he pulled me in.

The arms weren't weird or intrusive or overbearing. There was nothing unnatural or uncomfortable about it. Erik holding me felt right. The moment his arms went around me and my face went into his neck, I felt at peace and more steadied than I had been in quite some time.

I let myself have a few sobs into his soft shirt. Then I heard what he said and my heartache went away. Helena hadn't said anything truthful to me. Even if I didn't believe that, Erik did. And I was comforted.

As I took note of how firm his chest was under his thermal, how steady and strong his heartbeat was, I wondered what he thought of me. I almost didn't dare guess.

"What year is your car?" I asked in a ruined voice.

"1972," Erik replied gravely.

"Okay," I said, then gave a huge ugly sniff. I gasped out an embarrassed giggle. Erik chuckled and pulled a blue paisley handkerchief out of his pocket for me. I was about to blow my nose when I saw him watching. I turned a bit and tried to blow my nose as discreetly as possible when a large guy is towering over you.

"I'll wash this," I said lamely. I tucked the handkerchief in the pocket of my apron. Right then, an Irish band came over the surround sound system, singing about all they wanted, promising clear highways and priceless treasures.

And at that moment, all I wanted was him. The crystalline jangle of yearning came through the airwaves, and I fought the urge to leap across the counter to turn off the music that was being more honest than me.

Erik solemnly held out his hand. He made no more movement toward me, like he thought I might bolt. I knew that I was blushing furiously and fought the urge to crawl under one of the tables. This didn't seem odd to me, this big guy I barely knew silently asking me to dance. He was doing it to take my mind off the vicious words of one angry ex-girlfriend.

Still, the hand was there, and I really adored this song. Hesitantly, I put my hand in his. He pulled me close and set his other hand on my hip. The diner had excellent acoustics which were even better when the place wasn't filled with diners. The chiming, shimmering guitar chords of this live recording reverberated off the walls and floor of the room as this quiet boy led me in an easy, comfortable dance.

I had never really danced with a guy before. I'd never really danced with anyone before, unless you count silly-dancing with Mom in the living room. It stunned me how comfortable I was in this guy's arms. It was something I could easily get used to, feeling so safe.

Mom and I were used to creating our own safety, but this, this was someone freely offering me protection, someone wanting to keep me from harm.

I won't lie—it felt great. I wanted to stay.

We moved like we knew each other. It was so simple, easier than breathing.

****

After Erik left smiling, I took out the last of the trash. Erik had offered to do it, but I honestly thought that I had done it all. I had made him go home with the promise to call him tomorrow to talk more. I knew he was going to ask me out again, and I was going to say yes.

I found the last bag by Grandpa Doug's cutting board. He had run out the door before we really closed the kitchen. It wasn't a huge deal but my day had been awful and my night had been outrageously good. I just wanted to end on a high note. I guess I could handle a little bag of cutting board scraps.

Outside the back of the diner, I could still hear the music as I lifted the trashcan lid. I sensed him before I knew he was there. It felt like a heavy wet sponge hitting my neck and sliding down my spine.

"I thought he'd never leave," Freddy said. I gripped the lid and spun around. I somehow managed to keep the bag of trash in my other hand. I could use it, swing it, something. I was about to scream for Mom when Freddy held a finger to his lips.

"You don't want to do that, princess. George's watching your mom right now, and one scream will have him charging into her room. George is not what you'd call gentle to begin with. It could hurt. A lot."

I was very proud that I didn't scream, but I didn't put down the trashcan lid. I had no idea what to do but a vague idea formed in my mind of getting away from Freddy and into the kitchen at the knives.

My home. These bastards had invaded my sanctuary. This was the only place in the world I was completely safe, and the Janssens had violated that safety for me. Beneath my fear, I was angry, too. How dare they.

"Don't look so worried, lovely one. I just want to talk," Freddy said. He was a really good-looking guy. He could probably use a few healthy meals and chosen clothes from the thrift store that weren't so obviously worn, but he was a tall, strong-looking guy with a handsome face.

Freddy had driven the dark truck that had chased me from the hospital, and just for that, he was the ugliest jerk on the planet to me. It didn't matter what he wanted to say. I wasn't going to forget the attack.

"I have nothing to say to you," I said, moving a bit toward the door. "You can't be here. Please leave." Freddy threw out a hand and the heavy door closed behind the storm door, as if an invisible wind had pushed it. My fingers went nerveless and the trash bag dropped. The lid of the trashcan was looped through my hand or it would have dropped, too.

"What, how did you do that?" I asked. I hadn't seen him touch the door. There was no possible way he could have done that.

"Do you believe in magic, pretty girl?" Freddy said. My heart clenched in fear, but something sparked inside of me. I hated being talked down to, and Freddy's little cute nicknames were starting to irritate me. I had a name and we were not at the stage that I'd accept endearments from him.

It could have been coincidence or just my remarkable luck, but the wail of a man calling for helter skelter came on over the speakers.

"There's no such thing as magic. Look, why do you keep coming after me?" I demanded. "I don't know what drama you have with your cousins, but leave me out of it. I don't know you. I don't know what you think I've done to offend you, but it wasn't intentional. Just leave me alone!"

"They haven't told you anything, have they?" Freddy said, his face thoughtful. He was undeniably a very good-looking guy. However, he was also the malevolent sadist who kept wanting to hurt me.

"Told me what?" I snapped. Anger was more productive than fear. I pushed my fear down and fanned my anger. I would get out of this. I wouldn't freeze. I would not wring my hands. I had a plan. Get to the knives in the kitchen or get to Mom and lock the doors, call Lou.

"There's a story that I think you might know. It's about a fairy girl who finds a boy washed up on the shore. She saves him and they fall in love. Then his family comes to bring him home and he won't go home with them," Freddy said, his words turning me cold.

I did know this story. I dreamed about this story.

The world had just turned utterly bizarre, and I felt completely disoriented. How we got from this boy threatening me to weird tales was a path I didn't follow.

"I don't know what you're talking about," I protested, forcing my mind to seek options. Cell phone. Where was my phone? In my bag, which was in the upper cabinet in the kitchen.

"No, my lovely. This is your past. And it's happening again."

"You sound like you just went off your meds. I don't understand."

"Then I'll be clear," Freddy said. In the blink of an eye, the trashcan lid was batted aside. He shoved his forearm against my throat and shoved me up into the wall. I could get some weight on the tips of my toes, but I couldn't breathe well.

Somewhere in my confused brain, I recognized my embroidered scarf tied around his wrist. It was the same scarf I had lost at the hospital when I had biked away from them.

"You're the fairy girl. You're the witch who found my cousin. You're the reason he wanted to stay with you instead of going home with his family. You're the reason he died, and you're the one who stole our magic, made us mortal. Do you understand that?" Freddy said. "This time, he won't die first on the beach. This time, it'll be different."

His breath was hot on my face. I couldn't move, frozen in terror. His words sparked some connections in my brain, though. My dream. He was describing my dream.

"That's not me. It's a story, and it's not even real. It's all in my head," I gasped out, my eyes tearing up.

"No, little bitch, it's history. You ruined us all. We took the life that was rightfully ours to take and you, bastard of the Tuatha, laid the geas on us to relive this cycle for eternity as humans. Now, I'm going to stop it. I'm tired of living your nightmare. I have plans for this world, and it doesn't involve taking part of your soap opera again."

He hauled me away from the wall and used my body to shove the door open. Freddy threw me down onto the kitchen floor and put his foot on my throat. I was so desperately afraid and very tired of this guy beating me down. Alone in the dark kitchen, I struggled against the foot on my neck, but he was so much stronger than me.

"We are done being puppets to your story, little bird. You will give us back the magic you stole," he said, flipping on the gas burners of the stove. Then he took a knife and slashed behind the stove for good measure.

"I'll do it. Whatever it is, I'll do it," I gasped out. I swiped at his other leg, and he put more pressure on my throat. I started seeing dark spots before Freddy reached down and lifted me by my collar.

"Yes, you will, sweet girl. Because I'm going to rip your head off and eat your soul," Freddy whispered in my ear and licked the side of my face.

"Eat my soul?" I croaked through my bruised throat. "Eat my soul?" This was not happening. People in this day and age don't eat other people. I think he believed my soul was in my head. Of all the dangers in this world, keeping my brain from being consumed was not even on my top ten list of things to look out for.

"I'm going to break you like a wishbone and savor your face, bite by bite," Freddy told me seriously.

I hated this boy, more than I thought possible, more than I cared to admit. Oh, I was plenty scared, too, but hate was winning right now. And the knives were too far out of my reach, up on the counter.

"Can't we talk about this?" I said, inching for the rolling island. Some of Grandpa Doug's cast iron skillets on the lower shelf of the island.

"There is nothing to talk about. You stole our destiny from us. George will release his tail from between his teeth, and Ragnarök will begin. I was meant to kill the Allfather. You took my purpose from me, Tuatha slut. I'm going to take it back from you," Freddy said. He bunched up his shoulders and I shrank back. "Because you overreacted, I've been locked in this never-ending cycle of mundane for thousands of years. I am a god. I am going to fight at Ragnarök and watch the world burn."

"I'm sorry," I said tearfully, completely confused and desperately afraid. I wasn't apologetic, because I barely understood what he was talking about, but I wanted him to stop hurting me.

"Not enough. I want you prostrate with sorrow, wracked with regret and woe. Would it help if I said it louder? Maybe I should shout," Freddy said. "I hate you!" My ear drums were ringing, and I was on the floor again. I could smell the gas. Mom. Oh no, Mom. She had to get out of here. She must have heard this. We were making so much noise.

I lunged for the cast iron skillet and got my fingers around a Griswold. Blindly, aimlessly, I lunged at Freddy and managed a good smack across the face.

He barely budged. I dropped the cast iron skillet, my wrists and hands too hurt to hold it. He spat out a bit of blood and smirked at me, a bloody baring of teeth that did nothing to make me feel better. He looked like a cat who was enjoying playing with his food.

"I prefer the cold, but just this once, I think a little heat is in order," Freddy said.

I was running away before Freddy flicked the lighter. I went for the door. I didn't see the lighter ignite the gas, but brightness behind me illuminated the dark kitchen. I wasn't going to make it. I was going to burn to death. I felt the heat of the flames rise up behind me and saw the red glow brighten the walls.

Only for the flames to never reach me. One moment I was running for the door—without hope. In the next heartbeat, I was pressed against a hard chest and my nostrils were filled with the clean scent of the woods instead of my own scorched flesh. I knew this red thermal shirt. I knew the arms that held me so tightly. I knew this boy.

"Erik?" I asked, my voice rising octaves. I looked up from the red thermal and couldn't believe my eyes. Erik had his right arm around me and his left hand was palm-out to the kitchen. The flames from the gas-fire were curling and winding away from an invisible wall right in front of us. The heat was overwhelming but not enough to hurt me and certainly not enough to kill me. And Erik was holding it back somehow.

"Come on, let's go," Erik said, frowning at the flames currently being deflected off his force field or whatever it was. A silver bracelet encircled his left wrist. That was new.

"You're fire retardant?" I gaped.

"Just for today," Erik said and pulled me out of the kitchen. I shook myself. *Don't freeze up*, I reminded myself. *You can't freeze up.*

"Mom," I said and made for the stairs of the back porch. Erik grabbed my arm.

"Don't just rush up there."

"George is up there, and he's going to hurt my mom!"

"He can't hurt your mom in this house!"

"What?" I shouted. Erik and I were about to get into our first argument when we were both blasted off our feet by a gust more at home in Alaska than Michigan.

"Don't you," Freddy sang as he waltzed out the back door of my diner, "forget about me. No, no, no, no."

Erik staggered to his feet and faced his cousin. He swung his arm underhanded like he was serving a softball. A bolt of lightning flew from his palm, slamming Freddy square in the chest and temporarily blinding me.

Freddy jerked and convulsed with unthinkable voltage until Erik cut the electricity, and then Freddy slumped to the ground. For the moment, Freddy was out.

I tried to get to my feet, too, not yet willing to process the fact that I just saw a guy I grew up with throw a lightning bolt. I went for the porch again.

Before my foot touched the porch, the breath was knocked out of me and I was on the ground again. This was getting really old. I was already trying to get my breath back, the suffocating sensation gripping my lungs like a vise.

George Janssen stood over me, holding what looked like a piece of the wooden porch railing he had just hit me with. Before Erik could take care of him, George was lifted into the air. I was looking at a boy suspended in midair by nothing.

I wasn't looking at George, though, hanging in the air as if he was caught in an invisible noose. As Erik helped me up to my feet and kept me close to his side, my gaze stayed glued on the blonde figure standing on the top landing of the porch, her arm outstretched to George. Mom jerked her arm and George landed far away. I was distantly aware of him getting away as fast as his legs could carry him. I glanced at the diner and saw that Freddy was gone, too.

So much had happened tonight that I didn't know where to start. My world was upside down.

No. My world was gone. Erik's arms tightened around me, and I took comfort in the only thing that was solid and real to me right now, the firm reality of his arms holding me up.

I felt gentle hands on my face. I knew these hands; they had raised me. My mother looked at me, her sea-green eyes incredibly sad.

"Mom?" I croaked, using up what little breath I could pull back into my lungs. Then I started to cry.

CONSTANCE KERSAINT

Chapter Seven
New World

My mother, my very practical mother, put a cup of tea on the coffee table in front of me. I knew that it would be liberally laced with honey and perhaps a shot of Irish whiskey. I would not even question how she found any of these items at the Vanners' house.

After the attack, Erik and my mom had taken me over to the Vanners', while Norman and Duston did something to our house and the diner. Grandpa was still out with his buddies and probably wouldn't be back until the sun came up.

We were in Erik's living room, a homey, sparsely-decorated place that was a little sterile and sort of comforting to me. I was on Erik's couch, firmly ensconced in Erik's arms, with a soft old quilt around me. Mom kept this quilt in our car for emergencies.

I remember finding the quilt at a thrift store in Kalamazoo. It was so beautiful, with a fanciful pattern of a Viking ship and a mermaid under the waves, catching a whale's tale for a ride. I had laundered it carefully and made it ours. A non-tangential thought occurred to me that this quilt was very much at home here in the Vanner house.

"Mom," I said faintly. I stared up at the face I knew as well as my own and saw it blur through my tears. "What is going on?"

"Well, apparently, you started dating Erik Vanner and didn't tell me," she replied. I frowned and sat up a bit. Then I realized what it looked like, me on the couch with Erik's arms around me. There had been so little peace for me these past few days that I had automatically sought the comfort of his arms without thinking.

"We're not dating. He's protecting me from his crazy cousins," I said, but I made no move away from Erik. I was having a very weird day, and there seemed to be no safer place I could be than right next to Erik. "But tonight Erik threw lightning bolts, and you seemed to be able to move things with your mind, and no one is telling me anything. I'd really like someone to clue me in here. Freddy was babbling about some bedtime story."

"No. It's safer for you to not know," Erik said.

"I can't believe you're so dense," I muttered rudely.

"I agree with Callie on this one," Norman said, stepping into the living room. Duston came in right behind him, minutely examining how close Erik and I were on his couch. I couldn't tell if Duston disapproved of the way Erik was holding me or the fact that we were taking up the couch. He handed something to my mom. "I found this."

"Callie's scarf." My mom frowned. "It takes skill to use this to get past my wards, and your nephews are imbeciles. Someone's helping them."

"Your wards?" I asked.

"Protective spells. I set a ward on the diner so no one from Erik's family who intends us harm may enter. The wards can only be broken or altered by someone from our story, a Celtic god. Any other being would not be able to tune into our frequency, so to speak," Mom explained.

"That's why I said George couldn't hurt your mom inside your house and the diner," Erik said. "Freddy bypassed your wards with your scarf, making the ward think he was from your side instead of mine." Erik gave me a squeeze and got up. "Dad, our wards are up?" Norman opened his mouth to say something and stopped.

"You put on the torc," Norman said flatly, shock

sucking all emotion from his voice. His gaze was on the silver wolf torc on Erik's left wrist.

"Just for a bit. Look, I'm taking it off right now," Erik said, tugging at the bracelet. No, they called it a torc. I got a good look from where I was sitting. I think it was silver, or silver-colored metal. It was more like a cuff, a twisting rope of silver that ended in two alarmingly realistic wolf heads. The two wolf heads snapped and snarled at each other, not quite touching. Erik couldn't take it off.

"You put on the torc, Erik. The path is set. You have to take it to the end," Mom said, shaking her head slowly.

"No," Erik said, straining at the torc. "I put this on because I didn't want to lose it. I didn't accept anything."

"You shouldn't be worrying about Callie," Norman said. "It's you they'll kill."

"Wait, what?" I snapped. I couldn't keep the sharpness from my voice. "If the Janssens are going to try to kill Erik, we have to tell Sheriff Loggins." I ignored what Freddy had told me, how he had pulled my dream from my head and spoken of it like it was ancient history.

"That'll just get the sheriff killed and Erik murdered faster," Duston said, dropping onto the armrest of the couch. "Killed sooner? You know what I mean. You saw what happened tonight. You can't contain that kind of wrong with conventional law enforcement. This is a family matter."

"And what happened to you? Where were you during all of this?" I demanded.

"If I knew my brother was going to take on our cousins, I would have stopped him."

"Stop," Erik admonished his brother. "Don't blame her. I chose to do this."

"All of you stop," Mom ordered. The Vanner

boys quieted. Norman sat back, like he was content to let Mom drive. "Let's start from the beginning so that everyone is on the same page. Then we'll figure out what to do. And no one is to blame. This has happened before, and the story wants to happen again. We were never going to be able to stop it."

"Why? Why is all this happening?" I asked

"You did something, a long time ago," Mom said slowly. I shook my head.

"Like, when I was a kid?" I asked.

"No, in another lifetime. In a previous life," Mom said intently. She waved everyone down and we settled in for the explanation. "Long, long ago," Mom started, "there was a girl who lived in a village by the sea. One day, the girl found a boy washed up on the beach, the survivor of a shipwreck. She saved him, nursed him back to health, and they grew to love each other. His family found the village and demanded the boy come back with them, but he did not want to leave the girl. His family killed him for refusing to come home with them. The girl found them after the boy had been murdered and cursed them all to live the story over and over, so that they could never escape this mistake they had made. Then she turned to stone to seal the curse."

There was absolute silence after Mom's summary.

I looked around. No one was smirking. No one else was in on the joke.

"No," I slowly, gently. I think they all actually believed Mom's story. "This isn't real. Mom, this is my dream, the one I keep having. This isn't real."

"Dreams are memories," Erik said quietly. I stared at him and, oddly, had the urge to smack him in the arm.

"No, it can't be. It's just a dream. It's not real, not history. This isn't a true story, and even if it is, it happened centuries ago!" I heard hysteria in my voice. I didn't care.

"It's happened before," Mom told me gently.

"What do you mean?" I got up. I couldn't sit anymore. I paced a bit. My world was careening wildly out of control, and it didn't seem to be settling down anytime soon. The walking helped.

"I mean that we've lived this story before, over and over again, exactly as the geas cursed us to do. We're tied this cycle," Mom explained. I looked at them wildly.

"Why?"

"Because you made it that way. You set your geas upon us, remember?" Duston said.

"No, I don't remember! I don't even know where to start. How could I do that?"

"You took all our magic, all our immortality and power, and used it to fuel the geas and make us mortal. You tied us to the wheel of reincarnation or whatever we're calling it these days," Duston said.

"What is a geas?" I asked, still trying to make sense of their words.

"A geas is a magical prohibition, like a curse," Erik said.

"And if I, no, my past life person girl, took all our magic and used it to make a curse, how are you fire retardant and my mom can levitate people?" I asked, trying to understand.

"When we start to remember, we gain back a little of ourselves from past lives, a little bit of magic," Mom explained patiently. "Let's start from the very beginning. The girl in the story, her mother was Brigid."

"Brigid is the Celtic goddess you named the diner after. Wait a minute, what?" I said blankly, reaching into my shallow knowledge of mythology. "You're a goddess?"

"Not anymore, but I was her, once, long ago," Mom said. "It's hard to explain. Our family is very old. Some people call us Tuatha de Danaan. The person I used to be was what some people would call fae. The girl you were all those years ago, that girl was Brigid's daughter. And the boy that girl found on the beach, that boy's father was Njordr, cousin to Odin."

"Odin, the Viking god. Okay, no. You're mixing up stories here. The Celts and the Norse were two separate people. They barely interacted."

"Other than the raiding, and the battles, and the centuries of bloodshed and enmity between our people," Duston said. "Also, Norse is an adjective. You should probably say Norsemen or Nordic people."

"That is the heart of the matter," Norman broke in. "Your story, Callie, is Celtic. Our story is Norse. In the Nordic story, Odin's nephew calls Ragnarök, the Twilight of the Gods, and dies gloriously in the final battle. In the Celtic story, Brigid's daughter marries a hero from her own people and lives happily ever after. That's how it was supposed to play out. Nowhere does it allow for these stories to mix, except that there was a storm in the North Sea during the raiding season, and Odin's nephew was cast to sea. He was rescued by Brigid's daughter, you. That's why our family came back for the boy, because he didn't belong with the Tuatha."

"And that's why you killed him?" I asked. I was slowly digesting the information, and the conclusions I was making did not make me happy. "You're going to kill Erik?"

"Not us," Duston said in disgust. "Dad and I weren't the ones who killed Erik. It was our cousins, the jötnar. Frost giants, if that's easier for you to understand. Freddy and George Janssen's family. We're Vanir gods. They're jötnar. Different families. But related."

I sank back into Erik. The world was spinning, and I needed the solidity and warmth.

"This is insane. You're talking about gods. We don't even go to church, because gods don't exist," I insisted.

"Maybe they were gods, or maybe they made themselves gods, but they most certainly exist, little bird," Duston snapped. "This is all about the story and how you two screwed it up. If you two hadn't met, we wouldn't have spent the past few centuries living this same sequence of events over and over again. I don't want my brother to die for you!"

"Me neither, you moron!" I snapped at him.

"Duston, shut it," Erik said. "This is a lot of information. Just settle down."

Mom squeezed my hand comfortingly, then really squeezed my hand, her gaze narrowing. She was looking at something I was wearing and leaned forward to pull my pendant out from under my shirt.

"Honey, where did you get this?" Mom asked very seriously. Norman straightened abruptly, his eyes locked on the necklace like it was going to bite him.

"You gave it to me. It was in my bag. Didn't you?" I asked. Mom's hand fell into her lap, her eyes hollow. She shook her head slowly.

"I did not give this to you. I would never give this to you. It was in your bag?" she asked.

"Yes. I found it when I was changing in the hospital," I said, digging through my bag for the note and the box. I handed it to Mom, who frowned.

"I didn't write this note. I didn't give you the triskele," Mom said slowly.

"The geas is being forced, Brigid," Norm said. "Our cuimhne was triggered by accident. Looks like someone wants Callie to remember on purpose. You said you never found the triskele."

"That's right," Mom said. "Someone sent this to you." She set the box down and started dismantling it.

"Queevna?" I interrupted. "What's that?"

"Cuimhne," Mom said, pronouncing it the way I had heard it, "means to remember. It's when you remember your past life, a very rare occurrence."

"It's not meant to happen. A soul is wiped between lives to not remember what happened before," Norm said.

"But," I frowned, "the same thing keeps happening to us. We have to remember at some level."

"Our memories aren't making us relive the same events," Mom explained. "The spell you cast is doing that."

I would be proud of myself if first, I remembered what I had done, and second, I hadn't cursed us to never-ending desolation.

"The Janssens aren't forcing Callie to remember. They don't think that far ahead," Norm said, his fingers steepled in front of him. "There's someone else, someone who has been planning a long time."

"It's pretty, but I don't understand why a necklace is such a big deal," I said, taking the necklace back.

"There are anchors in the story, signals that another cycle has started. You put on the triskele, which belonged to the original Branwen. Erik puts on the torc, which belonged to the murdered boy, Vindler," Mom said. I winced. "The Vindler who loved Branwen in the first iteration," Mom amended.

"It's okay, Mrs. Redmond," Erik said. "I know the story. I died on a beach. She turned all the gods into humans and tied us to a reincarnation cycle."

"So we can all die and do this again later," I finished.

"All before Samhain of your eighteenth year," Mom clarified. "Samhain is November first, the day after Halloween."

"I'm eighteen right now. And Halloween is next month," I said in dawning horror.

"Bridget," Norm said in a weird voice, then handed her a piece of paper. He pulled a business card from underneath the cotton in the gift box

"Oh my lord," Mom whispered. I leaned in and read the card. Then I felt an intense need to vomit.

"Pritchard Poole?" I choked. "My father did this?"

****

We didn't say anything on the short drive back home. Home felt strange. I felt strange. I moved by habit, letting us into our house where recently frost giants from some Scandinavian myths had tried to kill me.

Erik assured us that the wards his family put around the diner would keep any jötnar out. Mom had scoffed, letting me know that it was our family wards that would actually do the real protecting.

I hadn't processed any of that yet. Mom being magic. Jötnar. Reincarnation. Norse frost giants. A generational curse. I still saw the Janssens as really creepy juvenile delinquents, and the Vanner family saw them as something out of ancient myths.

I walked past the smoking door leading to the destroyed diner kitchen and the stairs missing a wooden railing. I had no idea how we would explain that tomorrow, or get it fixed. Some things I just could not deal with right now. I felt numb. I had put my bag on the kitchen table when I just couldn't take it anymore.

"How long have you known this would happen?" I asked Mom.

Mom looked at me sadly, then put the tea kettle

on. Redmond women could fix the entire world, but only if we had a cup of tea in front of us. We settled down with some spiced vanilla tea and split a carrot muffin.

"The cuimhne happened to me about a year ago. We call remembering our past life the cuimhne," Mom began. "I didn't tell you because we didn't know where the raven triskele was. Without the triskele and the torc, the story doesn't start."

"Magical jewelry are triggers?"

"Yes. We were in a holding pattern, and I hoped that we would be able to skip the tragedy and move on. I didn't want to burden you."

"Has that ever happened before? Have we ever lived a life without tragedy?" I asked curiously. Mom paused, giving me my answer.

"No," Mom said slowly, sadly. "In the lives that you don't find each other, you both die young anyway. Influenza, shipwrecks, tuberculosis, a fall down the stairs, something ends your life early."

Stuck through eternity at eighteen. Lucky me.

"What does Pritchard Poole have to do with this?" I asked after a moment. I really didn't want to bring my phantom father into this conversation, but it seemed pertinent. It also felt very alien. I had spent a long, long time avoiding the thought of my father. Bringing him up willingly seemed foreign.

I had never asked for his full name. He had been Pritchard, always. I had wanted to ask for everything, but just mentioning him brought so much pain to my mother that I didn't. It wasn't worth it, I would tell myself. I couldn't hurt my mother by saying the name of the man who abandoned me.

And now it seemed that my father wanted me dead. Or, more accurately, eaten by Nordic ice giants.

"I don't know," Mom said after her own

hesitation. I never asked her how she felt about my father leaving us before I was born. Her face seemed carefully blank. "He has been out of our lives since before you were born. I found out just a few weeks ago that he died. I don't know how or why the necklace came to you in his name. I haven't been looking for it, but we didn't know where it was."

"Why don't I remember, cuimhne, whatever, like Erik remembers?" I asked.

"From what Norm told me, Erik remembered his past life four years ago, during the summer solstice," Mom said. "He got hit in the head."

"There's no summer solstice right now," I pointed out, frustrated. "Do we want to get ahead of things by giving me a concussion? I'm not crazy about letting someone punch my lights out."

"I know this is a lot," Mom said. "Please understand, we are all trying to keep you safe."

"Is this why you wanted me to go to Notre Dame so badly?" I asked, going over the past year in my head.

"We have family in South Bend. It's a protected place for our kind, like Bellhaven is safe for our kind," Mom said. "I had thought, with Erik so far away in Minnesota, that the danger was gone. I also want you to reach your potential, something that you have never been able to do because of the geas."

"My geas, my curse, that I don't remember casting, because I'm not a witch," I summarized. I think I was repeating myself, but the repetition helped me work through the ideas. I was never a fast learner, but I could keep at an idea until it made sense to me. The method has worked for me in every area except chemistry and my dating life. I gulped my tea and grimly poured myself another.

"Fairy, not witch," Mom corrected. "It's

reductive, but if you have to call us anything, fae is the more accurate term. The Tuatha are believed to be the inspiration for fairies."

"Fairy, whatever! And another thing, I don't believe Pritchard Poole sent me this necklace," I said, taking off the triskele. It was a piece of metal, a trinket that chained me to a curse. "A person doesn't spend a lifetime ignoring me and one day decide that I have to die." I tried to drop the triskele, but I couldn't. I shook my hand over the dining table and for some reason, I could not let go of the cursed thing.

"I don't believe Pritchard did either, but that's not the biggest issue right now. The curse is starting its cycle again, and we can't stop it."

"So was I super-powerful?" I asked. "I don't feel super-powerful. And from the story, it didn't sound like I had a whole lot going for me. How did I do this?"

"All of us are governed by rules. A higher power had decreed that you were entitled to this curse. Three insults avenged in blood. Erik's family had killed him, his dog, and set fire to Branwen's village," Mom said. "That's how you were able to take their magic to forge this geas."

"But it wasn't just Erik's murderers. I cursed us all," I pointed out.

"She cursed us all," Mom corrected me. "You two aren't the same person. You are Callie. She was Branwen."

"Branwen." I said the name slowly. "That was my name, before? Let me wrap my head around how we're not Catholic since I'm reincarnated, and then I'll work on fairies and Viking gods."

"For us, magic is real," Mom said, rubbing her forehead tiredly. When I was a kid, I used to go to Sunday school, but that fell away once the diner took off.

Being able to fund a roof over our heads and shoes that fit was more critical than praying to a deity of questionable existence. I may have to revisit my agnosticism at a later date.

I wasn't sure what the Catholic Church would have to say about my situation, but I couldn't imagine they would approve.

"I'm not Irish," I pointed out inanely. I only had to look in the mirror to verify that fact.

"You are, through me," Mom reminded me.

"That's not what I meant."

"That's what you said."

"Yeah, yes, I know, what I meant is," I paused, searching for words, "I don't look like what this Branwen would have looked like." This seemed like a very salient point to me.

"Why would that matter?" Mom said.

"Shouldn't it?"

"It has never mattered before. Did you notice that Erik doesn't look like a Viking?"

The thought took longer to make sense to me than it should have.

And that was the sticking point for me. I finally realized what was bothering me.

"Mom," I said. She looked at me, and I tried to find the right words to ask what I wanted to ask. "I'm sorry. I'm sorry I did this to you. I'm sure I didn't mean to, but it doesn't change the fact that I ruined … your eternity."

Mom was quiet so long that I wondered if I had finally broken her. She handled a teen pregnancy and single motherhood with aplomb, but my apology may be the last straw.

Then she took my hand and squeezed, and everything was okay again.

"I love you, Callie," Mom said, looking deep into my eyes. "Even if I hadn't been included in the geas, I would have found a way to bind myself to it. You don't do this without me. Now, you are Calliope Redmond. You are smart and strong, and you shouldn't punish yourself for what someone else did. We'll have to do what we always do: make the best of the situation."

"Any idea how we can break this cycle so we can just live our own lives?" I asked. Mom grinned faintly.

"Not a clue," Mom answered. We both jumped when we heard a thump. The kitchen door burst open to reveal Grandpa Doug, possibly drunk, beard sticking every which way.

"There be my girls!" he roared. "What's to eat? This old man is hungry!"

Chapter Eight
Walkabout

I woke up on Friday groggy as all get out. Mercifully, I didn't remember any dreams.

There was a clatter in the kitchen. I shot up in terror, my mouth dry. I searched my room for some sort of weapon before I heard Grandpa singing, and I could breathe again.

That's when I smelled it. Grandpa, who had fallen asleep on our couch after we had fed him, had whipped up some cheddar eggs. He always knew when I needed my comfort food.

I cleaned my plate in record time. I needed to clear my head, so I hugged Mom and Grandpa Doug before heading down the stairs for a walk.

Then I suddenly remembered that a frost giant had set my diner kitchen on fire last night. I cautiously descended and blinked at the scene.

The diner kitchen was fine. There was no sign of a fire. I peered into the back window. Billy the fry doing kitchen prep on a spotless counter. It was as if no one had tried to murder me last night.

I looked up the stairs, remembering another jötnar ripping off a section of railing, and that too was completely fine. Well, my mom could levitate giants. I'm sure house repairs were easier.

Then Erik texted. He was skipping class today and asked if I wanted to go for a walk. I almost cried with relief.

****

I rolled the window down for Garth to hang his head out as we headed to the pier. I laughed at the tongue lolling happily in the wind.

The Javelin drove like it had come off the AMC production line yesterday, notwithstanding dog slobber on the door. I found the dull roar of the powerful engine comforting, not overwhelming. It was like being cuddled by a purring cat, rather nice.

The pier was the defining landmark of Bellhaven. This was where the Coast Guard festival was held every summer, the same place every person escaped to once the weather warmed up, where half the town received their first kisses.

Erik and I had given up on making excuses to be around each other. I don't know how true my feelings are, but they're there. I like him and he likes me and for right now, for a walk down the pier, that was enough.

We had just passed the first red lighthouse when I felt my heart relax. Like I said, no thoughts of any kind of Nordic ice giant wanting to eat my soul, just sunshine and fresh air. Erik had magically produced pints from the Creamery, peanut butter pretzel and strawberry fudge, which had in turn magically raised my spirits.

"Wait, what is your team?" I laughed. Football was sacred in Michigan, and there were only two choices.

"Why is that a surprise to you?" Erik asked. "We do, after all, live in Michigan."

"I just expected you to be a Wolverine," I replied.

"No way. Spartans all the way."

"You're mixing up religions again. That's what got us in trouble in the first place."

"I don't see Leonidas and three hundred Spartans marching around in loincloth. I think we're safe on that front," Erik said. "What about you?"

"We're die-hard Notre Dame fans in my family."

"Right, no competitions on that front at all. Might not want to mention Notre Dame in my house," he said, watching Garth do a funny happy dance, flying in dopey circles.

"Do you notice that dogs are heroes, too? Not just people? I can't think of a heroic horse or cat or I don't know, elephant, but there are heroic dogs," I said.

"Cavall, King Arthur's dog," Erik said. "Cerberus, the three-headed guard dog to hell. Argos, who was the only one to recognize Odysseus when he returned to Ithaca after twenty years. Cu Sith, the Scottish demon dog. Anubis, the jackal-headed Egyptian god of the death. Church grims."

"I was thinking Toto and Lassie, but I like that you proved my point." I laughed. "Why the interest in mythology? Why not science fiction or horror?"

"Horror?" He laughed.

"Come on, I know you've read Stephen King," I postulated. "What else?"

"True-life and history," Erik said.

"Ah, here's the meat of things," I said and nodded wisely. "You know, reading isn't something to be ashamed of."

"In this day and age? It's considered quaint, and you know it," Erik said. "Yeah, I do read all the categories previously mentioned, and while I enjoyed them, they don't really do it for me. I can't explain it, but I can never get enough of mythology. And mythology feeds into horror and adventure, but it's the way these stories are shaped that gets me."

"Did Helena agree with you?" I said, then wanted to kick myself.

"Where did that come from?" Erik asked, his eyes steady on me. "Why is she even featuring in your thinking?" Well done, me. Way to make things awkward.

"Yes, I think about Helena. There's no way a girl harasses me this badly unless your relationship ended badly."

"I find it interesting that you know this. You didn't date during high school except for that one date." Erik dug at a pretzel in the ice cream.

"How do you know about that?" I laughed, covering my flushed cheeks with my hands.

"Like I wouldn't know that Manny took you bowling?" Erik asked.

"No, I didn't think you knew nor cared what I was doing. Erik, we didn't talk for four years. Four."

"We didn't talk because I didn't want us to go down this road," Erik said, looking at me in the way I had always wanted him to. "Everyone dies in our story, Callie, and you don't deserve that. You never deserved that. I stayed away, but I always knew where you were. I remember when you made first clarinets in band and went to State with that Weber concerto. I remember when you fell asleep on the soup cans because you had stayed up all night sorting the food donations. I remember when you got so frustrated that you had to retake chemistry. And yes, I remember Manuel." He got up to throw away our trash and I got up, too, because I wanted to be close to him. We started walking toward the giant red lighthouse.

I didn't know what to say. I regretted all of this, and it hadn't even been my choice to regret. We had wasted so many years.

Were we fated to die soon? Would I have felt more strongly about it had we been together all these years? Because I was pretty darned pissed as it was.

"I missed you," I said, because I couldn't think of anything truer. "I didn't want you to stay away."

"I don't want you to die because of me. Again," Erik said simply. We sat like that for a long time, letting the last of the autumn sun illuminate the waves and listening to the cormorants.

"So what you're saying is that I am not your rebound from Helena?" I asked. He blinked and then burst out laughing. I could see a faint blush on his tawny cheeks.

"I am going to confess something that I'm not at all proud of. She was my rebound from you. I don't know if you could classify what we had as 'love'. We hung out a lot and, on my side, it wasn't serious. Then I couldn't live with the lie anymore. It was always going to be you."

"Because of the story," I said. It all made sense now. To Helena, I was the girl who stole her boyfriend. I could almost sympathize if she hadn't gone out of her way to disrupt my life.

"I've known I would love you since I was fourteen," Erik said quietly. I tripped and the situation would have ended badly had Erik not caught me and lowered me carefully onto a bench.

My heart was beating so loud I could hear it. I didn't know what to think.

"How?"

"I visit our cousins in Minnesota every summer. We were playing flag football," Erik said.

"There's no way you guys weren't playing full-contact football," I said absently.

"You would be correct. It was full contact without pads. Freddy back then, he was still weird but not unstable, you know? With some help, he could have been different. He was obsessed with Vikings, TV shows, the mythology, all of it," Erik said. He stopped, staring at nothing, like he was remembering.

"Go on," I urged.

"We were playing, and I was on defense. Freddy had the ball, and George was clearing a path for him. God, I remember this as clear as day. Duston took out George, and I tackled Freddy. He went wild, like he always does, twisting and turning, and I was trying to grip anything I could. I got him on the ground and we rolled, and then George jumped on us. I hit my head pretty bad. I've had concussions before, I play football, but this was different. I started remembering right away, and there was the sound of thunder. The thunder was so loud that it shook the ground, and there was lightning. We all fell down like we were knocked down. Everything you had at homecoming happened to us."

I remembered the colossal headache and the pain all through my body, like I was being electrocuted. I wouldn't wish that on anyone, but I had people trying to help me. I put a hand on his arm, reaching out because I didn't know what to say.

What must it have been like that a family had gone through that alone and couldn't have understood what they were seeing?

"What happened after?" I asked.

"Not a lot. My grandpa gave me the torc, said that because of the summer solstice, and the head hit, the combo made us remember everything. Everyone was in shock. We had all just seen several different versions of my uncles, aunts, and cousins murdering me shoved into our brains. We didn't know what to do. Dad took us home right away. He shoved us into the car, and we were on the road twelve hours until we saw the garage. Wisconsin just flew by. I don't think he really believed they would kill me right then and there, but he wasn't taking any chances."

Erik stared out over the water and we were quiet. Then he pulled my hand through the crook of his elbow and kept his hand over mine, like he wanted to keep me there. We didn't look at each other, and I could savor the contact.

Garth chose that moment to let out a historic fart.

I burst out laughing.

"It sounds like a dying bagpipe," I observed.

"A walk by the sea with a beautiful girl and my farting dog." Erik laughed. "How can you resist me?"

"For our next date, maybe we should go somewhere and have dinner. You know, something simple," I said. I blinked. "Oh. I said that out loud." Then I tried to blend in with the background.

I stared out at the water because I didn't know what else to do. Erik walked in front of me, making me look at him.

"Can I ask you out now? Officially?"

"What?" I said. I am eloquent in times of deep embarrassment. "You want to?" I asked blankly. He laughed at my disbelief.

"Yeah, I do. I'd like to see you without having to make up excuses which, let's be honest, make me seem creepy and weird."

"But you are creepy and weird. That's why I like you," I protested. "You could come to the homecoming game tonight with me."

"I hate football games."

"You're joking."

"I played because we live in Michigan." Erik looked into my eyes. "I was never that into it."

"Oh," I realized. I worried my lower lip with my teeth. I wanted him to come with me.

"You're safe in a crowd," Erik assured me. "I'm not worried about you there. You should go. You haven't seen Trish and Marley in a week. Anyway, I want to give you time to miss me."

"I might panic in a crowd and need a steady hand," I teased.

"You are the farthest thing from panicky. Well, you're panicking a little now," Erik observed gently. "If you want to spend time with the awesomeness that is me, you just have to say so."

"I'm just not sure that this is the right time to be making decisions like this." Why was I protesting? I could not control my mouth. "What if we're letting the stress of the situation provoke abnormal reactions from us?"

"Tell yourself that until the cows come home. After the homecoming game, I'm going to ask you to dinner."

"What happened to not letting otherworldly forces make our decisions for us?" I joked, a little uneasy. Was he asking me because of fate or because he wanted to?

"I'm pretty sure this is me wanting to ask you out and not a previous version of me," Erik said.

"Okay, okay," I said, worried and not understanding why. "Let's see how the night goes. You may not want to ask me out after tonight."

I would give myself the night to be worried and make a decision tomorrow. I wanted to say yes, but something wasn't right.

Maybe it was me.

****

Football games are magic for me. The pageantry and being part of something so vast thrilled me. This was what an autumn Friday night was supposed to be like. The air was crisp and brought all the action on the field into sharp focus.

The bleachers smelled like kettle corn and hotdogs and cotton candy. The familiarity of it all pulled me out of the funk I had been in since I was attacked by ice giants.

This year, though, I wasn't in the marching band. I wasn't going over the music or settled in the bleachers with an eye on the drum major. I felt a twinge about that.

High school was over and it was time to move on. For tonight, I could enjoy myself.

The homecoming game was madness. Alumni from all years milled around, reliving glory days. I didn't want to be down there in the crowd. I was happy in the stands, watching.

Trish huddled next to me. She looked great in a dashing shearling coat and Fair Isle mittens. I was wearing probably the most unflattering red hoodie in all of creation and a beanie Marley had knitted for me years ago.

We passed a cup of hot chocolate between us, and Trish munched on popcorn. Michigan was already cold in September; snow wasn't far off. We had a clear view of the field.

Marley was working concessions since her mom still ran the booster club. We ran out of hot chocolate and I went for more.

Okay, so this next thing was my fault: I was looking at the new band uniforms and wasn't watching where I was going.

Naturally, I ran smack into Helena. She shoved me off, causing me to smack my head hard against a metal lamp post.

"Oh my god, idiot, you can't even walk?" Helena snapped, and her words rang in my ears. For a minute, there were two of her.

"Glad you're here to support the team," I managed to say. For a bad moment, words were hard. *Be civil, be civil*, I repeated in my head. Mom always told me to rise above and have integrity, even when others had none. Ow, my ears were ringing.

"I'm all about team spirit, girl," Helena said, flashing me a toothpaste commercial smile. "How does it feel to be the princess? Enjoy it while you can. You're just the flavor of the week."

"I'm not dating Erik," I told her quietly. "I didn't even start talking to him until after you guys broke up. I've never done anything to you. Can you just leave it?"

"Not," Helena leaned in close, violating every tenet of personal space that had ever existed, "on your life."

"Ladies, you are both looking gorgeous as ever," a deep, friendly voice intervened.

We both turned and stared at the bronze giant smiling benevolently at us. Manuel was wearing a warm plaid over his wrestler shoulders and still sported the most gloriously lush head of ink-black hair I had ever seen.

"Hey, Manuel," I said to my former fry cook and percussions first chair, who must have grown a foot since we graduated.

Helena responded by storming off in a truly glorious stomp of blonde hair. Manuel squinted at me.

"Antagonizing the cheerleaders again?" he asked.

"Not on purpose," I said plaintively. I waved a hand helplessly. "It's just girl crap."

"Since when do you do girl crap with Helena?" Manuel asked, tweaking my collar.

"She thinks I'm dating her ex," I explained. I frowned when I saw how still Manuel got. "It's a misunderstanding. I just wanted hot chocolate." Then I blinked when he handed me a cup, seemingly out of thin air.

"A tribute, dear lady," Manuel said grandly. I started to hand him money and stopped when I saw how insulted he was. I pocketed the cash and took the hot chocolate as graciously as possible.

"You and Erik? I didn't think you guys knew each other," Manuel said. I rolled my eyes.

"We went to elementary school together. It's not romantic. Anyway, forget about that. How are you? I thought you were doing a gap year." He used to wash dishes at the diner before manning the fryer so we knew each other well, probably too well. It was probably why our one date ended in a raucous videogame duel rather than a kiss.

"I made it as far as Guadalajara, visited my cousins, and ran out of money," Manuel admitted.

"Mexico, wow. I've never even made it to Ohio," I said.

"Why would you want to go to Ohio?" he said quizzically, walking me back to the stands.

"I don't actually want to go to Ohio. I meant that I haven't really been anywhere," I explained.

"You should try it sometime. Big, big world out there. As for myself, my days of wandering are at a pause. You know your mom gave me my old job back."

"You want to be our fry cook again? Sorry to tell you, we will not part with Billy the fry. He's ours now— and is unlikely to run off to Mexico."

"My heart bleeds that you won't throw over the newbie for your old faithful. Fear not. I'll be washing dishes, fry cooking, and in charge of the line," Manuel said proudly. "Your grandpa is going to teach me."

"Oh, that's great!" I said, genuinely pleased. Manuel was one of my favorite people in the world, and I had missed him when he was gone on his adventures this summer. Manuel waved as a group of his old buddies caught up with him, and I mouthed a thank-you for the drink.

I was settled back with Trish when I got another surprise visit.

"All right." Duston plopped down next to me, almost making me spill hot chocolate all over him.

"What's the spread?"

Chapter Nine
Homecoming

"Good god, Duston, no one gambles on a high school game," Trish admonished. Then she stared at him. "Do they?" One of Trish's exes popped over to say hi, and Trish left me for a bit to catch up.

"You look like a dweeb, little bird." Duston looked me up and down.

"You're not a sartorial wonder yourself," I snapped. Ooh, my head still hurt from the run-in with Helena. "Little bird?"

"Branwen means 'beautiful raven' in Welsh," Duston explained.

"That's nice. I don't care," I told him firmly. The more I learned about who I used to be, the more I wanted to roll my eyes. As far as I could tell, Branwen's main attributes had been a pretty face and self-pity. "What do you want?"

"I wanted to dwell among the mortals for a night and relive my days as a high school god."

"No, seriously."

"I'm here to watch over you, Callie. Hard as it may be to believe, but homecoming isn't important to me. You want to go to a real game? We should go to Ann Arbor and drink pilsner on the top bleachers. That's football."

"I'm good here, thanks. I don't believe this," I muttered, rubbing my forehead. I think Duston was giving me a migraine.

"You better believe, Callie. There's a chance that we can break from this cycle, and I need you on board."

"I meant that I don't believe I have a headache, not that we're trying to keep Norse giants from beheading me. On that note, you really don't have to sit here, Duston," I said in resignation.

"You're dating my baby brother apparently," Duston said. "I figured I should keep an eye on you."

"We're not dating. We're just keeping close. Strength in numbers."

"As you said, strength in numbers. Stay in sight, okay? We don't know if my cousins are going to come for you tonight, but I'd give it good odds."

"And you're going to stop them?" I asked in exasperation. Did I have aspirin in my bag? If not, I knew Marley had some in hers.

"Since you're refusing to accept your part in the story, I don't really have a choice, do I?"

"Pretend, just for once, that you're a normal person and then go over what you told me last night. Would you accept that?"

"Pretend that you saw my brother take a fire blast for you, and your mother magically levitated frost giants. For Erik's sake, try to make it right for once," Duston said.

"What are you talking about now? Other than criticizing me?" I accused harshly.

"You never change. You always stay stuck in the same rut. That's why you always die," Duston said, his eyes on the field.

"That's not fair," I spluttered. This could not be. Of course I would have fought it if I had known. If this was my mistake, I would have fixed it. Wouldn't I?

"Keep telling yourself that. Maybe you don't want to remember. If you're too scared to embrace that, then you're not the person I thought you were."

"What, not good enough for your brother?" I said without thinking. I almost bit my tongue. Those were Helena's words, not mine. God, my head.

I cared about what Duston thought of me. I cared about them all. Was I scared? I guess I was scared. The person I used to be had broken them all. How could I fix that? Where did I even start?

"I just don't want my brother hurt," Duston said quietly, after thinking for an insultingly long time. "Helena was supposed to be his off-ramp to a different life but he chose you, again. I have hopes for you, but we all need you to step up and fix this."

"When I want you to start making decisions for me, I'll tell you. Can you be quiet please? I want to see the half-time show," I said. I felt off. Something was wrong inside. I could power through it, though. Maybe. "What did I do to deserve you?" I asked rhetorically.

"All women deserve me," Duston said breezily.

"Totally not what I meant, Duston. And from where I'm sitting, you just insulted the entirety of the female gender." Duston's words bounced around my brain, making me cranky. Actually, I was more than cranky. It felt like PMS, but it wasn't the right time of month. I was all out of sorts. Something wasn't right.

"It's all about perspective, Calliope."

"Can you stop being patronizing for one minute?" I said distantly. Then the world went bright, and it was all I could do to stay upright.

"Callie? What's wrong?" I heard Duston say. It seemed like I was getting his words from across a long distance.

"I hit my head," I said vaguely.

Second quarter was almost finished, and people were getting ready to hit the concessions. I couldn't focus. There was a whine. No, it was a scream far, far away. It was getting closer.

That's when the world went mad and I lost my mind.

I convulsed, arching backward sharply. Duston caught me, so fast that it seemed he was waiting for this. He did something, like an illusion or a glamour. I was distantly aware that no one could see us now.

I couldn't really see anymore. Everything was in my head, but it was so real, it could have been a memory. This must be what hallucinating felt like. What I was seeing wasn't my life. It was like watching a movie on fast forward but with my head inside the television set. I was living a life, experiencing everything this other person experienced, in a compressed and increasingly painful fashion.

I don't know how he did it, but Duston slipped me between the seat and the foot boards, underneath the bleachers. Thank goodness, because I didn't have control of my body anymore.

Like a monkey, Duston carried me down, using the steel rebar as if it were a jungle gym. My beanie didn't survive the climb down, but I was in too much sensory overload to care. I was seeing a place I'd never been before, but I had known it my whole life. Green fields and lush woods and a shoreline that went on forever.

None of it was Michigan.

Duston hauled me away from the football field, from the lights and the noise as the halftime show started. My senses had gone so haywire that it all jumbled together into chaos for my brain. I didn't know what was going on, but I had the vague idea that we were headed toward his car.

"Callie?" I heard Trish say. She came running up and caught one side of me. In my head, though, all I could see was Branwen's childhood. A lifetime lived by another person was being shoved wholesale into my head and it was hurting me.

I was playing at my mom's feet by the fire at night. I was riding piggy-back on someone who loved me. I was gathering wildflowers in a meadow. I was walking along the beach on a rainy day.

"What on earth?" Marley demanded, coming up to take my other side as she was pulling on her jacket. "What's going on?" Duston had dragged me halfway across the parking lot.

"What day is it?" Duston suddenly asked. If I had any ounce of control over my body at that moment, I would have smacked him for that inane question. Couldn't he see I was dying?

"What does that have to do with anything?" Marley demanded. She put the back of her hand across my forehead and flinched. "She's ice-cold. What happened? Did she eat something?"

"Crap, it's the equinox." Duston gripped me harder as I jerked like I was having an epileptic fit. "I can't believe we missed this."

I could see a beach. I was on a beach. There was a man lying on the shoreline, wet and cold and unconscious. No, it was a boy. It was Erik. I was there, kneeling in the wet sand, trying to find a pulse on Erik. I was in the parking lot of Bellhaven High, and I was on a rain-swept beach long ago and far away.

Duston's head snapped up, as if he heard something. I heard it also, through the dense monstrosity of my hallucinations. A wolf howled, which didn't make sense because wolves didn't come near populated areas. And then we both felt the snap.

"What was that?" I gasped.

"That was someone breaking the ward on the school," Duston said grimly, baring his teeth against the pain. He seemed to expand. "It was set by my family. Man, that hurts."

"Freddy broke the ward?" I gritted out, swaying. I felt another hallucination coming.

"Seems like. Take her." Duston shoved me at Trish. He was scanning the parking lot. "Get her inside the school. No one can see her like this." Trish nearly let me fall and Marley came up on my other side. Just as they were getting a firm grip, I jerked so violently they both almost dropped me.

I was on the beach that was nowhere I had ever been, but I knew this beach. I had gotten the boy to wake up a bit because I couldn't carry him back, not by myself. It was raining that day. By the time I got him to the edge of my village, I was exhausted and my dress was soaked. My mother and others came running when they saw me.

"What's happening?" Marley gasped, trying to keep a hold of me as I twisted in agony.

"She's remembering her past life," Duston muttered. "One of you needs to get Erik, right now. She'll be fine. We just have to get her away from here." Duston suddenly cursed and shoved us through the glass double doors. Trish and Marley barely kept me from smashing my face into the floor before Duston was beset by a wolf the size of a piano.

Trish gave a little shriek, but my girls had the sense to keep going, away from Duston's struggle. I stared at the brawl between Duston and wolf with disinterest as my mind was completely elsewhere. Duston had a bit more magic, perhaps from the school ward breaking.

The girls got me onto a bench near the cafeteria and I collapsed bonelessly, desperately trying to clear my head. I heard a sharp howl outside and a muffled cheer from the football field. I fleetingly wondered if I had ever attended college in my past lives and if the past few months were the actual hallucination, not this moment of desolation. Then I doubled over in pain and sobbed.

Erik was thrashing, wild with fever. Mom was the best healer in the village, and she took it personally when someone got sick. If anyone could heal Erik, it was her.

Erik was eating, quick and savage, shoving food into his mouth and staring at me like I was going to hurt him or kill him.

Erik was hauling water for our household. He washed more often than we did.

Erik was mending tools and furniture by the fire, the back of one of my chairs, the spit-roast, nets.

I heard a low chuckle that was not at all reassuring. Trish and Marley jerked around. Freddy strode through the empty cafeteria and stared at me intently. George must have been fighting Duston outside the school. Trish moved between me and Freddy while Marley took a firm grip of my arms.

"In every lifetime, it's the same. When he dies, you take our magic and make us human, and then we wait until you put on the triskele again to repeat the curse. Can you imagine how boring that gets?" Freddy said. He ignored the girls, who were both very confused but not budging. Bless them.

"Go," I gasped to the girls. "Get away. You have to get away now!" I groaned and doubled over, again overwhelmed. Instead of the cafeteria, there was a shoreline. Viking ships and a band of men in fur and rough-woven cloth. I recognized Freddy but a dirtier, rougher Freddy. He held up a sword that was coated with blood. I knew whose blood was on the sword.

"Ladies, I don't think we've been properly introduced," Freddy said, strolling forward. The girls snapped into action. Marley hauled me up and Trish took my other arm. They hurried me away from Freddy and into a hallway of lockers. Freddy strolled along after us, whistling.

Marley turned to Freddy, braver than I ever will be.

"Leave or I will call security," she ordered grimly. I briefly lit up, so proud of her. She was going to be an amazing psychiatrist. Right now, she was just my glorious best friend.

"Marley, Marley, Marley, be nice," Freddy said, like they were having a coffee date. "My name is Frederick Janssen. I'm a Scorpio. I was born in Duluth this time because your best friend there destroyed my home, Jötunheimr, and now I'm going to eat Callie's soul. You're Marlene Sutter and here is Tricia Weise. Lovely to meet you both. Now! Let's all work together. Hand Callie over to me."

My vision blurred. Erik was dying. I could actually see dark silhouettes, shoving a sword through Erik's stomach, but at an angle so that they get his heart. I felt Branwen's pain. I was there. I was her.

I remember the terrible gravity in my chest as I stole their magic from them. Such murderers did not deserve their gifts. I could see myself weaving the torrential ocean of power into something different, something sharp, and then I had cast loose the curse that would make them all feel the pain I felt.

Tears were streaming down my face now. I was blinded and hurting.

"Callie, come on, you have to get with it!" Marley hissed in my ear. I was looking out over my village. I was on a cliff, not moving. I could not move. Everything was cold and hard. Then I was stone.

All was dark.

I was gone.

****

I came to as I was slammed into a locker. I wasn't

in a village or on a cliff or by the sea anymore. I was Callie Redmond and some asshole was bullying me in my old high school. Trish was holding me up by her shoulder and Marley was on my other side, staring at Freddy.

"Hurts, doesn't it, Branwen," Freddy growled. Then he lowered his jaw. A howl that hurt my eardrums and crippled my nervous system keened through the air, the wave of the scream hitting us with physical force.

The three of us flew back and slammed into the lockers. Lockers burst open, books, equipment, clothes, and pens spilled out into the hallway. We fell to the ground and were pressed against the lockers by some unseen force like we were being held.

"Don't call me that," I managed to grit out. I couldn't let myself be murdered in a high school of all places. The pain in my brain was still there, but it was more like someone's fingers digging relentlessly into my pressure points rather than a hammer to the head. Freddy bent over me and I could smell his breath. He had eaten sauerkraut recently.

I pushed his face away. We were both shocked when frost formed on his face where I touched him.

"There you are, little goddess," Freddy said tenderly.

"Hey crazy, go away!" Trish yelled, struggling to her feet. Freddy ignored her and reached for me. He almost touched me when a fire extinguisher slammed into the side of his head. I barely registered Erik dropping the fire extinguisher.

Erik yanked me up, and all the girls in turn.

"Get away from here," Erik ordered, but he didn't move to push me away.

"Does my distress summon you or something?" I asked incredulously, clinging to his chest. My legs would not cooperate.

"Kind of, yeah," Erik said. "Duston, get up here!" Duston limped up, the worse for wear from whatever he had been doing with George. He was carrying a red fire ax.

"Look out!" Duston shouted, right before Freddy swung the fire extinguisher at Erik's head. Erik was in motion the moment he heard his brother's voice, shoving me at Trish and Marley. He threw himself the other way so he only caught the fire extinguisher on a shoulder. Erik launched himself at Freddy and they tumbled over and over in the hallway.

"Go," Duston said, pushing me behind him toward the door. "Go now."

"Erik," I said faintly, hanging on to Trish's arm.

"Right behind you," Duston said. Then his knees buckled when George slammed his palms against either side of Duston's head, square on the ears. The fire ax clattered to the ground. George body-slammed Duston into the lockers.

"What are you doing?" Duston gasped blearily, George's forearm across his throat.

"We're going to eat Erik's girlfriend," George informed him gleefully. "I'm going to crack her head open like an egg and scoop out her brain with a melon-baller." At that disturbingly specific description, Duston kneed George in the side and both guys went down.

Marley scooped up the ax and swung the blunt end down into George's stomach like she was hitting a softball. We heard George's breath whoosh out of his lungs. With a viciousness I've never seen in her before, Marley whipped the ax around to slam the blunt end of the ax down on the back of George's head. He went down like a pile of rocks.

I heard Freddy roar. I turned and watched him grow before my eyes. I nearly fell over as another wave of dizziness hit me like slap in the face. I knew the word for these beasts, not because of a tale someone told me, but because I had trouble with them before. Jötunn. Giant.

Freddy's skin iced over and turn blue and gray with cold. Erik's breath chilled in the suddenly cold air and in a blink, Freddy rammed into Erik hard. Erik's head hit the wall with a sickening thud that chilled me more than the sudden atmospheric drop did.

Duston shouted and ran for his brother. I was moving, too, but my mind was not giving the orders. I snatched the ax away from Marley and hurled it down at Freddy, who was now completely blue. The blade of the ax caught Freddy in the shoulder, splattering blood everywhere, and he went down. Duston yanked the ax from Freddy's body before pulling an unsteady Erik toward us.

I have never thrown an ax in my life. I would certainly never throw an ax at an actual person. This was all quite uncharacteristic of me, as was the possible migraine building in my head.

Trish kicked George to the side and took Erik's other arm, which was slick with redness. Erik was bleeding. Duston shoved his brother at us and tossed his shiny new fire ax at Marley, who almost dropped it. He picked up the fire extinguisher and threw it at a column next to Freddy with tremendous force. It burst, spraying foam everywhere and blinding us.

In the distance, I heard the roar of the crowd at the football game. And the pressure in my head was overwhelming. I opened my mouth and screamed, wanting it all to stop, wanting everyone to just be still and relieve the pressure behind my eyes.

The force of an icy hurricane blew the Janssens and the fire extinguishant away from us. Freddy tried to get up, gripping a doorframe, and his lips drew back in a feral snarl.

Freddy and George flickered in my eyes, flipped in on themselves. Suddenly, I was looking at two gargantuan wolves, one with blood dripping from its shoulder. They growled in our direction and then were gone.

I stopped screaming, depleted and exhausted. I fell to my knees and stayed there until Trish and Marley took me by the arms. It took some doing, but they got me walking.

My friends bundled me into the backseat of Duston's Eliminator and Duston threw his brother across the seat, Erik's head landing on my lap. I was present in the now. I was Callie again, not Branwen.

I steadied Erik as best I could, being careful with his head. His height made orienting him a logistical difficulty.

"Look at me," I urged with concern. "How many of me do you see?" Bleary hazel eyes gazed up at me.

"I will love you until the end of the world, even if it's tonight," Erik said, a bit unsteadily. I pushed his hair out of his unfocused eyes.

He gave me a loopy, lop-sided grin.

"I might have a concussion," Erik said.

Chapter Ten
Concussed

"You think?" I said drily. The first time a boy says he loves me and he might have a concussion. It was also questionable if he could call me by the correct name right now.

"They want to eat your soul?" Marley said hysterically. Marley was one of the most composed, assured people I knew, and right now she was holding on to the Eliminator like she was going to fall over. Not five minutes ago, she had beaten down our attacker with a fire ax, and now she was letting the fear bubble up.

"Why did the weird icky guy say that?" Trish demanded. She was shaking and covering it with brash and sass.

"I'll explain," I told the girls. They deserved that. "Just not here." I craned my neck to look back at the school, which did my headache no favors. There was no sign of pursuit. I was not the least bit remorseful that I had thrown an ax at another human being. "Duston, the other people here," I started.

"The jötnar are after you, not alumni and the Booster Club," Duston said. "They're not strong enough to take on that many people. Our shop, it's closed right now, and safe. We can talk there. Trish, follow me."

****

Duston had me call his dad while we were on the way to the shop to tell him where we would be. With a pragmatism that I didn't know he had, Duston bundled us all to the back of the shop, where there was a minimalist seating area.

I was under Erik's arm, urging him on. Duston came up beside me and got Erik into a chair. I wet a rag and fetched the first aid kit from the bathroom for Duston. Distantly, I noted that Duston had braced the fire ax against a cabinet. The school was going to have a heck of a time searching for a missing fire ax and fixing the damage we had caused.

Erik kept an extra shirt in his locker at the shop which I claimed, pretty sure Erik wouldn't mind. I didn't relish running around in bloody clothes, no matter that the blood wasn't mine. The shirt was a very soft faded blue flannel and I swam in it, but Erik's extra belt took care of that. I looked ridiculous, but it was better than looking like I had been run through a wood-chipper.

Duston was not-gently cleaning the back of Erik's head and lecturing him on dropping his weapon. It told me how out of it Erik was that he wasn't making a sound as his brother rubbed away at his open head wound.

I took the rag away from Duston and cleaned Erik's head wound myself, then moved on to the antiseptic. It didn't look like Erik would need stitches. As I finished up, I took stock of my friends. They looked shaken and scared. Marley was sort of listless in her chair, and Trish had gotten up but seemed unsure as to where to go.

"Are you guys okay?" I asked them as I washed my hands in the sink and got Erik some water, after which I then hovered to make sure he could drink on his own.

"I threw up in my mouth a bit," Marley said bemusedly. Then she made a huge shaking, sobbing noise. I threw my arms around her and held her tight. I held her until the shaking went away. The sleeve of Erik's shirt was very good at wiping away tears.

"The whole world's crazy right now," I said. "I'm so sorry."

"Is this your fault?" Trish asked. She was pacing.

Her normal high energy had worked up to a point that it needed physical release, any release.

"Yeah, it sort of is. I'm still trying to get a handle on it myself," I said.

"You better explain what on earth this was all about." Marley faced down Erik.

"Don't yell at him," I said.

"Yeah, we've been protecting her so don't make us the bad guys here," Duston said.

"Yell at him." I indicated Duston.

"Callie, do you know what's going on?" Trish said to me, swiping her blonde hair out of her face.

"Yeah," I said, going over to check on Erik again. It was a cheap excuse to touch him, but I had to reassure myself he was okay.

"And you didn't tell us," Marley said. I finally caught the tone and looked up.

"Correct," I affirmed.

"Right now, you're a terrible friend," Trish said. "Tell us now."

"Can you ladies not do this right now?" Erik said, standing up woozily and abruptly sitting back down again.

"No, we have to tell them," I interjected. "Your cousins went after them tonight."

"Sweetheart, they went after you. Your friends got in their way," Erik said.

"They have a right to know. What they don't know *will* hurt them," I said. Then I turned to my two best friends on earth, who at that moment were as equally interested in my interaction with Erik as with my explanation of why we were just attacked by two psychotic giants.

"Okay, so, a long time ago, a Celtic girl found a Viking boy washed up on the beach," I began. I told them everything I knew as I understood it, from the dreams to the frost giants all the way up to tonight's grand entertainment, and remembering a life I never lived.

Then they stared at me and Erik for a good solid minute of silence.

"Where did this happen the first time?" Marley asked.

"Huh?" I grunted, surprised.

"British Isles? Normandy? Was it Ireland or Scotland?" she pressed.

"I don't know," I said slowly. Marley seemed to be taking this pretty well.

"So, super-basic question." Trish held up a finger. "I thought the Celts and the Vikings were about the same? What's the difference?" I opened my mouth, then shut it with a click. I looked at the brothers.

They both blinked back owlishly.

"There is a difference," I started and stopped again.

"Viking sailors, Celtic farmers," Marley piped up. "That's glossing over a ton of fine points. The Celts also had prodigious interactions with the Roman Empire and had a touch more sophistication."

"Hey now," Duston protested, then paused. "Never mind. We are proud to be barbarians. Makes us tougher than her lot."

"Can we not debate that right now?" I snapped at him. "I just had the mother of all migraines, and your frost giant cousins tried to kill my friends."

"I am sufficiently assured that there is a difference between your two families," Trish interrupted before we started brawling. "Thank you for clarifying."

"When were you going to tell me jötnar can turn into wolves?" I asked.

"Just Freddy and George. The rest of the giants

are only giants, not werewolves."

"Still, that is a mighty big detail I should have known."

"How does Callie have the power to turn gods into mortals?" Marley broke in, still chewing over the story in her mind.

"Three insults avenged in blood," Erik said. "The Vikings insulted Branwen three times, so she was allowed to take her revenge. She took all the magic that made us gods and used it to curse us all."

"What happens when you try to do something else?" Marley said. She frowned at Duston. "Why do you have a constipated look on your face?"

"You think we haven't tried?" Duston said. "I tried to go to Africa last month to volunteer. My flight kept getting canceled, and the refugee camp I was supposed to work at was dismantled. We have no control over our own lives. We don't make our own decisions. The fairy princess here hijacked out destiny."

"And what are you?" Trish demanded. "Are you a god? Were you gods?"

"I don't think god is the right term. We were something else, something magical. When Erik remembered, we all started to remember, and we get fun updates like my cousin going from a world-class jerk to a full-blown demigod. All the gods are waking up before we get to the reset point, which has never happened before," Duston said dourly.

"If humanly possible," Trish said, "you make less sense than usual. Who are you when you're at home?"

"I've had a hundred names, but I used to be Víðarr," Duston said thoughtfully. "Whatever my name, I'm still awesome."

Trish snorted, then fell into a chair, her blue eyes staring off into the distance.

"I hate your cousins," Trish said raggedly.

"So do we," Duston said.

"And I'm still very confused here," Marley declared.

"Yeah, that doesn't go away," I said, fidgeting with the hem of the over-big shirt I was wearing.

"Well, what now?" Marley said. I shrugged.

"Now we try to keep the frost giants from eating Callie's soul," Erik said quietly.

"And if they don't eat my soul," I said, "there's a good chance your family will kill you and then I curse us all to this nightmare again." Erik stroked my hair and I leaned my chin onto his shoulder.

Duston's head snapped up as if he sensed something, and he hurried to the front of the shop to peer out the windows.

"My dad's here," Duston called back. Oh, good. "Callie, your mom's here, too." I covered my eyes with my hands.

"Oh crap," I muttered.

****

Norman hardly blinked when he saw what shape Erik was in, which made me wonder how often the Vanner boys came home with concussions.

Mom came in and did a quick check of the girls and me, then moved on to Erik. Erik was a little surprised to be mothered, but he looked like he needed it. The girls turned on me while Mom clinically checked Erik's head wound.

"Let me be the one to say it out loud: you messed up," Marley said a little sympathetically. "You should have told us. It's out in the open now. We all accept it. Let's move on. Any problems with that?"

I shook my head mutely.

"Hand to god, er, gods," Trish corrected herself,

then shook her head. "Whatever, we'll get through this. Together." She squeezed my hand.

"Marley, call your mom and tell her you're with us," Mom told Marley. "You missed your pick-up." It was Marley's turn to have a constipated look on her face, and she hurried to a corner with her cell phone. Mom put her hand on my shoulder.

"I'm okay," I said faintly. "It hurt when I started remembering, but now, I'm just sort of achy. I'm okay. Do we need a head injury and a celestial event to jog our memory? Is that how this is happening?"

"Your guess is as good as ours," Norm said. "That's what happened to Erik, and it happened to you tonight."

"You're both the main players of the geas," Mom said.

"Players," I said, not a little bitterly. "Someone is playing games with my life."

"That someone may be trying to help," Mom said. "I don't think there has been a single reincarnation in which you both remembered. Intent is an integral part of our magic."

"I would greatly like this visualization exercise to end before my chakras get more out of whack," I tried to joke.

"We can discuss it tomorrow," Mom said. "Let's go home."

"Actually, Mom, Norman," I started. Erik's father looked over. He seemed so tired. "Can I stay with Erik tonight? We have to make sure he wakes up every hour, right?" Marley and Trish stopped preparing to leave to stare at me. Duston had that constipated expression on his face again.

Mom and Norman looked at each other. They had an entire conversation in that one long look.

"I promise, no funny business. He has a traumatic head injury for heaven's sake. He can barely stand," I said. If I could make the issue pre-marital sex as opposed to eons of blood vengeance, I would have won half the battle.

"Erik is about as dangerous as a puppy right now," Duston pointed out.

"I'm the most dangerous of the Æsir," Erik said seriously. "I am Vindler, he of the golden teeth, blower of Gjallarhorn, and your protector from the wind." Then he winced and closed his eyes. Mom sighed and nodded.

Marley squashed a giggle, and I was gifted with a group hug from the best girlfriends this side of heaven.

"You are cuckoo bananas, girl, and I love you," Marley said.

"I second that," Trish said. She took my face in her hands like she used to do when she was teaching me to be aggressive in soccer. "Homecoming prep tomorrow, starting at two. We'll see you soon." Trish pointed at me and waggled her eyebrows evilly.

"Are you having a good day?" Marley asked, squeezing my shoulders.

"Fantastic. I went to a football game, remembered a life I never lived, found out I'm not quite human, and my best friends almost got killed," I summarized drily, my voice low.

"Maybe you'll even lose your virginity tonight," Trish assured me. We all looked at Erik, who may have been asleep on the sofa.

"Let's not get ahead of ourselves," I said. "This homecoming has been too exciting already."

"It's been epic," Marley declared. "Let's try to top it next year." A traitorous voice in my head wondered if there was going to be a next year for me. I quashed that voice ruthlessly.

"My daughter will be very safe tonight." Mom pointed at Norm. There was a warning and a promise of retribution in her voice. Norman gave a little sigh.

"My boys will behave," Norman promised. He then frowned at the fire ax that had inexplicably appeared in his living room.

"Speak for," Duston started, then abruptly grunted when Erik kicked his calf. "Always," Duston amended, with an angelic head-tilt.

The door had to stay open the entire time I was on the Vanner property. Erik wanted to give me his bed, but I stood firm. He was the one with the head wound. Therefore, he was sleeping on the bed.

Duston cleared random guy stuff off the futon in Erik's room, shoving it behind the surfboard in the corner. I felt a deep warmth in my chest. Duston didn't put down a sheet. I suspect he had pulled the lumpy pillow and quilt off his own bed, but it was the effort that counted. I was very thankful that at least this family of Viking gods didn't want to eat my soul and kill me, in that order.

Finally, Erik chased his brother out. And then he wouldn't quit pacing. I settled down on the futon and asked Erik where he went this summer. The guy who was destined to be the love of my life was slightly concussed, and I felt no remorse at leveraging my advantage.

"And no more of those sort-of answers please," I insisted gently. "Why did you want to get away?" Erik stared at me blearily for a moment. He was either going to pass out or be angry at my presumption. Then he plopped down on his desk chair.

"I left because I didn't want this, you know? Freddy was furious when he remembered. He said it should have been him, and he was going to break the cycle and change everything, change our lives. Once I remembered, I kept thinking of all the things that I wanted to do. I wanted to get a scholarship to a decent college and maybe go into engineering. I wouldn't have to play football anymore, I would be the first in my family to get a degree, and I could get a job in Detroit, get out of Bellhaven, but I can't because I'm supposed to die before I can legally drink. Every life we live, it always ends the same way—we fall in love and we die. That's not what I wanted for us," Erik said. I wondered if this was the first time he was confessing out loud.

"Not what you wanted for us. Yes, I remember that conversation distinctly," I said sarcastically, the pain in my heart making my words sharp. He gave me a look and I didn't interrupt him again. He got a good glare from me, though.

"I'm not finished. After graduation, I left town. I went to Duluth and stayed with my cousins. Minnesota is jötnar country, the new Jötunheimr. You can't throw a rock in Duluth without hitting a jötnar. It's something I had been considering for a while. If I stayed away, then we could avoid destiny. Then Freddy and I got into a fight, over what I don't even remember, but that did it for me. That's when I was done fighting. I didn't plan on coming back to see you, but I needed to know if you were okay. And then I would leave Bellhaven for good. None of it, none of this curse would happen if I'm not here. And you'd be happy. And safe."

"And ignorant," I shot back. "I'd be alone, wondering why all these things were happening, why I was feeling these things, and you wouldn't be here." I stopped. Was this me talking or a girl long gone? I had no idea, but I felt like I needed to say it. "I don't know yet if we're going to… Oh, this is ridiculous. We don't even know each other. I don't understand how I could feel this for you. I don't know you anymore."

"And I don't know you. But I remember you," Erik said, squinting because he knew how stupid he sounded.

"This is beyond ridiculous, that we are the way we are because it's how we were in, quite literally, a past life," I said, still trying to reason it out. "That's all in the past. None of this has any bearing on the present. We are not the same people."

"Listen, sweetheart, I don't want this either. I'm not looking forward to a force completely beyond my power telling me who I'm going to love and what I'm going to do. I hate this. I hate having no control over my life."

CONSTANCE KERSAINT

Chapter Eleven
Open Door Policy

The head wound must have shaken something up. Erik would never say something like this if he was in full control.

He stopped and looked at me, really looked at me. My hands were shaking. I could feel it and he could see it. I felt lightheaded and knew that I was paler than usual.

"Hey," Erik said gruffly. "Hey, are you okay?"

"No," I said quietly, secretly delighted that my voice was steadier than I felt. "I am most definitely not okay. You do not yell at me, do you understand? I will not be shouted at."

"Sorry, I'm so sorry," Erik said. I heard the truth in his voice. Stupid head wound. "I didn't mean to yell. I'm not a yeller."

"They went after my friends," I stated. I willed him to understand me and, miraculously, he seemed to.

"It's different when it's just you," Erik said. "I get it. You weren't as shook up after they attacked you, but this time, they went after Trish and Marley, and they can't defend themselves."

I felt one side of my mouth curve up in spite of me.

"You didn't see Marley with the fire ax," I said.

"Well, they won't go down without a fight," Erik amended. "Still, they're normal girls. If my cousins decide to come after them, they don't stand much of a chance."

He knelt down in front of me and took my ice-cold hands in his. He started rubbing my hands between his so that the blood started flowing into my fingers again. My blood was pumping everywhere else at a more

127

rapid pace. I hate to admit that he had that effect on me, but you have a handsome dark Viking rubbing your hands and then you can judge me.

And that was the sticking point, one of many. I didn't know if I was attracted to him because he was an attractive man who was good to me or because in a past life I had cursed us to fall in love again.

"I almost lost them." My voice broke. "They're more than friends. We've been together for as long as I remember. I can't let those monsters come after them. What do I do?"

"You fight, Callie. It's the only thing to do if you want your life back," Erik said.

"Will that end this?" I asked. "So, we find some way to stop your cousins, then what happens? Will things go back to the way they were? You'll be alive. I'll be alive. Then what?"

"Are you talking about us or college?" Erik asked.

"There's an 'us'?" I said frankly. "Erik, are you back in Bellhaven to break a curse or because of me? I won't hold it against you if you just want to be free, but don't lie to me. I'm pretty fed up with being lied to."

"I don't know," Erik said. "That's the truth, Callie. I have no idea if what I feel for you is true or a magic spell. The only thing I know for certain is that the Janssens want to hurt you, and I won't let them."

"Thank you, but I am not your responsibility," I pointed out. "We don't owe each other anything."

"Agree to disagree," Erik said, standing not quite steadily. "I woke up the Janssens. They want to kill you so yes, it is my duty to protect you. I've been doing it for the last four years, and I will keep doing it."

"You ignored me!" I lashed out.

"I was trying to keep you safe! If we never fall in love, you don't have to watch me die," Erik said.

"Does not compute, Erik," I snapped. "We don't die until we're eighteen, so high school doesn't count."

"But I knew!" Erik snapped back. "I knew what would happen. I remember it, Callie, I remember them killing me, over and over again. And that's it for me. I don't ever see you die. I never want to see you die, but I know that you do. And I couldn't take it. Maybe that makes me a coward, but I can't be close to you only to remember that we end badly."

I closed my eyes. I wanted honesty. Way to torture the guy with a concussion.

"Okay," I said. "Okay. We're both awake. We will break the geas together. And then we figure us out, okay? When we're both alive the day after Halloween."

Erik nodded, still not steady on his feet.

"That, I agree to," Erik said.

"You're about to fall down. Will you sit down please?" I begged

"Nah, I got this. Excuse me," he said and wobbled away.

Erik went off into the bathroom across the hall and swung the door closed. The door didn't latch and swung back open, letting me peek into the bathroom. If I had any decency, I would look away. Then Erik pulled off his shirt and threw it in the hamper, which may sound mundane but warmed my stomach in funny ways.

"I don't remember this from my dreams," I muttered.

"What was that?" Erik asked, coming back in and rooting around for a clean t-shirt. I shook my head, averting my eyes. I wondered if he would be this blasé about being shirtless if he was in his right mind.

"I've been dreaming about you. I didn't think those dreams were real," I told him.

"Memories?" Erik asked as he took off his shoes.

"Yeah, memories. Hints of everything I got from the cuimhne tonight."

"Like what?"

"Like in one, we were walking by a lake. In another one, I was cooking and you were building something."

"Were you making a stew or baking?" Erik asked. I blinked.

"Making a stew, rabbit and vegetables. How did you know?" I asked. He looked at me and I nodded. "Memories. Gotcha."

"I was fixing your mom's loom," Erik said distantly. He rubbed his forehead and looked at me. "How's your head now?" Erik asked. I snorted, finding this comment funny coming from the guy with a concussion.

"Better. I'm not being overwhelmed by someone else's memories. Well, they still pop up but only in spurts as opposed to this deluge that floors me," I said. "How did you know I had a headache?"

"I can tell. I know when you're upset."

"Uh," I stuttered, unsure of how creeped out I should be.

"I can't read your mind. I can just tell when you're feeling something strongly," he reassured me. I was a little mollified. Mostly I was overwhelmed. But it was almost eleven at night, and that meant one thing.

"Listen," I said, holding up a finger. Erik tilted his head and then he heard it, the train whistle. Every night, my entire life, I heard a train whistle at eleven. It was usually a sign that I was up too late and needed to sleep before my mom came in and caught me reading. It was also something that marked the end of my day, a constant that never failed. I would hear the train whistle at eleven at night, and all was right with the world.

"Every night, like clockwork," I said. I turned around and saw Erik's chin resting against his chest.

I snorted and gently pushed Erik down into the bed. He plopped back softly and didn't wake up. I pulled his legs up and covered him up with his comforter.

Garth trotted into the room. The enormous hound leapt onto the bed and eventually found his comfortable spot. I appreciated my new chaperon and gave him a quick scratch behind his ear.

I am not a saint, so I made no apologies for poking around Erik's room. It was fairly neat and organized, where I had expected a violent disarray. Garth watched me for a while with his muzzle between his paws, then fell asleep.

Clearly, my old crush and partner in destiny had a curious mind and a thorough work ethic. He had connector sets and Xbox games huddled up against ancient science fiction books. I picked up a palm-sized hunk of crystal to peruse the science magazines underneath. His e-reader was low on charge and I plugged it in.

Pulling out a book of Norse myths for myself, I let my fingers drift over Erik one last time, just to check on him, I told myself. Brushing his hair back from his forehead, I settled down on the futon with the book and set my phone alarm to check on Erik in an hour.

I had family and friends I could depend on. Hopes and dreams. There were people in the world who didn't want to kill me. Thank the gods for small favors.

****

After waking Erik up again at seven in the morning, I whipped up some French toast and corned beef hash for the Vanners. No one was more shocked than the Vanner men that all the ingredients were present in the Vanner kitchen. Garth begged so politely that I had to give him some hash.

Norman checked Erik and proclaimed the concussion too slight to warrant my attention any longer. With no pretext to stay, I made my excuses and Duston dropped me off at home, chomping on French toast folded with crunchy peanut butter. Erik had pressed a book in my hands before I left, so he could still be a touch concussed. A book is not really what a girl wants after a night in a guy's room.

Mom sent me straight to bed when she saw me sleep-walking through the kitchen, and then I was awoken promptly at one thirty by the two harpies I called friends. They had broken into my bedroom to politely make sure I would be on time for homecoming prep. Marley had fired up her mom's tablet so we could research while we primped. Never let it be said that we couldn't multi-task.

"Okay, says here that tribes in Norway used to practice ritual human sacrifice," Marley said, tapping delicately to not ruin the fresh manicure I had just given her.

"Skip it," I said as I tottered around in heels.

"You're dating a Viking, whose cousin wants to make you a ritual sacrifice. You should know these things," Marley pointed out.

"No ritual human sacrifice," I said firmly. "Skip it for right now. And we're not dating." Trish's snort could have put a horse to shame, and she caught me before I fell over an ottoman.

"How does anyone walk in these things?" I asked.

"Like dancing, you don't overthink it. Look, you have to loosen up." Trish slipped on a pair of four-inch teal pumps and walked toward me like she was in tennis shoes. "You want to step down at the center of the foot, not the heel or the toe. Sway your hips with it. Later we'll work on the clomping issue."

I aimed for my dresser and was surprised I made it without falling over. Trish insisted I try with the three-inch heels first. I asked if she had anything more sensible and she looked at me blankly, asking what the point would be. I said my boots would be fine tonight, to Trish's deep disappointment.

Trish made me sit down so she could straighten my hair. Marley patted me on the shoulder, then leaned forward to look at something on me.

"This is the triskele?" Marley asked, pulling my triskele out from my collar.

"Yup. It's like a cursed object. My father, who died a few months ago, mailed this to me a few days ago. I put on the necklace and boom! Groundhog day," I said, keeping very still for fear of the curling iron.

Marley set the triskele down on my shirt, and I felt the heavy weight on my chest. I wondered then about the other wearers, my previous incarnations. What had those girls been like? Had they been loved? What had they hoped to do with their lives before they died tragically?

"You put on the cursed necklace and live out the crappy fairy tale?" Trish summarized.

"And your father, who has been deceased for a few months, mailed this to you last week?" Marley frowned. "That doesn't sound right."

"Yup, that is my life right now." I sighed. "How are you guys taking this so well? I sound insane."

"You are insane," Marley said. "However, we saw your boyfriend punch a werewolf across a hallway."

"Erik's not my boyfriend," I insisted. "And the Janssens are frost giants, not werewolves. I don't know why they can turn into wolves but they can."

"It's just easier for us to say 'boyfriend' as

opposed to 'reincarnation of Viking demigod who is destined to die because he fell in love with you'. Now, dangly earrings or swingy drops?" Trish asked, holding up my options.

****

We cruised Main Street. It had taken enormous effort on the part of my friends and the Vanner boys, but Mom finally relented with multiple conditions pertaining to safety. I didn't even have to play my trump card, the fact that I'm eighteen and legally an adult.

Anyway, I thought this would be the one and only time we would do this. Trish and Marley were off with their future and soon, they would be beyond small-town traditions. Soon, I would be beyond this, too, but I wanted to indulge in a bit of nostalgia first.

I grew up here, Bellhaven being all I have ever known. I knew exactly what would happen every single day. I knew I couldn't stay here forever, but I would miss it.

This was nice, though. I felt like I was saying goodbye. I breathed in my last cool breath of childhood. It felt like an ending of something anyway.

I was lucky to be in good company.

I leaned my head against my arm and caught my reflection in the side mirror. The triskele was visible underneath my collar. It was always heavier than it looked. Apparently the other incarnations never remembered the geas. I remembered. Maybe this time would be different. Then the limestone gothic façade of the Caledonian appeared and I put all thoughts of curses away.

The homecoming dance was always at our town's one and only hotel, the Caledonian. I don't know which millionaire decided to construct an art deco-style hotel in our tiny seaside town, but we put it to good use. I had many dances and my high school graduation here.

We cruised slowly past the hotel along with the caravan of other cars, watching the kids arriving like kings and queens. This was their night, not ours.

We couldn't even think about sneaking into a bar because we knew everyone. Trish was tapping away at her phone with much determination and then ordered us to park behind the Caledonian. It was, not shockingly, packed and we found a spot quite a walk away. When we entered, we were engulfed in a deluge of acquaintances.

A group of alumni, including half of our high school class, were holding an impromptu gathering in the hotel restaurant. Once inside, the girls tried to stay with me, but I shoved them off to talk to everyone else, who all wanted to catch up on what had happened in the whole four months since we had all last seen each other.

"Are you okay?" Erik asked, handing me some punch. I took a sip to buy time and then focused on not spewing punch all over my date.

"This is spiked," I informed him, coughing.

"Really?" he said blandly, taking a huge quaff. "I hadn't noticed Duston pouring gin into the bowl." I made a wheezing noise because I hated gin and resolved to hold the punch, as opposed to getting trashed. I wanted to save that experience for a time when no one was actively trying to kill me.

"Yeah," I said. "Still a little shaky, but fine. You're the one with the concussion. I'm more concerned about you." He looked at me closely, and I knew he saw bags under my eyes. It had been a few nights since I had some good sleep. Every time I closed my eyes, generations of homicide awaited me.

"I promise, you'll be okay today," Erik swore.

"What have we here?" a brittle voice asked. My contentment turned to abject dislike in an instant. Helena surveyed all of us with hard eyes. She was so gorgeous, pageant-level stunning, but those eyes were what you noticed first. It's hard to think of a person as beautiful when they clearly wanted to vivisect you alive.

"Hi, Helena," I said in resignation. She didn't even look at me. Her eyes were on the tall, handsome guy that we most certainly were not fighting over.

"You are so adorable," Helena cooed. I noted, with much respect for the game, that she was wearing a silky silver top that kept threatening to fall off her shoulders. She had a silver chain wrapped several times around her neck. I would have looked ridiculous in that outfit, and she looked like she belonged on a magazine cover. I could never look like that.

"I'm about to vomit all over my shoes, you're so cute. I can't believe you're so brave to be seen in public with," here Helena paused for dramatic affect as she eyed me up and down, "trailer-park trash."

"That's enough, Helena," Erik snapped.

"Not even close, babes," Helena shot back. "The least you could do is save me some face by hitting on the rebound girl in private. I don't need this drama."

She's jealous and hurt, I realized. And Erik still cared enough that he didn't want to offend her unnecessarily. How on earth was I supposed to rise above this?

Erik and Helena were both staring at me. I knew I had the sleepy look on my face I always got when I was speculating. I think they both knew what I was thinking, though, because Helena looked even more enraged than I thought possible, and Erik looked faintly worried.

Sweet boy. I think I'll keep him.

And my posse swept in at exactly that moment to help me out. Trish came over with perhaps three ex-boyfriends in tow. Marley suddenly appeared with most of her old cheer squad and what was most certainly not a mocktail.

"Oh, girl," Trish said sweetly to Helena, "you might want to look into adding wheatgrass to your diet or something. You look a little green."

Helena left abruptly, causing the cheer group to murmur. We stared at Trish.

"You fight bitch with bitch," Trish murmured to us. I hugged her, and Erik whistled reverently. "I mean, honestly, what was she going to say? This is her version of taking the high road as opposed to getting into a catfight with me. These are basics, people."

"Is there anything better than my girl here?" I said to Erik proudly.

"Me." Duston popped up next to Marley, like a good-looking jack-in-the-box. Marley yelped in surprise, smacked his arm hard, and almost splashed her drink on him.

"No, no, don't hurt the handsome one!" Duston cried in mock-horror. He deftly rescued Marley's drink and took a sip. "Is there bourbon in here?"

"Mine." Trish took the drink as her own and turned to her coterie of love-slaves.

"I don't know what I did to deserve that." Duston rubbed his arm.

"It beggars the imagination," Marley agreed with him. She let Erik tease his brother and took me a little apart from the others. Marley put her palms on my cheeks, just like she had when we were eight and I was too timid to go up against a particularly aggressive forward in soccer. She repeated the same words she said to me then.

"Do *not* let her push you around," Marley said firmly. I took her hands in mine and squeezed. "You understand me, Redmond?"

"Oh, yes, ma'am," I said grimly.

"Excellent. Now, the banquet rooms down the hall are empty and unlocked. Go get some privacy," Marley said.

"Marley!" I laughed and we hugged. Then Marley winced.

"What's up?" I murmured.

"Cramps," she said ruefully.

"You already took Motrin?"

"This morning," she said. "I was fine until just now."

"None in your bag?"

"Nope. I'm okay."

"Yes, you will be," I said. "I left some in your car last month. I'll be back." I couldn't see Erik anymore. I assumed his old teammates had found him.

"Callie," Marley said warningly. I took the keys from her bag anyway.

"We're in public. Nothing's going to happen here. It'll be okay," I reassured her. I made my way out of the hotel restaurant and to the parking lot at the back of the hotel. I was almost to the doors when I noticed something out of the windows and stopped.

Erik was in the parking lot, walking behind a copse of trees. When had he left the party? Why was he there? Following the unease in my gut, I quickly texted Duston, then pushed out through the door.

I wasn't being jealous. I was being careful with a possibly homicidal, definitely vengeful ex-girlfriend.

Every light in the parking lot was on, and I could see as clear as day. There were still enough shadows for me to follow unobtrusively. I kept close to the edges and paused by the bollards of the parking lot entrance. I had the same pressure behind my eyes that I had last night at the school. I kept a tight lid on it because I didn't need a headache right this second.

Erik stopped between two rows of cars and looked around. Then she suddenly appeared. Helena, again. Her silver necklace gleamed brightly in the halogen light as she waited for her ex-boyfriend.

CONSTANCE KERSAINT

Chapter Twelve
Secrets We Keep

I hated her. What was the point of taking the high road? The world was so supremely unfair to gift her, the one born into privilege, with so many gifts while I was given scraps and made to fight for what I have. The pressure in my head grew and I fisted my hands.

They were talking and I felt some shame. I shouldn't have texted Duston. My gut had lied to me. There was nothing going on here, just two exes having a friendly conversation, alone in the moonlight.

I was still angry, though, and I hated this whole situation. Look at me, skulking around a parking lot, spying on my date and his ex. How much lower could I go?

As I pondered how to maturely deal with this, Helena moved in close to Erik. And he let her. Absently, I noted that she very pointedly wasn't wearing a bra.

They looked ridiculously good together. Him, with his tall, dark, and handsomeness. She, in all her blonde, former homecoming queen glory.

Helena put a palm on Erik's chest. He didn't move. I didn't breathe.

I was about to leave and find my way home when Helena whipped the silver chain off her neck. In a flash, the necklace seemed to lengthen. With a quick wrist flick, she had the silver chain wrapped around Erik's neck, where it tightened on its own.

Apparently, I wasn't the only one with a magic necklace. *Game on, bitch.*

I didn't even notice the cool pressure in my head releasing as I gripped a bollard, letting me break the thick concrete pole from the ground. I threw the heavy thing at

Helena. I'm a terrible aim, but I wanted the bollard to smack her hard and avoid Erik, and it did exactly what I wanted it to.

Helena wasn't even on the ground when I reached Erik's side. I started to unwrap the chain from his neck, but surprisingly, Helena was moving. I abandoned my date and dashed over to her, shoving her back down hard and pinning her with the bollard.

It was savage and I did not apologize. Being nice had taken no affect previously.

In the back of my head, I knew I should not have been able to lift the bollard. None of this was possible. I ignored that fact because I was sick to death of being on the defensive.

"We're going to talk," I said, a little angry. I squinted. There was something about her face that was bugging me, other than its perfection.

"What is it about you? Why does he keep coming back to you and not me? You're so bland." Helena didn't even sound winded with the heavy concrete bollard weighing her down. Definitely magic. I'm going to guess she was a Valkyrie or something cooler than me.

Seriously. Fairy. Ugh.

"I find it odd that you keep personally insulting me," I told Helena. It struck me: she looked like the Janssens. "Makes me think that you don't feel so good about yourself. And you're not talking like this is the first time Erik has come back to me. How are you related to the Janssens?" The blonde had the nerve to laugh at me. She wasn't even fazed.

"He didn't tell you? Well done, babes," Helena said to Erik. Poor guy was still not one hundred percent from his concussion. The chain glowing around his neck might also have had something to do with it.

I looked closer and saw a glaze over his eyes. The

bitch was hurting him. Oh, of all the ways to make me angrier.

I lifted the bollard, then viciously slammed it down on Helena again. She grunted and I heard something snap. I think I snapped her rib, but I would not apologize.

"What's going on?" Erik asked unsteadily. I ignored him and twisted the bollard down on Helena. She took it well, better than a normal person should. She glared at me like I smelled bad and tried to get a grip on the bollard.

I could not let this become a tug-of-war, metaphorically or physically.

"The Janssens," I said grimly. "Are you one of them? You seem to know an awful lot about what's going on."

"They're my cousins," Helena spat.

I blinked. That was not what I expected. Also, *ew*.

"You know," I realized. "You know what's going on. Are you helping them?"

Helena's face twisted and became ugly. With a mighty scream, she twisted the bollard off herself and swung it at my head. I ducked low. The concrete pillar whooshed over my head, ruffling my hair. Then her back was to me.

I shoved my shoulder into her back and slammed her hard into a car. That should have knocked the wind out of her, but Helena twisted. Then I was busy keeping her from clawing my eyes out. I slammed a palm up against her jaw and was gratified to see a tooth go flying.

I have never been a violent person. My body was fighting Helena, but I wasn't driving it. This instinct toward immediate aggression was not something I ever had. I would have a breakdown about this later.

"Who were you that first time?" I said, shoving

my foot against her abdomen. She landed on her butt and I tried to flip her over with my foot. Helena grabbed my foot and twisted. I flipped myself with it to keep my ankle bones intact and ended up on the ground.

Manuel had been a wrestler. I learned a thing or two between shifts from my fry cook, specifically that I did not want to be flat on my back in a fight.

Helena straddled me and I bucked my hips hard, throwing her to the side. She landed on her shoulder, and I quickly got on top of her back. I drove my elbow between her shoulder blades.

"Valkyrie? Farmer? Princess? Who were you?" I shouted.

"I am the most dread of goddesses," Helena hissed. "I housed the dead and my servants are legion." I frowned at her until my brain found the correct reference. It took a few moments because Norse mythology is not my strong suit.

"Hel," I realized. "You were the ruler of Hel? Why on earth are you so obsessed with Erik?"

"We were betrothed! There was an understanding! Silver and livestock had changed hands," Helena snapped at me, struggling to her feet. I ruthlessly snaked an arm under one of her armpits from behind, then put my palm on the back of her head, like Lou had shown me once. Her other shoulder was grinding against the pavement. I thought I could break it.

"Well, if he traded cows for you, of course you were engaged!" I snapped, then heaved a big breath. A little class, I reminded myself. From the way she was speaking, I wasn't even sure she remembered who Helena was anymore. "Do you think he'll take you back after this, you moron?" I asked. "Lying to a guy and killing his date isn't winning you any points here."

"Welcome to the last thousand years of my life,"

Helena snapped at me. Then she started to sob, which made me feel horrible. "He was supposed to be with me. He was always meant to find me and love me. Then you stole him, you slut. He would have been happy with me. I could have made him happy. He could have lived if he had chosen me."

I opened my mouth to calm her down when suddenly my brain pieced it all together.

Oh shit. *That bitch.*

I released my hold and flipped her over. I dug my heel against her throat and used the leverage to get up.

"Is that what happened?" I asked. "Did you give him that choice on the beach? Choose you and live or choose me and die?"

Helena stopped fighting. Her stillness answered my question. I looked up at Erik. I could see so much betrayal and horror on his face that I had to look away.

"Did you?" Erik asked quietly. Helena sobbed.

"You lured Erik to the beach that night, the night they killed him," I said. I read the way her face abruptly twisted, and I knew it to be true. "Just like tonight, when you lured Erik to the parking lot."

Helena said nothing, and her crying became sobs.

"How could you?" Erik said. "I never remembered why I went to my own death, but this makes sense. I would have come to meet you, of course I would have. Have you always known that you caused my murder?"

"Please listen to me. I'm trying to save you. Just come with me. Choose me and it will be fine. Everything will be fine. Please, it's the only way they won't kill you," Helena wept desperately.

I heard Helena draw ragged breaths under my heel, but I didn't care. I was worried about Erik. His face had the stony cast it took on when he was trying to control his emotions.

Duston came up with Helena's silver chain wrapped around a wrist and the fire ax in hand. He better give that ax back to the school at some point because petty theft is the start of a slippery slope.

"You gave the signal for the jötnar to attack me. You killed me," Erik said slowly.

"I only told them where you'd be," Helena said. "I swear, babes, I didn't know they were going to kill you. Erik, I thought we were going to snatch you and bring you home, with us, where you belong."

"Lie," Duston said. He sounded tired. "When Erik rejected you, you lit the bonfire with magic and called your brothers. You had me tied to a tree. Don't you remember that? I watched it all."

Erik gave his brother a look, and I knew they would have it out later.

"You betrayed us then. You betrayed us every time since," Erik accused. Duston came over to me, ax at the ready.

"Can't you see that she's wrong for you! She's not one of us. I'm the one you're meant to be with! I'm your destiny. I don't know why you keep choosing her, every time!" Helena pleaded, her eyes wet with tears.

"Helena." Erik shook his head. "We're over. We've been over for a long time. You have to let it go."

The look on her face almost broke my heart.

"You don't mean that," Helena pleaded. The beautiful blonde who had been homecoming queen and head cheerleader was on her knees, begging. I would have been heartless not to feel a little bad for her.

"You keep trying to hurt the people I care for. Helena, you betrayed me. You had me killed. We're never coming back from that," Erik said with finality. Helena's face twisted and she threw me off like I weighed nothing.

A car hood broke my fall. It hurt, to say the least.

As I was remembering how to breathe, I watched Duston advance toward the crying blonde. He fared about the same as me.

Helena shoved at his stomach, and Duston smacked into a truck, his momentum shoving the truck a good three feet into the car on the other side of it. Nordic gods are made of stern stuff.

The goddess of the dead turned to her ex-boyfriend. There was something else in her face now, tear-stained and mascara-streaked as it was.

"I tell Freddy where to find her and he keeps screwing it up," Helena said to Erik. "Maybe you're right. Maybe we are done. If so, all I want now is for them to hunt you down and make you pay." Ah, there she was. This was the girl who had been gunning for me since day one.

I slid slowly down the hood, because heaven knows I hurt too much to get down on my own. Maybe I would be okay by the time my boots hit the ground.

My boots hit the ground. Then I was blindsided by what I suspected was a frost giant in wolf form. Its shoulder slammed into my ribs, because I think it missed what it was aiming for.

I gripped my hands together and brought my elbow down on the head of the wolf, who was snapping at me. I grabbed the scruff of his neck and threw myself over his back.

I wrapped my arm around the wolf's neck. It had to be George. I was almost certain of it, from the light fur to the dumb look in his eyes, present even when he was an actual animal. I caught a glimpse of Duston struggling with a darker wolf with a bloody shoulder, who must be Freddy. I was a little pleased that the wound I had given him was still there.

I couldn't make out what Erik and Helena were doing, but she was hanging on to his arm and he was, if I was not mistaken, trying to get her off without hurting her.

George-wolf attempted a death roll. He was so much stronger than me, so I went with it and added some weight of my own into the roll. Our momentum let me slam George's head into the nose of a truck. He went limp. It was very difficult to extricate myself from his dead weight.

I felt it again, that pressure in my head. This was all new to me, having been born yesterday, but I had a new tool and I would use it.

"I don't want us to be like this," Helena pleaded with Erik.

"We don't give a good goddamn what you want," I said as I took her hand off of Erik and twisted hard, hearing a dull break, then her screaming. She had been begging for a fight, and I felt like giving her one. I threw her away with sudden god-like strength, and she landed hard on the cement.

I started walking toward her as she got to her feet, one arm dangling uselessly. Helena then ripped a bike rack from the ground and threw it at me. I barely dodged it.

"I am the goddess of the dead!" Helena snarled at me. "You can't take me, you little bitch."

"What you are is a pain," I gritted out. The pressure in my head was now coursing down my limbs, and I got a good grip on the wheel well of a car. Bracing my feet, I pivoted and threw a car at her.

The car came crashing down, breaking the pavement. I ran to the overturned car and couldn't find a trace of her. I pushed the car to the side and there was nothing, no blood, no body, nothing.

"That's enough!"

I whipped around and saw something horrifying.

Sheriff Lou Loggins was there, staring at me. I turned back to the tableau and saw the Janssens on the ground, the cars wrecked, the bollards in pieces, but there was one detail that stuck out to me.

Helena was gone.

****

"Let's get something straight," I said evenly, "you dated your cousin?"

"We're not related by blood," Erik protested. "Her aunt married my uncle's son-in-law. There is no blood relation here."

"You can think that if you want," Duston said. "It's still gross." Erik growled at his brother. "What? We always thought so, but you wouldn't listen."

I sat down hard in a plastic chair. We were once again in the waiting area of Vanner Automotive. Earlier, in the parking lot, we had all frozen, not knowing how to explain the chaos to the sheriff. Lou had stared at me, after surveying the damage and the two delinquents on the ground, and had told the three of us to leave immediately before the deputies arrived.

I had stared at Lou, uncomprehending, until the Vanner brothers had hurried me away. I had texted Trish and Marley about tucking the car keys under the floor mat on the driver side. They were supposed to sleep over at my place that night, but I wasn't thinking that far ahead.

Why did Lou let us go? Was he one of us? Or did he do it because he knew me, had watched me grow up?

Erik marched over to hand me a cup of hot tea. Duston followed more leisurely, ax slung over his shoulder.

"You look like hell," Duston said to me.

"Shut up," I told him, then looked at Erik. "You could have told me your ex was the goddess of the dead and, more importantly, related to you," I said. He opened his mouth, then closed it again. Smart boy. "I don't understand how you could date her after how she betrayed you."

"He never knew," Duston said, working the vending machine.

"What?" I snapped.

"He never knew Helena lured Erik to the beach that night, in the storm, so that her cousins could murder him," Duston shouted at me, his face contorted.

I wasn't the only person who was angry. In fact, I had less reason to be upset than them. I had unearthed a secret held for eons. Yay, me.

"I'm sorry." Duston rubbed his face roughly, then tapped the vending machine. Two bags of chips dropped down, as if by magic, and he tossed me a bag.

"You could have warned me," Erik told his brother, his eyes far away. "I didn't know she betrayed me. That part of the story was never clear."

At any other time, I would be trying to empathize with his betrayal, but I was numb. I still felt a heaviness around my heart and this was too much, far too much. How could so much change in two weeks.

"Are you okay?" Erik asked me. I stared up at him. I was still trying to come to grips with the power coursing through my veins, but he had just discovered the source of an old betrayal. He stepped closer to me. "Where do you feel it? In your head, behind your eyes?"

I stared at him, eyes round.

"In my head. There's like a weight or pressure inside my head," I tried to explain. He nodded.

"That's how it builds. You have to let it go. You

can't keep it inside of you. Let it flow down."

I was doing it before he finished speaking. I let it all flow out of me, dissipating into the ground. Soon, I was just boneless. I didn't think I could bring it back, whatever it was.

"Lou shouldn't have let us go," Duston said, gnawing on a pretzel. "We should be at the station right now."

"He probably let us go because of Callie," Erik said.

"It shouldn't have mattered if she's his favorite person in the world. You find suspicious people with two unconscious bodies in a wrecked parking lot, you bring them in for questioning. Lou is not incompetent."

"It doesn't matter," I said. "He did, and we won't mention it again."

"The town sheriff lets three suspects leave a crime scene and we're not going to mention it again?" Duston scoffed.

"Exactly," I snapped, "because in the grand scheme of things, that's just one less problem to deal with. Listen, can someone take me home?" Surprisingly, I had finished the tea and chips.

"I'll drive you home," Erik said. I nodded.

CONSTANCE KERSAINT

Chapter Thirteen
The Old Way

"This is a tragedy wrapped in a horror story then set on fire." I looked up from my book. I was sitting at the couch with my books, working on my second pot of tea.

I had texted with Erik, who reported that the Janssens were in county lock-up and Helena was nowhere to be found. I was doing more research with Mom while she made lunch. I don't think she quite enjoyed me talking about murder, death, and curses, but I was woefully behind the curve and I needed her brain.

"Branwen was a victim her entire life. She got everyone killed. Literally. An entire country was decimated because of her. This is a tragedy. I'm a reincarnated tragedy." I looked at my notes. I mapped out destinies with my pencil, my lines crossing each other until I had a spiderweb all over my notebook.

"The previous incarnations of Branwen were tragedies, yes." Mom set a cudighi in front of me. She looked me in the eye. "Then one day, a Branwen saved the life of a Viking boy."

"And then I became a different tragedy. How do I go from battered housewife to perpetual bastard?" I complained, setting the book aside.

"Language," Mom warned, biting into her sandwich

"I use the word in the technical sense, not the derogatory," I sulked, then bit into my own sandwich. The spicy sausage and marinara lifted my spirits.

"You should be proud that you've proven our destiny isn't set in stone. It's an achievement."

"Very glass half full, Mom." I chuckled around a

bite of sandwich.

"Don't talk with your mouth full. Are you done feeling sorry for yourself?" Mom asked. I chewed thoughtfully.

"I guess. It makes me wonder, what would we be like if we were still locked in the old story? Would I be dating a brain surgeon who would eventually lock me in his kitchen?"

"Let us be grateful you were raised better than that," Mom said drily. "Sometimes we surprise destiny. I fell in love with your father, a Welsh prince. We had you and you outdid all of us by falling in love with a Viking god," Mom finished. "You are no longer in the Mabinogion. You are not a princess sold into marriage and abused by her husband. You are not the daughter of the village witch. You are Calliope Redmond, born and raised in Bellhaven. Your destiny is yours to write, and that is frightening to everyone else."

We ate in silence for a while, and I digested the idea.

"Do you know what is actually frightening? I have super-strength. I ripped up a parking lot like it was nothing. I fought another person, actually fought, and I don't have a scratch on me. I didn't mean to do any of that," I said slowly.

"You'll do it again, because you won't stand on the sidelines when people are coming for you and those you love. This is who you are," Mom said.

"I don't want to be a monster," I insisted. "That was horrible. I deliberately hurt someone."

"Who was trying to hurt you," Mom pointed out. "You are Tuatha. You have the power to do anything you want. Protecting your friends isn't a horrible thing."

"It's too much," I said, washing my plate. "Things are going too fast and this is all too much. No. I'm not using some mystical energy I have no right to."

"Listen to me." Mom squeezed my hand. "You're not a monster. You're Callie. Just because you remembered you're a fairy doesn't make you a monster. It just adds to you. This doesn't change who you are, just what you can do."

"I'm a fairy?" I said blankly. "Oh yeah, Tuatha. I'll be honest, that's not very encouraging. I don't like glitter, and I don't plan on flying around granting wishes."

"That's not how this works," Mom said. "I will show you. Put on some pants. We're going to the woods."

****

An hour later, Mom and I emerged into a clearing, deep in the green. We had parked a quarter mile back. I had no idea where we were.

"Don't lose me," I said, looking around. It was so beautiful and peaceful here.

"You'll never be lost again," Mom said as a breeze swirled around us. I squinted. I couldn't see what she was doing, but I could feel it.

"That's you, isn't it?" I said, turning. The breeze gently ruffled my hair and batted at my jacket. I remembered the stray breeze I had thrown at the Janssens wildly. This was different, but similar.

"The most basic truth you have to learn is that you aren't wedded to the land or a tree hugger or someone who enjoys nature. You *are* the land. Nature is you," Mom said. "The Tuatha are of the earth, and the air, and the sunlight, and the water. You've been tapping into the essence of our kind unconsciously, and now it's time to do it on purpose. Callie, close your eyes," Mom said. I obeyed my mother. "Take a deep breath and think of your breathing. Breathe in all that is good in the world and breathe out all your problems, everything that troubles you. Your breathing is the engine of your body and your connection to the world."

I was conscious of my breathing, strong and steady. I started listening to it, filling my lungs and the whoosh of it leaving my body. Suddenly, I saw the world around me even though my eyes were closed. This was new.

"I see every blade of grass," I said to my mother, my eyes still closed. "I see all the birds in the trees, every leaf, the worms in the earth. I feel it all."

"Never try to force anything and always know your limit. If you have to force it, it probably wasn't meant to be and you've wasted your energy. If you don't set a limit, you can burn yourself out. You said on Friday night, you felt tired after using the wind to knock Helena down, right? You were tired because you ripped the breeze from where it was originally going and forced it to knock her over. It would have been easier to lead the breeze to where you wanted it to go and then ask it to speed up. You also didn't limit yourself to what you were taking in. Try it now," Mom said.

"I didn't understand half of what you said," I protested.

"Try it," Mom insisted. My first attempt was futile. My second attempt was just clumsy.

"Don't try to be gentle. Be firm," Mom suggested. She made it sound so easy. My third attempt was still miserable. In half an hour, I was covered in sweat and could move my mom's hair a bit. It was exhausting.

"It takes time and practice," Mom said.

"Yes, but someone is trying to kill me now," I said plaintively, Then I turned toward the east, sensing an approach. A very fast approach.

"Mom," I managed to say before the wolf burst

into the clearing. It never got to us. Tree branches whipped down and smacked the wolf back.

Mom guided the trees with such grace and finesse that I felt like an amateur.

"George," my mother said. She tilted her head, and I felt her change George back into his human form through sheer force of will. She didn't force her will on the jötnar, but just expected it to be done. Then an angry blond boy was shouting at us from where trees had wrapped their branches implacably around his limbs and torso.

"Stop that," Mom said, and George was silent even though his mouth thrashed and snarled. "Callie, did you see how I did that?"

"Yes," I said slowly, completely in awe. My mother was a badass. I never knew.

"Then undo it," Mom said. I blinked, then concentrated on Mom's binding. I willed for George to be able to speak again—and felt a warmth briefly spark in my head. Then George was talking, hurling invectives and ungentlemanly slurs at us.

I could see that he despised me, but I wanted to know how he knew how to find us.

"How did you know we were here?" I asked George. He snarled at me and refused to answer. I reached out a hand, because it helped me focus, and probed into his mind with my own. "Tell me."

"Helena tracked you for us," George spat out. "She's been very useful, giving us the scarf to get past your wards, feeding us your whereabouts. You never leave Bellhaven, little bird, so you are not hard to track."

"We," I repeated. "We who? Where's Freddy?" Then I felt something cold and terrible on the other side of me. I desperately lashed out and tossed up some sort of ice shield a bare second before the frost giant slammed

157

into it.

I fell down in fright and stared at a man two stories high with skin made of what I imagine an iceberg is made of. And he was slamming against my ice shield, trying to batter his way through. It cracked immediately.

"Callie, lower the shield," Mom said.

I let the ice shield shatter, and a fireball the size of a bowling ball appeared from behind me and slammed into the frost giant's chest.

"Back away from him, Callie," my mom said. "Get clear so I can get a shot."

Get a shot. I tried to parse that out in my head as I scrambled away. I swung around to see my mom advancing, a deadly determined expression on her face. Mom pulled her arm back like she was winding up for a softball pitch and threw another fireball at the giant.

He laughed.

"I don't remember you being so weak, Brigid!" The frost giant curled his lips derisively, showing sharp teeth. "This will be no sport at all."

"Try working with what you have, Callie," Mom said. Then I realized that Mom was keeping him occupied so I could practice.

I remembered how Mom had spun the fireball into existence, pulling the ambient heat from the air and rapidly swirling it into a small conflagration, and I repeated it. I failed.

I kept trying and the only thing I could come up with was a jagged, ugly spear of ice, which I threw. It shattered in a puff at the frost giant, who laughed in my face.

That made me mad. I called up another ice spear and threw this one harder at the frost giant. This ice spear slammed into his chest and made him back him up a step. He grunted and glared at me.

"Don't get angry," Mom warned. "Whatever you feel, use it, feed it into your work to fuel your focus."

"Can we take care of the giant first and train later?" I gasped.

"Do it," Mom ordered.

Don't get angry, Mom says. *Okay, I won't get angry. I'll use my anger to focus maybe shielding us.* Unintentionally, I made a ring of frost around us. Mom tried not to look disappointed.

I tried again and it was like lifting a car. I was panting and sweating, but finally I had a short, spiky ice fence around us. Out of pettiness, I ripped off an ice spike and threw it at George. He screamed at me, and it made me angry enough to hurl more ice spikes at him, which apparently, I could not do on purpose. He started to scream.

"Enough," Mom said. I looked at her. "That's enough for today, Callie." I started to protest and Mom gave me a look.

"Okay?" I asked. Mom nodded and waved her hand. George blinked out of existence. I blinked.

"I didn't catch that," I said. "Where did you send him?"

"I didn't send him anywhere," Mom said. "It was an illusion." I gaped at her.

"But he was here," I said. "I could smell the frost giant burning. I could hear him."

"Do you really think I'd let you practice on the real thing? It's your first day, Callie. These were very real illusions but not real nonetheless. You still need practice. That's enough for today," Mom said. We hiked back to the truck in silence. As we drove back home, I turned to Mom.

"Lou let us go last night," I said.

"Yes," was Mom's only response.

"Mom, who is he?"

"He's Lou, someone who has loved you since before you were born," Mom said. "Don't worry about him. Worry about learning your craft."

"Okay, fine. Can we put wards on Trish and Marley's house?" I asked.

"Of course," she answered. "I have minor protection on their houses now, but we can expand them. It'll be good practice for you."

"Me?" I blinked.

"Yes, definitely you. I'll show you the basics with our own wards when we get back to the house."

"And wards for the city? I was thinking something that could keep the Janssens out completely. Can I even do that?"

"Why don't you practice on something a bit less prodigious," Mom said. "Let's start with the block. You'll need Norman's help. He'll probably say yes. That can be your project for tomorrow." Of course, because Mom never saw the point to sitting on a task.

"Well, Erik and I were thinking of going out tomorrow," I hedged.

"And I think, with everything that's been going on this past week, that you should stay home tomorrow instead of traipsing around the woods. Erik is welcome to come over," Mom said.

"Nothing is going to happen, Mom. He really does want to protect me," I pointed out.

"I'm not worried about Erik," Mom said. I looked at her suspiciously.

"Really? Why is it that you're the only mother in Bellhaven who is never worried about my dating life?"

"Maybe I trust my eighteen-year-old, legally adult daughter to make good choices," Mom replied.

"Or maybe you know something," I said slowly.

My jaw dropped. "In my previous lives, have I ever had sex?" Mom winced, and I knew. "I die a virgin?!"

****

"Training was that hard?" Erik asked. We were in his kitchen, and I was researching his family. I looked it up. Njordr's house was called Noatun, so technically we were in the kitchen of Noatun.

"Training was that bad." I set down our drinks on the kitchen counter and hopped up on the stool next to him. I think my greatest super-power is selective memory. I choose to forget that I have not had sex in hundreds of years. "It's like I'm banging on a wall or something. Bad metaphor, I know. I don't know why it's so difficult."

"Give it time," Erik said. "You just remembered. You can't expect to be an expert right away."

"I don't think the people coming to kill me are going to give me the courtesy of waiting until I can defend myself," I said. "But that wasn't the mortifying part. Mom gave me the bird and the bees speech. Stop laughing. It's not funny."

"It's a little funny." He chuckled. "My dad gave me the talk when I turned thirteen. It cracks me up that it took this long for you to get the talk."

"It must be the company I'm keeping," I said drily as I clicked a website on Norse mythology. Erik was giving me a crash course in mythology.

"No, it's not that," Erik said absently. "She said so."

"What was that?" I asked. He looked a little uncomfortable.

"It was when I first dropped you off. Your mom and I chatted for a bit," Erik said. He looked very uncomfortable. "Basically, I have permission to see you if I'm a perfect gentleman."

I was speechless. After a moment, I mentally checked to make sure my mouth wasn't hanging open.

"Did you have plans to *not* be a gentleman?" I asked haltingly.

"God, no!" he exclaimed. Deep down, I was a little disappointed. I was going to die a virgin.

"Erik, let's order." Duston came in. "Hi, Callie. Staying for dinner?"

"Maybe?" I said slowly. "What's dinner?"

"You can pick. Pizza or Chinese?" Erik asked.

"Chinese sounds good," I said. Twenty minutes later, Erik was paying the delivery guy. I went to get Duston.

"Duston, the food is he—ah!" I screamed and ran out the door again, the image of Duston in orange and blue striped boxer briefs engraved in my brain. "You couldn't close your door, jerk? I'm going to have to scrub steel wool over my brain now!"

"You wander around a house of bachelors, what did you expect?" Duston asked, wandering into the hallway with briefs on and nothing else. I glared at him, my eyes fixed firmly on his face and not anywhere else.

"You knew I was here. Don't play games. And get used to wearing pants!" I ordered and marched away.

"Did you want something?" Duston called.

"Food is here!" I yelled back.

Chapter Fourteen
The Cost of Love

We had an uneventful dinner, other than me cutting my hands washing the dishes. Fairy princesses can be klutzes, too, and it's hard to see in soapy dishwater.

"I better get going," I told Norm. I had something else in mind, but I didn't tell him that.

"I'll give you a ride," Erik said.

"Really? You're not going to make her bike home?" Duston rolled his eyes. Norm lifted an eyebrow at him.

"I can take my bike. Actually, I want to set the wards around the school," I said, then hesitated. "Can I do that?"

"Theoretically yes, though you were technically born last week," Norm said. "It took me months to remember how to do it, and another month before I could build enough strength to set a ward. You will want Duston for that."

I turned to stare at the older Vanner brother, who actually blushed.

"Are you the king of wards?" I asked.

"Maybe," Duston said warily.

"He is," Erik said.

Fifteen minutes later, I stared at the soccer field where I had spent so many afternoons. The street was lonely and quiet. It was almost full dark.

"Okay, did your mom talk you through how to make basic wards?" Duston asked as we got out of the Eliminator.

"Yes," I said, looking around.

"Then start with that and then I'll work around

you," Duston said. "Let's make it the edges the walls of the school."

"What about the parking lots?"

"Listen, I doubt they'll come back to the school. They're stupid, but that's just a special kind of stupid. I'm ready whenever you are," Duston said, leaning back against the car.

I took a deep breath and let it out, releasing all the bad with it. I took a few more breaths until I felt energized and clear-minded. I envisioned my heartbeat beating in the band room, since that was the place I found most peace at school.

After a few minutes, Duston cleared his throat.

"Yes?" I snapped.

"Nothing's happening," Duston pointed out.

"I realize this," I said and opened my eyes.

"Do you want me to do it?" Duston asked.

"Can you ward against your own kind?"

"Not really, but has your mom shown you how to transfer someone else's magic?" Duston asked.

"That sounds not right," I said warily.

"It's not encouraged, but sometimes necessity is an excuse, you know? If you want, I could set the wards with your magic."

"I can't even use my magic."

"I know. I can explain or I can do it."

"Whatever. Just do it," I said.

Duston rolled his eyes, then stared up to the dark night sky. I waited, and was about to say something when I felt it. *Oh, I get it now.* I could almost see how he was turning his magic into a magnet which tugged at me.

He held out a hand, and I didn't hesitate to take it. Duston would never hurt me. Then he peeled back one side of my bandage and put his mouth on the back of my hand where the cut was.

It was shockingly intimate and made me feel uneasy. Duston kept his gaze on the field and, with a little suck, put the bandage back in place.

Then I felt a tiny tug and my hair shifted, like a breeze was blowing at me from behind. I understood then that my blood was linking Duston to my magic.

As gentle as a summer breeze, Duston drew my magic through me and into himself. Then he wove it around me and showed me what I was supposed to do. He was like a tutor teaching me with his hand over mine.

My heartbeat was a swirling ball of power and intent, to which nothing bad or with ill-intent could penetrate. With every beat of my heart, the dome of magic around me expanded, my intent pulsing with it. The protective dome grew into a sphere of protection that extended above the school, down into the water-pipes, and outward toward the perimeter Duston had suggested.

When my ward had reached the perimeter, Duston whispered to it, strengthening it with my own prayers and intent. I felt the grass and the birds and the earth and the sky hear my prayer, that none who wished harm could cross into this space. I imagined different colors swirling around—

"Callie, stop the snow," Duston interjected. I bobbled and almost lost the shield. I didn't even realize I was holding it, that Duston had handed it to me earlier. It wavered for a moment before I could yank the ward back into place through sheer will. It wasn't graceful or as easy as leading it to where it needed to be, but I was new.

"What?" I snapped at him.

"You were thinking protection. I think that protection manifested in snow," Duston pointed out. "Or didn't you notice that the grass near the soccer field is frozen?" With shock, I realized he was right. I let go, hoping I hadn't killed the grass.

"I'm almost there," I said. "I was thinking colors and we got snow."

"Focus on protection," Duston suggested. I went back to work. Instead of layering level upon level of different colors of protection, I focused on making it strong. Then I felt something wild and passionate slide beside my shield.

I held steady this time and felt Duston call up his particular brand of magic to bolster mine. I was amazed. I had expected Nordic magic to be as natural and nature-based as Tuatha magic, but it was very different.

I felt wild heat and smelled cold sea air as Duston chanted quietly. When I could make out his words. I thought it was similar to kenning, the way the Norsemen described something in ultra-literal terms, such as a sword being a wound-hoe.

Then Duston pulled the sword Hfud out of the air and sliced his left hand along the blade. His blood spilled to the ground and soaked in blindingly fast. I felt Duston's side of the ward solidify as his blood fed it. We tied off the binding of the ward together.

"You almost lost the ward," Duston said, almost accusingly. He wiped the broadsword against his pant leg and slid it back into invisibility. The wound on his hand had already healed.

"I'm new to this," I said unsteadily. "I was a little surprised when you starting slicing yourself with a broadsword. Cut me some slack."

"No," Duston said, opening his door. "You're in this now, and any slack I cut you could end up getting someone killed."

"You mean Erik. You don't want me to get Erik killed," I corrected, getting into the Eliminator.

"Exactly," Duston said, starting up the engine. "And I know this isn't fair. If it makes you feel better, I feel bad about this, but I only have the one brother. He's more important to me."

"Thank you for clarifying," I said. And I meant it. I appreciated the honesty.

I was very, very tired. Maybe after more practice, magic wouldn't drain me as much.

As I watched the houses pass by, I slumped in the seat. Apparently, there was a trap waiting for me this weekend. I didn't feel ready to figure out what to do.

"This wouldn't be so bad if I felt more responsible," I complained suddenly, "but this wasn't me. I wouldn't take out my emotions on other people."

"You're talking about everything?"

"I'm talking about what started this all, about Branwen cursing the Norsemen to repeat this story as punishment. I mean, that's so juvenile! I would never do that."

"How would you know?" Duston asked, watching the traffic light. "You've never been in that situation. You have no idea how you'd react."

"I think I know myself well enough that I wouldn't curse people to eternal damnation."

"It was vengeance. They killed the man you love. Revenge is something universal. You'd get yours, raven girl. I know you would."

"You don't know me."

"No, I don't," Duston said thoughtfully as he pulled up behind the diner. It was only eight o'clock, so the diner was almost empty.

I ran inside without saying thank you.

****

Every muscle in my body ached. My head hurt. My eyelashes were tired. Training and the school wards had taken a lot out of me. I shouldn't have come to my hospital shift today, but I needed that bit of normal for a while. I could be Callie, the volunteer, rather than Callie, harbinger of doom.

I trudged through the halls after my shift and waved goodbye to Hamad, the security guard. I wondered if this was what my life would be like from here on out, crisis after crisis. It was exhausting. I wanted things to go back to normal, but I think we all have a good sense of my luck by now. Luck of the Irish, my butt.

I stepped outside of the hospital and breathed in the cold autumn air. The chill re-energized me after a long six hours. I looked around, really looked around, and squinted. It probably wouldn't be a bad idea to ward the hospital, too.

But should I? The wards held off most gods, but shouldn't benevolent gods be allowed in? We didn't want to keep out those who could help, right?

I checked my phone. Mom was coming to get me because she didn't want me riding my bike around town anymore. I did up the buttons of my coat as I stared at the sky. October was coming in hard. The wind was picking up, and the sun was already under the horizon.

Mom's car appeared and moved to the curb.

"Callie, what are you still doing here?"

I turned to Dr. Wyndham, who was tying his scarf as he exited the hospital.

"My mom just pulled up. Hey, speaking of which, how come you've never been to our diner? You should stop by sometime," I said and turned back to Mom, who had just pulled up.

Her face froze in shock and I frowned. Something was wrong. Mom was shocked. No, she was horrified. Terrified? I started to turn to see what she was staring at.

Then the building fell over on us. I had time to have one nonsensical thought about this being a different disaster that what I had experienced lately. Then my vision was filled with broken concrete, and I knew nothing.

****

I woke up in a hospital room. I distinctly remembered a building collapsing on me, but that must have been only my part of the hospital, the patient drop. This part of the hospital must have survived and looked to be in good working order.

I had fainted. Twice. I never faint. I could call the first time getting knocked out by bricks, but it still equated to fainting. I couldn't believe a building fell on me.

My grandpa was sitting next to me, looking like ten miles of bad road. He wore every year of his age tonight. His black watch-cap was a bit crooked, letting wisps of white hair poke out. When had his beard turned so gray?

"Good!" a deep voice boomed. I jerked, then groaned as the noise bounced around the inside of my skull. Everything was pain. I glared at the giant with wild red hair sitting on the other side of the bed from Grandpa, then decided to ignore him.

"Mom?" I croaked at Grandpa. Grandpa reached out and gripped my hand.

"I pushed her conveyance out of the way. She was not in the impact area, and thus survived," the giant said. He looked so odd with his wild barbarian beard and a suit that was, to my untrained eye, Italian.

"You rolled the car across the parking lot into a wall," Grandpa grunted at him. "Sweet pea, your mom is out cold, but nothing is broken."

A coma. My heart dropped. My mom was unconscious. How bad must it be that she could not wake up? That was bad, right?

"It was not the most elegant solution, but I saved

her life, Eochu." The giant redhead looked at his nails.

"Who are you?" I interrupted. "What did you call Grandpa?" This stranger was working my last nerve. The big man took my hand solicitously. I yanked my hand back and glared. He chuckled.

"Tyrone Osmont, Esquire, at your service," he said. "And I am only giving the old man his due. Rest assured, I utter his title with the utmost respect." He was probably trying to look engaging and friendly, but the show of teeth instead made him look decidedly psychotic.

Erik came in with two cups of coffee and saw that I was awake. He set both coffees down abruptly in front of Grandpa. I reached for him, and he had me in a bear hug. Finally, someone steady. The hug hurt because every part of me was bruised, but I wasn't broken. Yet.

"You were instructed to keep the peace, battle god." Grandpa Doug's stare bore into Tyrone grimly. I lifted my head to look at him.

"With all respect, Eochaid Ollathair, the young lady seems quite hale and hearty," Tyrone pointed out.

"You let a hospital collapse on top of her. People may still yet die. That is not 'fine', son of Odin."

"I would like to point out that, miraculously, no one has died. That was my doing. You also failed to mention that your own people are working to kill your granddaughter, not only my kin," Tyrone said coldly. "We were lucky today is my day, or your daughter and granddaughter would both be dead now."

"Uncle Ty," Erik said warningly.

"What do you mean my own people?" Grandpa snapped.

"The hospital was warded by the Tuatha. The Janssens could not have broken it. They're too dumb. The magic used to break the ward was distinctly Celtic. You have a traitor in your midst, Striker. And I am not beholden to defend the little goddess from other Tuatha."

"First off," I snapped, "never speak to my grandfather like that. Second, who are your kin and what does your birthday have to do with anything?"

"My apologies, Branwen." Tyrone dipped his head at Grandpa. "I am uncle to the Vanners and Janssens. My job is to keep the peace, and the Janssens broke that when they attacked the Vanners."

"You're here because Freddy fought Erik? They attacked me, too," I said.

"You're the enemy. You are fair game," Tyrone said.

"His job as Tyr, the god of war, is to make sure there is no in-fighting. He polices the boundaries and uphold the truce," Grandpa said flatly. "And today is Tuesday, named after him. Tysdagr. Tyr's day."

I looked back and forth between the men. Grandpa Doug was talking about gods. I turned away from Tyrone and zoned in on Grandpa.

"You don't look Irish." Tyrone eyed me casually. "You've always looked Irish before."

"Shut up," I said absently, focused on the old man in overalls. Tyrone drew himself up with indignation, and Erik went to talk him down.

Grandpa Doug was staring into a foam cup of coffee, saying nothing. His face was expressionless, and he was lost in thought.

I should have guessed. My mother was a goddess. Why not my grandfather? Mom said that cuimhne was when we remembered our past lives. Who else had I trapped in the curse? Who else was remembering?

My mother had been Brigid once, worshiped by countless as a goddess. This was her father, my grandfather. This was the man who made me fluffy silver dollar pancakes with cinnamon, who made sure my bacon was always super-crispy because it should be no other way. This was the man who has been more of a father to me than a grandfather.

This was a stranger.

Chapter Fifteen
Tumbling Down

"Grandpa?" I asked faintly.

"Yeah, sweet pea," Grandpa Doug said absently. Then he focused on me, as sharp as a laser. My grandpa was harmless, a sweet old fart. I loved my grandpa to bits, even when he embarrassed me. This man, though, I didn't know this man. He looked fierce. He looked like a soldier or a king.

Previous to this, I had been treading water, keeping my head at a good level. Now, I was ashamed to admit, I was completely overwhelmed. I wanted to lie there and cry, but I couldn't do that with a strange god in my hospital room.

Hospital room. We didn't have enough insurance to cover this.

"The Dagda," Erik said suddenly. At least someone had a clue. Did it count as mythology if it was standing next to my hospital bed?

"The Dagda," I repeated stupidly. "The Irish trickster?"

"The king of your pantheon," Erik said. "He's your Odin or Zeus."

"What? Why didn't you tell me?" I asked Grandpa Doug, shaking my head. I regretted the movement; it hurt badly, but I felt so betrayed. "Are you even really my grandpa?"

Please don't hesitate, I pled silently. *I won't be able to bear it if you're not my family.*

"Of course I'm your grandfather," Grandpa said immediately. He sounded offended. I let out the shaky breath I was holding, then hauled myself up.

"Hey now," Erik said. "Don't push it."

"Other than bruises, is there anything physically wrong with me?" I asked, lurching to my feet. Erik steadied me, and I thanked my stars for the hospital gown that tied in the back.

"No, but a building did collapse on you," Erik said.

"I need to see Mom," I said, ignoring the protests. Grandpa and I looked at each other. He had an expression I had never seen directed at me before, the same look he had when he was taking the measure of a new firefighter, or right before he hauled some troublemaker out of the diner.

"No point in arguing with her," Grandpa said.

"Mom said *we*," I thought out loud. "She said *we* were trying to protect me, and I thought she was talking about herself and the Vanners, but it was you, too, wasn't it. You knew you were a god this whole time."

"Remember when I hit my head back in March?" Grandpa asked.

"Yeah, when you got knocked down during the St. Patrick's Day race," I remembered. Grandpa had manned a checkpoint at the halfway mark with the firehouse, and a runner ran right into him. The medics had cleared him.

"It was the spring equinox and that hit jogged my memory. Listen, sweet pea, Michigan is about to host a whole convention of gods. I'm on your side," Grandpa Doug said. There was no change in his tone, but at that moment, my grandfather scared me a little. "Erik, get her that wheelchair."

Ten minutes later, we were in Mom's room. I was only a little surprised to see Norm sitting next to her.

Mom's eyes were closed. There was a nasty bruise on her cheek and a cut on her forehead. She was so still. If it weren't for the machine beeping, she could have been asleep.

"Mom's unconscious. They shouldn't have been able to hurt her. She's your real daughter, right? How could you let this happen?" I said, frustrated and scared.

Grandpa said nothing. I couldn't look at him, ashamed of myself. I felt his hand on my shoulder. He pressed a scratchy beard-kiss to my temple, like he always did. I still had my grandpa.

"What are you going to do about your brethren?" Grandpa said quietly. I was confused until I saw Norman's face.

"I'm going to Duluth to talk to Sutherland," Norm said grimly.

"Do you truly believe the fire jötnar will side with the Tuatha against their own kind? Because you asked nicely?" Tyrone said derisively.

"The jötnar have attacked the Vanners," Norm said. "I have been damaged. I will be recompensed. Sutherland has no choice but to comply or he will be destroyed. That is the rule of law."

"That sounds like a balancing of the scales that the arbiter of justice should be doing." Erik looked at Tyrone.

"I'm still not clear why you are here," Norm said blandly to Tyrone. I looked at the scruffy mechanic in an ancient jean jacket staring down the wild specimen in a three-piece suit and wondered how they could be related. I was curious, too—why gods from the same pantheon seemed so completely opposite, if not antagonistic toward each other, but I had other things to worry about.

"I am here to perform my duties as arbiter since the truce has been broken. I will oversee the formalities of war and ensure that both sides follow the agreed-upon terms. As a personal favor to the Dagda," Tyrone explained.

"At the very least, Tyr," Grandpa Doug said warningly.

"As such I will render my protection to the girl until Brigid is again capable of protecting her daughter. By my very presence, I shall shield the Tuatha from harm. Even from other Tuatha," Tyrone said smoothly. His voice was built for poetry. It flowed over the words like a river. "You reaching out to Sutherland, that's active diplomacy. I'm more of a judge or peacekeeper."

"As long as your goal is to keep the peace and not start a war," Norm warned.

"No, I shall leave the latter to the Janssen boys, little heathens," Tyrone said distastefully.

"Well, you can stay with us. We've got a room for you," Norm said, looking not at all happy about it.

"Ah, no, I believe I shall explore the local amenities, but thank you for the invitation," Tyrone said. "I've seen Noatun before."

"You'll stay with me," Grandpa said. Tyrone looked like he had stepped in cat poop. "I insist you partake of my hospitality, lord of justice," Grandpa said evilly. Tyrone nodded reluctantly.

"I don't want to leave Mom alone here," I told Grandpa. "I'll stay."

"You are going to be discharged—and then I'm taking you home," Grandpa said.

"I'm staying," I insisted.

"I'll stay," Duston said. I turned in my wheelchair. He had been sitting in the corner the whole time. He had been watching over my mother for me.

"Are you sure?" I asked. He shrugged, typical Duston.

"Erik should be with you. Dad's going to Duluth. I'll stay with your mom," Duston said quietly, his usual brashness absent. "You know I'm good for it." Yes, I knew what kind of a fighter he was. My mom would be safe.

"Come on," Grandpa said. I looked back at Mom again and promised myself I would be back tomorrow.

****

Later, I was scrubbing the diner bar top because I thought I would scream if I sat in my dining room a moment longer. I had scones going in the oven. I don't know why I chose scones, I just felt like it.

"That smells glorious, young lady," Tyrone said, his silky smooth voice booming through the empty diner. I had no music on tonight because it didn't feel right so the space felt hollow, even more so with the god's voice filling it.

I didn't jerk or jump. I simply looked at him.

"Have you eaten?" I asked politely. This was a diner, and I was my mother's daughter. This was my grandfather's guest. I would feed him if it killed me.

"Why now that you mentioned it, it has been a minute," Tyrone said. I invited him to sit, then slid a bowl of beef and vegetable soup in front of him. I sliced up some soda bread and set out the butter.

"Freddy and George," I said after Tyrone had demolished half of his bowl and a good chunk of bread. "They're wolves and frost giants, right? What were their names before?"

Tyrone dabbed at his mouth delicately with a napkin.

"Freddy was Fenrir and George was Jörmungandr, the world serpent," Tyrone said and continued to eat his soup, dipping chunks of buttered soda bread into the steaming broth. I didn't move. I had been catching these surprises left and right for weeks now, so I was starting to get numb to it.

"So Freddy is the wolf who ends the world," I

said. "And Helena?"

"Hel, goddess of the dead. All three were the children of Loki, but as they were reborn, they drifted. They're cousins now but still quite close," Tyrone explained amiably, lifting the lid off of the pie tray to examine the contents.

That's great. I guess I pissed off the whole family.

I went to switch out scone trays. I took a moment to reached out with my mind. I felt Grandpa Doug plucking at his guitar in his place. He was tired, but we needed to have this out.

"Grandpa, can you come in here please?" I said quietly, but I was quite certain he heard me. I was proven right when Grandpa Doug wandered in a few minutes later, a carton of vanilla bean frozen yogurt in hand.

I put a pot of coffee on while they warmed up mixed-berry pie and dished it out à la mode. I politely declined. My appetite had run away and showed no signs of coming home.

"You can enter the diner. Does that mean you were invited or that you mean us no harm?" I asked Ty. Grandpa said nothing and continued to eat his pie. Tyrone looked at me with something akin to pity.

"The wards your mother and the Vanners placed on your sanctuary ensure that only those who mean you no harm can enter. In addition, as a guest of your grandfather, I am prohibited from harming those who live here. Those are the laws of frið, which are binding and unbreakable. You are safe, young raven," Ty said.

"Freddy could enter the diner," I pointed out.

"They had a token of yours. There is a way to bypass the wards with personal possessions. They tricked the wards into thinking they were you, magic which is quite a bit more sophisticated than I expected from them," Tyrone said, neatly scooping an astounding amount of pie and frozen yogurt up into his mouth.

"And the triskele. Did you know that the necklace showed up in my bag at the hospital? The hospital that fell on me yesterday?" I pressed.

"Yes, I had noticed. Interesting coincidence, that."

"Tell me what you're trying to tell me without actually telling me," I said. "No more evasions, no more silence. Something or someone is coming for me, someone other than the Janssens, and I have the right to know who and why."

"Don't worry about it," Tyrone said.

"If I didn't worry about it, I wouldn't ask, God of Battles," I snapped. The name came out of nowhere. This usually bothered me, things I didn't understand coming out of my mouth, but right now my subconscious apparently knew more of what was going on than me so I gave it free rein.

"I hold your memory and thought, Fosterer of the Wolf, and I don't wish to make demands. That is why, inside my mother's threshold, I'm extending you my hospitality and the courtesy of asking." I didn't understand half of what I was saying, but I stared down the old god like I was confident in what I was doing.

Tyr, the champion of justice, measured me with consideration. He looked like a thug that had been shoved into a nice suit, but a thug nonetheless.

"There may be something of Branwen left in you after all," Tyrone said. I had been a little horrified that I was speaking to an adult in this way, but at that moment, I decided that the situation needed truth more than decorum. And I am an adult. Legally.

Erik chose that moment to walk into the diner. He paused when he felt the tension in the room, then continued to my side. I got a Vanner hug, which was the best place to be in the whole world.

Erik tried to hand Tyrone the silver chain that Helena had used to trap Erik and didn't have the strength to ask what was going on.

"That goes to Duston, remember," Tyrone said.

"Are you sure?" Erik frowned.

"It always has before. Give it to your brother."

Grandpa Doug and Tyrone dished Erik some pie while I poured him a glass of milk. I almost wished I was hungry. The pie smelled so good.

"It's Gwydion," Grandpa Doug explained, pushing his watch-cap up off his forehead to scratch. "This has Gwydion's fingerprints all over it."

I waited a moment, hoping someone would explain. They kept eating pie.

"Yeah, I have no idea who that is. Please elaborate," I said.

"Gwydion killed your father," Tyrone said quietly.

****

Without a word, I left the room. Mechanically, I took out the last tray of scones to cool down on the counter. The familiar task and the homey aroma helped me a little.

I brought out a tray of scones and made myself butter one. I even took a bite. It tasted like chalk. They watched me carefully, probably wondering if I was going to cry or throw something. Both were solid options.

"I take it you know what happened to my father after he left Mom," I said to them. Grandpa sat back and took a big gulp of coffee. He could drink three pots and go right to sleep. Thirty years working shifts at the fire house made a person immune to caffeine.

"Pritchard Poole was the reincarnation of Pryderi. Your mother fell in love with him right out of high school. He was still in the Coast Guard then. You know what happened next. He left while your mom was pregnant," Grandpa said.

"And Gwydion?" I forced myself to ask.

"We don't know where Pritchard met up with Gwydion. We didn't even know he was stuck in the geas," Grandpa explained.

"But you think it could be him," I pressed. Grandpa nodded slowly and I leaned back in my chair. "Why did he kill my father?"

"Because that's the story," Grandpa Doug said. "Gwydion kills Pryderi."

"No. There has to be a reason. People just don't kill other people without a good reason," I said, a little desperate.

"In the story, Gwydion killed Pryderi to stop a war. Now, today, we don't know, Callie. Gwydion doesn't need much justification to do what he does," Grandpa Doug said.

"So you're saying he's a psychopath, like Freddy Janssen." Freddy Janssen was Fenrir in Erik's story, I reminded myself. I probably needed to make flashcards to keep everyone straight. I didn't want to dwell on the homicidal ice giants, but they were my only basis for comparison. Bellhaven doesn't attract many psychopaths, but nowadays, they were popping up out of the woodwork.

"He's much worse than Freddy," Tyrone said. "Gwydion is one of the most intelligent people among us. He is, to a great extent, smarter and more devious than anyone you've ever met."

"That's just fantastic. How do we stop him?"

"Sweet pea, I don't even know what he wants." Grandpa Doug poured himself more coffee.

"I think it's a pretty safe bet to say that he's coming after me," I pointed out. "I don't know why."

"Maybe it's for the same reason my cousins are doing this," Erik said. "He probably wants to break the geas, too."

"Congratulations, princess." Tyrone toasted me with his coffee mug. "How does it feel to be the most important person in a city full of gods?"

"That was juvenile." I glared at him.

"Have you met my family?" Erik muttered. "My cousins are juvenile delinquents."

"Ugh, don't remind me. Those pups have absolutely no sense of style. I hate the skulking," Tyrone said in disgust. "Give me a good, honest battle. This skullduggery is so tawdry."

"They're your nephews," Grandpa pointed out.

"Not by choice, Ruad Rofhessa," Tyrone said. He nodded at me. "She's the one who kept it that way. We're supposed to grow with each incarnation. Branwen locked us into a never-ending cycle of mediocrity."

The phone on the counter rang, making me jump and probably saving me from testing my new fairy powers on Tyrone.

It was late. No one should be calling. Unless it was about Mom?

I made for the phone, but Grandpa beat me. He answered and talked quietly for a bit.

When he hung up and turned back, he looked at me.

"Is it Mom? Is Mom okay?" I asked, my voice breaking.

"Your mom is fine. That was the sheriff," Grandpa said evenly. "The Janssens broke out of jail."

****

The next day, Erik and I swapped with Duston at the hospital. Duston went home, but not before relaying us an intensely thorough run-down of medication and happenings since we had last been there.

I worked in a hospital. I knew how to read a patient chart, but I listened to Duston gravely. He'd watched over my mother and I was grateful.

I held Mom's hand for a bit. She had just gotten a sponge bath and seemed cold. I pulled the blanket over her and neatened her hair as best I could. There was a comfortable change of clothes for when she was discharged. I would accept no doubt; she would be discharged.

One problem at a time. I just wanted Mom back. I didn't want to think about the Janssens, who had mysteriously escaped from Lou's holding cell. I didn't want to think about the god arguing with Grandpa about whether or not dishes needed to be scraped and rinsed before being put in the dishwasher or if coffee grinds can go in the garbage disposal.

I focused on my mom. Her color was good and she was breathing fine. The nurse said there had been some swelling on her brain, but she was healing fine. It just took time, they said.

When I looked out of the window, I could see the ruin of the patient pick-up lane that I always used. I didn't let myself think about the security guards I waved at all the time, or the nurse with the pretty smile at the intake desk. There was a limit to how much I could handle. I was at that limit.

Erik had brought a backpack full of snacks and books. He settled in next to Mom and seemed ready for the long haul. I told him he didn't need to come and he said he knew. He was here anyway. I had never had that before from anyone other than the girls. I could love this guy.

I was still restless and troubled, and he saw that.

"I don't want to talk about it," I said. He nodded.

"This is so silly," I said, dangerously close to tears. "My mom is unconscious in a hospital, my grandpa is planning something possibly violent, and all I can think is once, just once, I'd like to go on a date without having to worry about ice giants or homicidal Celtic deities or the end of the world. I just want to put on a dress and go to dinner and a movie with my boyfriend."

Erik wrapped his arms around me.

"After your mom is home, we'll go on a date and not be interrupted, I promise." Erik nuzzled my hair. "I like the promotion. Being your friend was agonizing."

"I didn't mean to say that," I said, quite miserable. "Is that okay?"

"Yes, it's good. Do you want to go for a walk?" Erik asked. "I'm okay here." I nodded and left my new boyfriend with my comatose mother.

It felt better to walk because at least I was doing something. I found quiet places to text the girls. Marley called and I had a quick conversation with her. I couldn't make Mom wake up any faster, and I believed with all my soul that she would wake up, so I walked.

I did not know this part of the hospital well. I briefly wondered what happened to all the patients on the other side, the destroyed side. Where was Nurse Angie? I quickly shoved that thought away. One problem at a time.

When I saw the stain glass window with the shamrocks and the Celtic cross, I smiled. Well, here was a sign if there ever was one.

And then I felt something. I couldn't describe it, but there was something to be wary of. A heaviness start to build in my head in response—and an urge to be careful.

I drew myself up straight. This was a conversation that needed to happen, and I was not about to run away.

I entered the chapel. I had not been inside a

church for years and certainly never inside the hospital chapel. It was a bit dark, lit only by candles. Everything felt off, even sacrilegious.

I was a creature of magic from a different time and place. I did not belong here. There was someone else present who had even less right to be there.

"Don't do this," I said to the shadows. "You're better than cheap theatrics."

CONSTANCE KERSAINT

Chapter Sixteen
Selling Sanctuary

There was silence and the shadows seemed to lengthen. I watched and waited. I had power, too, and I would not be cowed.

"Oh now, let an old dog run through his tricks," he said, stepping out into the light. The shadows seemed to stretch and cling to his back, like he was pulling a dark cape behind him. Dr. Gerald Wyndham looked at me from behind wire-rimmed glasses. The dear old mentor was gone; this person was no friend of mine. "It's one of the reasons I like you."

"If you actually liked me, you wouldn't have sent the Janssens to kill me and eat my soul." I kept my voice casual. I needed answers. I needed to control this conversation. The deep hurt and frustration inside would need to stay bottled up for later.

"You need the full picture, little raven," Dr. Wyndham said. He walked to the front of the chapel and looked up at the altar, his face illuminated by the candlelight. He wore a doctor's coat and loafers.

"You never came to the diner. Your face was the last thing Mom saw before the hospital came down on us. You don't look like you just crawled out of a collapsed building. And the name, so close. Gwydion fab Dôn. God of tricks," I summarized.

"And premier physiatrist of Michigan, don't forget," Gwydion added, not taking his eyes off me. I felt like prey.

I knew he was really a doctor. I knew his bio, and I'd seen him work. As much I hated to admit it, I really was missing the whole picture.

"We're in the old part of the hospital, right?" I

said banally. "The part that used to be a school? I heard it burned down in 1901. Do you blame me for that, too? Because that's what this is all about, right? You hate me taking away your godhood and trapping you in the curse."

"No, Callie, I don't hate you. Do you know where I was before Trinity?" Dr. Wyndham walked forward and leaned against the altar. That struck me as highly disrespectful, if not sacrilegious.

"No, I don't know. Edify me," I said, leaning against a pew.

"I was in Duluth. I had a practice there. I liked it. It was a good life. Then, about four years ago, I fell to the ground with a blinding headache and saw hundreds and hundreds of lifetimes in which I lived and died unremarkably. I knew then what I used to be and should be and exactly where it all simply stops," Dr. Wyndham enunciated carefully.

"Four years ago," I said slowly. "When the jötnar regained their memories. I thought you were on my side of the house."

"I am. I am in your father's story and in yours. I don't know who crossed the wires of fate, but as luck would have it, the jötnar cuimhne triggered mine also. I remembered it all. Now, what do you think that does to a person, Callie?" Dr. Wyndham took off his glasses to polish them.

I worked in a diner. I knew when someone wanted to hear themselves talk.

"Why don't you tell me?" I invited.

"Faced with knowledge that you never had before, and an advantage, why wouldn't I try to make a difference? As much as I loved your father, Callie, I was not going to be a puppet in his daughter's play," Gwydion said. He saw the blankness in my face. "Your father and I were in the Coast Guard together. He was my best friend. I was there when he met your mother."

If I hadn't been leaning on a pew, I would have fallen over. The pieces clicked for me.

"She saw you. Mom saw you and recognized who you were. She's never met Dr. Wyndham before. She only started remembering last year." I tried to understand. "Does she know you're Gwydion?"

"She does now. Don't worry, Brigid will wake up. Seeing her after so long was a shock. I am truly sorry for that. It was an unforgivable mistake—one of many, I'm afraid," Gwydion said. What did that mean? What else?

"You gave me the triskele," I realized. *My fear will be anger. My anger will fuel me.* I would not be controlled by my fear. I kept the mantra running through my head, willing it to be true. "That's why it was in my locker at the hospital. You put it there."

"Yes."

"You remembered it all, same as the other side. You could have helped me," I said.

"I'm going to repeat myself because you seem to be having issues keeping up: I'm not going to be your puppet anymore," Gwydion said.

"There is no need to be an ass," I snapped. "You want the same thing as Fenrir does, to be free of my geas. Why didn't you kill me then? Why make me remember?"

"Killing a woman only kills the woman. You must kill the goddess and take her magic. Then you may break her curse. If you died before remembering, the story would reset and we would do it again in thirty, forty, fifty years. It's happened before when you or your young man died before he could be slaughtered by the right people. Sometimes it's an accident. Sometimes it's the Black Plague. Sometimes it's leukemia. No, a more novel approach was called for this time. To take a goddess' power at the crux of her manifestation, now that has a chance of breaking the geas. So first, you have to be a goddess."

"The triskele," I said dully. It sat heavy around my neck, with the weight of so many dead Branwens. I wondered what they had been like. Were they all like me, or variations thereof?

"I pried it out of your father's hands after the Janssens killed him," Gwydion said. "The moment he regained his memories, he started looking for that necklace because he wanted to keep it from you. He wanted you to be free to live your own life. He should have known that your life is forfeit. You put us here, so you are ours."

"I belong to me," I said, my voice trembling. Oh god. Oh god, oh no. The Janssens killed Pritchard. No, Dr. Wyndham had them kill my father. My father had tried to protect me. He had died trying to protect my right to choose my own future, my own path.

I felt very close to tears and fought to keep control of myself. I needed this ride to stop and let me off.

"I know you're scared. I know you're overwhelmed. This will all end soon," Gwydion said, like he was trying to reassure me.

"Why did you involve the Janssens? You could have come for me yourself," I said woodenly.

"No, I couldn't. The rules of the story are that you cannot attack your own kind without invoking the wrath of the arbiters. Had I killed your father, Lugus would have had my head on a platter, just as Tyr is protecting the Vanners. The Janssens were not difficult to convince," he explained. I stared at Dr. Gerald Wyndham, the foremost physiatrist in Michigan and pure monster, and said nothing, too sick to answer.

I closed my eyes.

"Did you get some sort of weird kick out of watching me all this time? Did you enjoy that? Because you're done," I said.

"You look so much like your mother right now." He stared at me. "It is so interesting to see her eyes in your father's face."

"I'm not my parents."

"I truly hope not or this will be shooting fish in a barrel. Your father was a fool. He deserved what I did to him, Branwen. He left your family," he said pointedly.

"There's always more to the story," I said. "I'm not that Branwen."

"Same product, different packaging."

"You may not have received the memo, but that story is over. This is a new century and a new me," I said.

"Are you eighteen? Is it dawn of All Hallows' and your lover stands alive? Then this isn't over. We are driving toward the inevitable, unless I stop it. I will free us all. I will free your mother. The geas will be broken and we will be gods again. This isn't about revenge. It's about making the world right again. Trust me, this is for the best."

"I don't trust you. You're the liar who killed my father. And you want to kill me. Tell me the truth. You're here to kill us all, aren't you?" I said, knowing as I said it that it must be true.

"Very good." Gwydion said, miming applause. I saw Dr. Wyndham then, the costume of a person who wanted me to succeed. "They deserve it. Your grandfather wanted to murder you before you were even born. Did you know that?" Gwydion asked.

"How do you know that?" I asked. Then I shook myself. "He doesn't want me dead now."

"Perhaps not now but before that you were the end of all your mother's dreams," Gwydion pointed out.

"Every time we are reborn, every time your mother falls pregnant and your father leaves her, every time, your grandfather tells your mother to get rid of the pregnancy."

I closed my eyes against the pain. And the weight, the heavy, crushing weight. I tried to convince myself that it didn't matter anymore, but what I believed and what I felt were two very different things.

"I'm awake now," I said. "We're all awake. We're not walking into the story blindly. Tell me, what part of your plan included you trying to kill my mother?"

"I would never hurt Bridget!" Gwydion shouted suddenly. I jerked. Oh. Okay. "All good stories end in death or tears. Our stories, especially, rarely deviate from this pattern."

"It is still my story, Gwydion fab Dôn," I said. "You will not eat my soul." I cannot explain what I did next. I perhaps flexed my brain and the windows shattered, spraying us with broken stain glass.

Neither of us moved. Him by the altar, me by the pews. The glass cut us, made us bleed, and we stared at each other, plotting how to kill the other.

"A little ostentatious there, raven." Gwydion picked a shard out of his brown hair. "That was good. I'm glad you're in this."

"Did you think I would roll over and let you kill me?"

"Yes," he admitted. "Branwen was like that."

"You are not listening to anything I'm saying. I'm not Branwen," I said.

"We will see." Gwydion blinked slowly, his brows seeming to pull up his eyes. "You may be better. I'm very proud of you, young lady."

Then he turned into a raven and flew away.

I stared at the glass, at my blood dripping onto the floor of the chapel, and took a deep breath. I looked up and saw Grandpa standing at the chapel doors. He was holding a paper cup of coffee and watching me with no expression.

Then Duston poked his head around Grandpa and sighed.

"Did you have to destroy a church?" Duston asked in exasperation.

"Duston," I said, then paused out of a loss for words. "I can be insecure all by my lonesome, thank you very much. No comment is needed from your peanut gallery."

Duston made his way inside gingerly, trying to step around glass.

"Did you hear all of that?" I asked Grandpa.

"I heard enough. That's not important right now," Grandpa said.

"What do you mean it's not important? He killed my father, and he almost killed my mother," I said tightly. "Isn't he one of us?" I had never felt as impotent as I did right then. I had responsibilities though. Mom was out, so I had to protect us. I had to fix this. I really wanted to cry. "I want his head."

"While I fully endorse your feelings on the matter, I came here to tell you something important," Grandpa Doug said.

"Unless it's a way to kill every fairy tale monster in Michigan, I'm not interested."

"We will talk about that later. Right now, get down to the ICU. Your mother's awake."

I started running toward the door when Grandpa stepped in front of me. He took a hold of my arm, and I felt all my cuts close. Even the bruises I had left over from the hospital collapse went away. I looked down and saw that I was once again presentable. Even the decorative holes at the knees of my jeans were gone.

I wondered what else Grandpa could do. I would ask him soon.

Grandpa got a big kiss on the cheek from me. Then I was out the door.

"Don't mind me!" Duston called from behind me. "I'll just clean up your mess. Again."

****

I arranged the flowers artfully and surveyed Mom's bedroom. It looked as if a florist shop had vomited over every surface. Perfect.

On second thought, I moved three vases to the living room. The house was aired out and warm, but not too stuffy. I had decluttered and cleaned it within in an inch of its life the minute the doctor had cleared Mom to come home.

People had brought over casseroles, even though we own a diner. Trish and Marley had organized the meal train. The matzo ball soup was warming on the stove. I think someone from Mom's book club had brought that.

We were set on food, so my biggest challenge was keeping Mom entertained while she healed. The doctors had said that there was a minor contusion on her brain but no swelling. All scans were clear. She had a checkup scheduled in a few days.

I glanced out the window and saw Grandpa's truck pull up. I hurried outside and saw the Norse god of law and justice opening Grandpa's front door.

"Na-ah," I warned Tyrone as I trotted across the driveway. "Back inside." He looked like he would protest, then saw my face. He closed the door without a fuss.

Mom waved at me, and I waved back as I rounded the front of the truck. Erik had pulled up behind them. He had taken over sentry duty for Duston while I, naturally, had been sent ahead to nest.

I got the door open, and Erik, after ascertaining that his actions would not be misconstrued, gently picked my mom up and brought her up the stairs to our apartment. I didn't know if he did it so easily because he was just that strong or because he was a god, but either way, I was grateful. Mom insisted Erik set her down near the bedroom, then firmly shut the door on all of us while she took a shower.

Her color looked good for having been in a rollover, I noted as I checked on the matzo ball soup. Erik gave me a big bear hug that made all my worries float away. Mom was home and taking a shower. Grandpa was home and also taking a shower. My boyfriend was nuzzling the spot right behind my ear. Things were going to be okay.

I dished Erik some soup, and he updated me on his dad. Norm was making very little headway with the jötnar, but the fact that Tyrone was staying with us was a big deal. From how Erik explained it, an attack on us would be tantamount to suicide.

I kind of wanted them to come. I knew I wasn't ready, not even close, but there is no better way to learn than on the job.

Mom came out of her bedroom with wet hair and wearing a warm cardigan. I gave her a big hug and she took her soup at the table.

"This is so much better than hospital food. Thank you, sweetie. Are you okay?" Mom squeezed my arm.

"Am I okay?" I asked incredulously. "I wasn't in a coma in the hospital."

"No, but a building fell on you," Erik interjected. I made a face at him and he squeezed my hand, completely immune to my annoyance. "She's doing better than I expected. She heals very fast now."

"The Tuatha have always healed quickly," Mom

said, sipping her tea. "I'll be right as rain in time for the Fall Festival."

"I am so happy you are feeling better," I said carefully, "but we still have a psychopath, sorry, several psychopaths, after us. I think that is more important."

"The Redmonds have been part of the Fall Festival for fifteen years, and we will not let something like this keep us from fulfilling our commitment to this community," Mom said firmly. She looked a lot better. I guess us fairies really do heal fast.

"Okay," I relented. "I'll pull out the decorations and start prepping while you nap. While you nap," I repeated firmly. Mom sighed dramatically.

I looked at her carefully and decided I could ask.

"Can we talk about Gwydion, please?" I said slowly. Mom was quiet for a long moment, her thoughts far away.

"He didn't expect to see me," Mom said, sounding weary. "He was quick on his feet, I'll give him that. I underestimated him, but then I always did."

"He said many, many things." I waved a hand helplessly.

"Hold that thought. Let's get everyone in here so you don't have to tell the tale twice," Mom said. "Erik, be a dear and bring me the teapot please. Callie, we'll need coffee. God of war," Mom said sternly, not even raising her voice, "on your best behavior. Be welcome in my home."

My kitchen door swung open on its own accord, and Tyr strolled in as if he had been waiting outside. He spread his hand, showing his palms, and smiled with all his teeth at my mother.

"Dearest Brigid, how lovely to see you again. It has been an age since we last dined," Tyr said, his eyes twinkling.

"Don't trust a word that man says," Mom murmured to me.

"I heard that," Tyr said, taking a seat at the island.

The fridge opened behind where I was putting on the coffee. The apple cake I had made before the hospital fell on us floated to the kitchen table.

I don't think I could have done it with that much control. I could blow things up or smash them really hard. This only showed me that I needed more practice.

"Do sit," Mom said. "We have cake and coffee for you."

Grandpa thumped into the kitchen, which was almost at capacity. I could not remember the last time we had this many people in our kitchen. He gave me a quick shoulder squeeze, and I handed him a bowl of soup.

"Why, that looks delicious," Ty said.

"Coffee," Mom said, as a steaming mug floated gently down in front of him, "and cake."

"Brigid, my heart bleeds," Tyrone said mockingly, scooping a slice of apple cake for Erik. "How are you feeling?"

"Better, despite the fact that you threw me into a concrete wall," Mom responded drily.

"I saved your life," he protested.

"You gave her a concussion," Grandpa said. "Don't give yourself too much credit, Tyrone." Then I was truly done with this word play.

"I have a few questions for you," I said to Tyrone. "Why would you protect Mom and me when you belong to the family that wants to kill us?"

He looked down his nose at me, and his eyes widened crazily. I think he was trying to reassure me, but it wasn't working. That expression accentuated his resemblance to his homicidal nephews.

"I am Æsir. I have no quarrel with the Tuatha,

same as the Vanir here. The jötnar are our more garrulous cousins. As for my responsibility to you, Branwen, your grandfather is to thank for that," Tyrone said. "I owe a favor. This was the debt to be paid."

"Ha," I scoffed. "I'm sure your sense of equity drives you to such charity. Why are you really here?"

The lawyer looked at me with an unwarranted amount of arrogance.

"Little raven," Tyrone said silkily. "I like you, but there's only so much attitude I will tolerate from a child."

Maybe it was the exhaustion, but I just snapped.

"I'm tired of all these secrets and lies. And they are lies. In case you haven't noticed, what I don't know can hurt me and has been trying to kill me. So I ask you again, one-armed god, why are you here?"

Chapter Seventeen
Answers in the Mail

"It's true that Ty owes your grandfather a favor. Also, this was the only agreement Sutherland and I could come to, to have an arbiter present in order for the proceedings to be legitimate and sanctioned," Norm said, coming inside. "We need the law on our side. Why was the door open?"

"That was Ty. The Vanners have chosen a side, uncle Ty. We will defend her. We will fight for her. The jötnar won't get her head," Erik said grimly. Ah yes, about that.

"If we're not expecting anyone else, let me start from the top," I said. I told them all about what Gwydion had said about waking up four years ago when Erik's family had their cuimhne. I told them about Gwydion approaching the Janssens with his plan and how they had taken the triskele from Pritchard. I explained that Gwydion wanted me to remember my past lives and be a full-blown goddess again that they could take my power by eating my soul and break the curse.

"Not that we're going to let them, but is that even plausible? That sounds like crazy talk." I asked the question that had been haunting me.

"For the Tuatha, our soul rests in the mind." Grandpa Doug tapped his temple. "You take a person's head, you take their power. The basic tenet of all magic is that you make the world into what you want it to be. If they believe that consuming your soul would allow them to also consume and steal your power, then that is what will be."

"It's also very illegal," Ty lectured, sipping his coffee. "Theophagy was banned even before Branwen cast the geas. There used to be problems with headhunter tribes."

"And you brought in the Æsir gods why?" I asked Grandpa and Norm.

"Because we need something more powerful than just your family or mine. I'm limited against Gwydion, and so is your mom and Norman. There's not much in the world who can stand against the Æsir, especially when they're teamed up with the Vanir." Grandpa sipped his coffee moodily.

I looked to Erik for clarification.

"The Æsir are more pugnacious than the Vanir. My family is more cerebral, and Æsir love a good fight. It took both our families combined to defeat the Jötunn, and it could come to that here. Separately, Vanir or Æsir alone are strong but limited. Together, we're pretty formidable. Or so I remembered. We haven't had a battle in eons," Erik said.

"And what do you get out of this?" I asked Tyrone. He smiled disingenuously. "Oh, don't even try. You never do anything without some gain, and there is no way on this earth that you're helping us out just because your old war buddy called in a favor."

"Maybe I want your goodwill. Maybe I want to kill the dog that takes my hand," Tyrone said. Ah okay. In the old legends, Fenrir takes Tyr's hand. Then his face hardened. "Maybe I want something of mine back that you have."

"I have nothing of yours, Son of Odin," I said. I swear, my mouth has a direct line to my subconscious, sometimes completely circumventing my brain. I don't know how I know Tyrone's names.

"We'll see," he grumbled behind his bushy red beard.

"How do we attack them?" Erik asked.

"You will attack no one." Tyrone turned to his nephew. "You are prohibited, on pain of death or destruction, from attacking those of your own kind in anything other than self-defense."

"Are we going to sit around and wait for the next attack?" I asked Mom. "I can't live my life waiting for someone to cut off my head and eat my soul."

"You are not going to live like that. You are going to live. Once you start giving in to the what-ifs and maybes, you may as well be dead. You are going to finish applying for the pathway program. You are going to college. We have a diner to run and a Fall Festival to prepare for. They will come at us, and when they do, we will be ready." Mom took my face in her hands. "Don't let them push you around."

I blew air out of my nostrils, and my forehead touched Mom's.

"I wish we weren't fairy goddesses," I said plaintively.

"If wishes were horses," Tyrone started.

"Beggars would ride," I finished. "Original."

"And with that, I will abscond to my humble abode to catch up on some work. Au revoir, my temporary compatriots," Tyrone sang and danced out the door. We stared after him.

"That is a very strange man," I said.

****

Later, when it was just family in the condo, Mom set an envelope in front of me. Grandpa had brought his guitar and was quietly strumming.

I stared at the innocuous-looking envelope. Grandpa patted my hand a few times before I realized I was squeezing his arm to death.

"It's from the same college in Muskegon Erik attends," Mom said pointedly.

I couldn't speak. I had sent the application in two weeks ago. This was a rejection. It had to be. Two weeks was not any amount of time for an acceptance. I looked at them both, then back at the envelope.

With great gravity, I picked up the envelope and opened it. My eyes zeroed in on the phrase "with great pleasure that I offer you admissions" and then I couldn't see through my tears.

Grandpa slapped me on the shoulder gruffly and slung his guitar behind his back by the strap. He went over to the sink to stand for a minute and wouldn't look at us. It wouldn't do for us to see him crying.

"I am so proud of you." My mom hugged me, though she had no idea one minute ago that I had even applied.

"Thank you. Thank you for being happy for me. I'm not ready to move to a different state, Mom," I said.

"I know. I didn't want to be selfish by keeping you here," Mom said, her voice breaking.

"Are you okay with me staying here a bit longer?" I asked, my voice shaking.

"This is your home, Calliope. We made this home for you. You will always have a place here," she said, full-out crying.

"We'll celebrate." Grandpa Doug slapped the sink. "By gods, we'll celebrate. We'll go out."

"Mom was in a coma two days ago," I reminded him.

"Then we're celebrating tomorrow!" Grandpa insisted. "We'll have cake and no church."

"We never go to church. The church crowd comes here," I pointed out.

"Naturally," Grandpa Doug said with more dignity than I ever knew he possessed. He swung his guitar back around his front so he could play a jaunty tune. "We are gods after all."

****

I chained my bike to the outside of the library and adjusted my scarf. Outside, by the sculpture of the two birds in flight I always loved, I stopped to look around. It was a cold, overcast day in Bellhaven.

There were things I wanted to look into, and I was terrible at concentrating at home. There was always something to do. The part of the hospital I volunteered at was gone. The town had been shocked, then marshaled on like it always did in a crisis.

Flood? Rebuild the dam, feed the crowd, move on. Tornado? Feed the crowd, rebuild houses, move on. Death? Mourn it, feed the crowd, move on. Freak hospital collapse? Shake your head, feed the crowd, make plans to clear the rubble and transfer medical care to a different location.

I walked in to the library, through the metal detector, and waved at Mr. Ogden. The ancient librarian was older than Grandpa and so thin that a strong breeze could blow him away.

The last I heard, patients were being transferred to Muskegon. I'm sure it was a nuisance for some of the patients, but at least they would continue receiving treatment. My services, such as they were, were no longer necessary. Dani and Agnes had insisted they were good at the diner for today and tomorrow, so I had some time to sort out my life.

I was curled up in a sofa chair by the fireplace, deep in thought. I loved the library, not just the part with the comfortable chairs and the fireplace. It wasn't the most beautiful or prestigious library around, but it was welcoming, well-lit, and well-stocked. Having grown up poor, the library had always been my happy place.

The community college had accepted me for the

winter semester, which was a few months away. I knew which classes I wanted to take, but—and here was the kicker—I was not certain how I was going to pay for it. Mom and Grandpa Doug had a college fund for me, of course, but it wasn't going to last very long. I had to live at home. We could not afford for me to go to the dorm.

And I still needed to get to school. Looking at the bus schedule, I was going to have to get up at the crack of dawn to get to Muskegon, then wait until my classes started. Maybe I could do work study, but then I would still have to wait for the last bus back to Bellhaven. I could perhaps get a car, but could I afford the gas if I wasn't working as much?

Did I want to take a full course load? To start with, it was just the basics that could go with any program, so I didn't have to commit to the Pathway right away if I changed my mind.

We're not poor. We've got a home. We've got jobs. We've got some put away. Still, forging a new path takes resources that I am direly short on. I didn't want to take out loans. Mom was adamantly anti-loan, but I didn't see any other choice.

Freddy sat down across from me.

I don't know how I did it, but I felt the unusual chill behind my eyes. If he came at me, I would hit him until he stayed down.

"We came to talk," Gwydion said, sitting down in another chair by the fire. "You will note that the wards are still in place here."

"You had to bring your pet dog for a 'talk'?" I asked my former mentor. Gwydion still looked like Dr. Wyndham, wearing the same nebbish sweater vest and loafers under that old coat from some department store. I had such respect for Dr. Gerald Wyndham. Now I looked at this person wearing Dr. Wyndham's clothes and I wondered if I could kill him.

"I truly wish things were different. There are things I could have taught you. I was surprised that you'd be so promising in physiatry, but you were always going to gravitate toward healing. You get that from your mother. Apologies, I digress. Mr. Janssen here is merely ornamental, I assure you, though he is a key part to our negotiations," Gwydion said.

"Negotiations. You want to cut off my head and eat my soul." I clarified as I looked Gwydion in the eye.

"The blood sacrifice called a blót. It is quite specific. It is for the good of all, you must understand," Gwydion rationalized.

"How, exactly?" I pressed. I wanted all the details from the criminal mastermind.

"I can't quite summarize how sacrificing you will release the power of the geas back to the gods you stole all magic from and return us to our natural state, so perhaps take my word for it."

"You never could answer a simple damn question, Son of Don. Don't start now," I enunciated sarcastically. I didn't know where the words came from.

"This crassness is new." Gwydion raised an affronted eyebrow at me. "I see the Norsemen are rubbing off on you. Bear in mind we are a different breed. We have a reputation for refinement."

"Celts hunted with sticks and painted themselves with animal blood," I pointed out. "No one is winning deportment prizes around here."

Freddy shifted in his chair, and I glanced at him derisively. He glared back at me and did nothing, only raked me up and down with his eyes like I was a piece of meat. I focused on the man in charge.

"You're saying I stole your power?" I asked. "How is that possible? You were all gods."

"And you are outside the story," Gwydion said. There was that term again. "That means you were the wildcard, with no set path. You came into being without a legend or destiny, so you could shape your own path, weave a new set of actions. All those years ago, you, the bastard daughter of Brigid de Danaan and Pryderi fab Pwyll, fell in love with a Viking god. And you broke us."

"Not by myself," I said angrily. "Three insults avenged in blood. You gave me the power to hurt you. It was my right to choose the punishment, and I chose to make you human, so you could feel what I felt. You needed to lose everything, just like me."

Again, I didn't know where the words came from, but they were all true.

Being a bastard made me a superhero. It was very cool and quite terrifying.

"If I did it before, I can undo it. Have you thought of that?" I tried to think through it.

"In all of our lives before, you never did."

"Was I awake, like this, empowered?" I pressed.

"No, this is the first time Branwen has fully manifested."

"My name is not Branwen. I am Calliope, and I'm not going to let you murder me."

"Not for nothing," Gwydion said. "Your family will be well-compensated."

I blinked. I could not have heard that correctly.

"Come again?" I asked.

"Nothing so crass as a check, you understand. Pritchard Poole came from a well-to-do family and never married. What do you think will happen to his estate?" Gwydion steepled his fingers.

I opened my mouth and closed it again. I had spent much time and energy not thinking about my biological father, so this question took me by surprise.

"Do enlighten me," I said.

"He has no will, so the estate will go to his next of kin," Gwydion said. "That is you, by the way. Now, listen closely: you will die. That, you cannot change. When you die, Pritchard's estate will go into probate and will eventually go nowhere. It could go to your mother instead."

I got up and paced. It made me look weak. I didn't care.

I believe this is the definition of ironic. Here I was wondering how to pay for college when I was actually heir to funds, but the super team of Celtic and Nordic villains were definitely going to kill me, so perhaps that money could go to my mother instead, who I could guarantee would not want blood money.

"How would my mother get Pritchard's estate. Is there a will?" I asked to buy time.

"I just said that the estate would go into probate, so there is no will. What do they teach in schools these days?"

"Estate law isn't taught in high school, Gwydion."

"More's the pity. Tyrone is a lawyer. And we're gods. We can handle a little paperwork." Gwydion took off his glasses to polish them, perfectly at peace with the world.

"You'd forge a will," I guessed. Gwydion squinted as if in thought.

"In so many words, yes. Think of it: your mother and grandfather would never have to worry about money ever again, never work again if they wished. Security is not a small thing, Callie, not in this day and age."

"And all I'd have to do is lay my head on the chopping block for you," I scoffed.

"Nothing so pretty, little bird." Freddy showed his hideous teeth. I felt the cold coil tightly inside me as I looked at him. I could see it all in my head as I targeted him. Between the eyes. That's where I would skewer him.

"Go," Gwydion said. His voice was quiet, but the command was unmistakable. I nearly followed the order, even though it was directed to Freddy.

The wolf looked belligerent, but Gwydion was implacable. That was some stare-down. I believed Gwydion would have killed Freddy if he hadn't jolted to his feet and stalked off.

"The beast of slaughter." Gwydion shook his head. "That boy is supposed to grow up to be the death of so many gods. I cannot believe it. He must have been neglected his entire life. Now where were we?"

"You were saying you would pay off my mother if I let you kill me," I reminded him.

"Ah, the freshly-hatched fairy princess thinks she has a say in the matter," Gwydion mocked. Oh, this was new from him. Not new to me, though. Sweater-vest here had nothing on high school girls.

"You didn't have to go out of your way to annoy everyone. Or to ruse your way into the volunteer program. Or this pathetic excuse for a meeting when all you're doing is attempting to intimidate me."

"Emotional maturity isn't my strong suit, little raven. I choose to be a bitter malcontent. It's easier than taking the high road."

"How admirable," I retorted.

"I never pretended to be admirable. I know my faults and I own them all."

"As do I. Know this, born of trees, you will not have me willingly. You killed my father. You tried to kill my mother."

"I didn't try to kill your mother. I would never hurt Brigid. Never," Gwydion said fiercely.

I heard something. There was a fervent conviction in his voice. I recognized the way he said my mother's name. Sometimes Erik said my name the same way.

Oh. Oh, you've got to be kidding me.

"Is it because you were army buddies with Pritchard?" I asked.

"Coast Guard. You understand nothing. This has always been the story: Gwydion kills Pryderi. The fact that your father was an idiot has nothing to do with it. And you, little fool, are the anthropomorphization, my misery made flesh. Your death is necessary and will free us. With your curse broken, perhaps I won't have to kill him next time."

"You didn't have to kill him this time! No one made you do it! No one forced you to his house. This is all your doing!"

"Foolish girl to think I had a choice. Just like your father. Too bad you never knew him. Or maybe you should have known him. Then you would have known all the bad traits you needed to avoid, blatant ignorance being the most prevalent," he said.

"Let's get something straight right now. Whatever happened between you and Pritchard has nothing to do with me. He didn't raise me. He left before I was born, and he has no place in this story. I do not need Pritchard Poole's money, and you will not bribe me into lying down and dying for you. I don't know what satisfaction you think you'll get from hurting me, but I guarantee there won't be any satisfaction for you. He was just a man. I don't even carry his name."

"Your generation is so entitled," Gwydion said through gritted teeth. "This may come as a surprise, but not everything is about you."

"I'm starting to realize that. This isn't about me at all. It was never about me. This is about you and

Pritchard."

"I don't care about your father," Gwydion said, apparently bored. My mentor was gone. This man, this hateful man, was a creature beyond my ken.

"Then why did you kill him?" I gasped, the words torn from my mouth before I could stop them. A pain that I didn't know existed swelled inside me and made itself known. Huh. Didn't even realize my daddy issues were that bad. "I thought you were friends. You could have taken the triskele from him without killing him. And don't give me that bullshit about Pritchard's death being a foregone conclusion, that you always kill him in the stories. Of any one of us, you know that it is always a choice, that destiny and fate are lazy excuses for those who are afraid. So you tell me, right now, why did you kill my father?"

"Because he had everything I wanted and threw it away!" Gwydion shouted in my face.

Chapter Eighteen
Quiet in the Library

Oh. I hadn't expected it to come out like that. I couldn't speak. I was frozen, my mouth hanging open like an idiot.

"Your father was a fool. He was loved and beloved by the most glorious women of the ages, and he threw it all away. He threw it away. If I was as beloved as Pritchard was, how magnificent I could have been. If only she'd have loved me. I could have shone like the sun."

"If only who had loved you?" I asked. I was trying to process the thought of this man possibly loving my mother, and my brain wasn't cooperating.

He beamed at me proudly.

"Now that is a fine question, little goddess," Gwydion said. I stared at him, weak in the knees.

"My mom?" I said the words with not a little nausea. "You loved Mom, too? She wasn't even in your story." The moment the words left my mouth, I could have kicked myself. "Everyone keeps saying it about me. It just came out."

"Your mother has standards, and Pryderi was the hero, the king. I was the redheaded stepchild no one wanted and everyone forgot."

"Then Mom chose Pryderi, and not you." I pieced the story together.

Gwydion looked at me with immense pain in his eyes. I almost sympathized.

"I didn't tell her, not until he left. Given the choice between me and the big damned hero, it was no contest. I should have known better. She wasn't in the mood for my confession, and I admit, I underestimated her. I thought that a woman, pregnant, alone, would be open to me, but even then, Bridget had standards. She wasn't about to commit to a life of less than what she wanted," Gwydion said tonelessly.

I wanted to apologize. I felt badly for him.

"You don't sound like you blame her," I said.

"I don't disagree with your mother. I wouldn't settle for me either. However, I am vindictive enough to be hurt by it. I can admit my faults," Gwydion said. Oh thank goodness. He gave me a reason to be angry again.

"So you're going to take it out on me?" I asked.

"Nothing personal, Callie," Gwydion said. My temper snapped.

"That is such crap! Why do people keep saying that to me? Trying to kill me is very personal. And you, this is completely personal for you—don't try to deny it."

"I am Gwydion. I am owed," he snarled.

"All of this because my mom didn't settle for you a lifetime ago? You vindictive little bitch. She hurt you, I get that, and now you're going to hurt me. You're smart enough to see how twisted this is."

"I do, little raven. I see exactly how petty this is. And I just. Don't. Care. If it weren't for your father, I would have been your father. I deserved your mother," he said. I don't know if I was horrified or intrigued, but this needed to end.

"Realize, please, that women are not trophies. It was her choice, Gwydion. You can't win a tournament and claim a person as a prize. What does it matter anyway? Pryderi left. My mother was pregnant and my father left us. No one got a happy ending, so I don't understand the point to your revenge scheme. You made it happen because you are bitter and awful."

"Death before revenge, little goddess," Gwydion said.

"What does that even mean?" I wondered. "It makes zero sense. You created a saying to justify murdering me. Coming up with a slogan doesn't make you the hero of this story."

"And now I have decided you are going to die screaming."

"There's no reason for that," I started.

"Do I need a reason? Maybe I just want to smash it all to pieces, you ever think of that?"

From somewhere in the library, someone started to clap slowly. I forgot that we were shouting at each other in a library

Mr. Ogden walked out from behind the stacks. His scalp reflected the light through his bad comb over.

Oh no. Panic crept into my chest. I had to get him away from the mad gods.

"I think that's enough," Mr. Ogden said. "You know the rules, Gwydion. You cannot harm Tuatha on these grounds. The threats I just witnessed are evidence of intent, and your impunity is revoked."

I stared at the librarian I had known since I first came to this library as a toddler. Was this one of my gods or Erik's gods?

"Do those rules apply to me?" I asked the librarian.

"The wards are against those who would do the Tuatha harm. You, being a princess of our people, can do as you wish," Mr. Ogden explained dogmatically.

"Thank you," I said to him, then turned to Gwydion. "Leave."

They came from everywhere, singly and in swarms. The black birds materialized from every bookshelf and from behind stacks. I let the murder of crows chase Gwydion and Freddy out of the library.

****

Once I had somewhat processed what had happened, I decided to ask Mom while we were working on our festival station. I was icing the Fall Festival snacks, and Mom was sorting the last of the crepe paper. Grandpa had gone to fetch the balloon arch and the dry ice.

"I met another god," I said, setting the rice krispie Jack-O-Lantern to dry.

"Oh?" Mom asked absently, finally finding the cauldron she had been looking for.

"Yup, Mr. Ogden at the library."

"Oh right, Ogmios," Mom said, still distracted. I waited.

"What is an Ogmios?" I prompted. Mom handed me the cauldron, which I put near the pile of decorations overwhelming the kitchen loveseat.

"Ogmios, the sun-faced, the shining sage, is our god of binding and eloquence. He is usually a soldier or an adventurer. This incarnation is actually quite amusing," Mom said.

I rubbed my forehead and got icing on my face instead of clarity.

"Are there any other gods in Bellhaven I should know about?" I asked finally. Mom looked at me.

"I don't know how many, but they reveal themselves when they're ready," Mom explained. It wasn't quite a scold, but it wanted to be. Did I sound like I was whining?

No, I wasn't entitled to anything, but I was the one battling the mother of all curses. Maybe my mom could cut me some slack. She started making tea instead.

"How is that fair?" I exclaimed. "Everyone seems to know about me and I know nothing."

"We are all still catching up with the rules. I'm not sure there are any. Why did Ogmios reveal himself to you? There must have been a reason."

"I ran into Gwydion at the library," I said. I spread my hands to pacify Mom when she swung around in alarm. "He just wanted to talk. He started getting testy and Mr. Ogden stepped in. Then I created or transported a bunch of black birds to chase Gwydion and Freddy out."

"Oh, that old trick." Mom shook her head, handing me a cup of tea.

"Yes, the old trick I did for the first time without knowing I could call a flock of birds to chase away my enemies," I said, sipping my tea. Mmm, coconut ginger green tea.

"You used to be able to talk to birds. You lost that gift, long ago. You could bring an entire forest to life in the middle of winter in the space of a breath, blooming green and warmth in the dreary cold. It was wondrous," Mom said, her eyes faraway.

I said nothing. That didn't feel like me. I could actually picture what she was saying in my head. I could see it like it was a memory, but it felt like someone else's memory. I was pretty sure I could do it again, but it would be like wearing someone else's clothes.

"Trish and Marley should be here soon," I said. "They said they're going to skip their morning classes tomorrow."

"I don't think that's a good use of their time," Mom said.

"Apparently, college freshman do not always have to do what their friends' parents say," I said drily. "Anyway, it's the Fall Festival."

"Fine. You have your costumes?" Mom asked.

"We do." I smiled devilishly. "You'll see."

****

Per tradition, all the businesses on Bellhaven's main street took part in the Fall Festival the weekend before Halloween. Several other businesses set up stations along the main strip, too. Everyone in the community was welcome.

A good chunk of the proceeds went to charity but most importantly, this was a giant excuse for a block party with costumes. This year, the donated funds were going directly to the families affected by the hospital collapse, so we had a bigger crowd than usual. The neighboring towns had driven in specifically to support us.

The Bridget's Cross station was to the left side of our front door. I had the dry ice going in the cauldron, and Mom was moving the balloon arch to frame our entrance. Like every year, she wore her black witch costume.

Grandpa walked by in a leprechaun costume, followed by Tyrone, dressed as a lawyer. Grandpa had a Notre Dame jersey over his green suit.

"What?" I said blankly.

"I bleed maize and blue," Grandpa Doug proclaimed. Tyrone snorted around the candy apple he was eating. I have never seen a candy apple eaten neatly, much less by an adult with a full red beard and a three-piece suit, but it was happening in front of me now.

"Grandpa, I will never go to Notre Dame," I said in exasperation. "I have no wish to live in Indiana."

"It's not a place. It's a state of mind."

"Have you been drinking?" I asked suspiciously. Grandpa blew a raspberry on his palm, because he was so mature, and went to see the fire crew. The firefighters had parked the truck by the library and were dishing chili.

The firefighters were helping kids crawl all over the fire truck and pretend to be firefighters, shouting out orders for ladders and hoses. Mr. Ogden sat sedately eating a cup of chili as he watched the next generation of firefighters, and I waved at him. He nodded back gravely.

"Is there drinking?" Duston asked. I moved around a balloon pillar to see Erik and Duston. Duston had a mouthful of spider cupcakes, the ones I had painstakingly filled with peanut buttercream. Helena's silver chain was wrapped around his wrist. I'm sure it was important, but it was my personal day, so I didn't ask.

"He will only have one," Erik assured me, looking so delicious that I would have gladly given him all of the cupcakes. I didn't understand their costumes. I think they were both adventurers, but from separate video games. I gave Erik a big hug, shedding glitter all over his camp shirt and lasso.

"You are so lost down the path of romance that I'm about to give you an otter to hold on to so that you won't float away," Duston said in disgust. At least that's what I thought he said as crumbs flew everywhere.

"*One* cupcake," I warned. "Those are for the trick or treaters. You, you're doing the punch." I shooed Duston over to Mom, who showed him how to pour punch into paper cups.

Erik eyed my costume, and he tried, he really tried to say nothing.

"You can say it." I grinned. I gave a twirl in my ice fairy costume, glitter cheerfully flying everywhere.

"That's a little on the nose," Erik said finally.

"I am who I am, and anyone who has a problem with it can get stuffed," I said airily.

"That does not sound like something a fairy princess would say."

"If you are consorting with any other fairy princesses, you need to tell me now. Listen, I want one night, just one night of normal," I pleaded. Erik looked pointedly at the Fall Festival, with the turnout of almost the entire population of Bellhaven, and everyone in costume.

"Okay," Erik said. "But for normal, we should have hit Oktoberfest in Frankenmuth last month. It would have been less work."

"You weren't talking to me last month. Doesn't Frankenmuth have a Christmas store?"

"The largest Christmas store in the world. I'll take you," he promised. I smiled helplessly. If it weren't for the divine forces at play, this would have been easy. Being with Erik was like falling in love, to use squishy idioms. I didn't have to put any effort into being with him.

"All right, break it up, you two." Trish wrapped gold-and-green-clad arms around me. The summer fairy had arrived. "There's money to be raised and no one is going to buy cookies with you too yukking it up here."

"Duston," Marley the spring fairy said warningly, the flower crown I made for her holding back her auburn hair. "You better not be spiking that punch."

I let the Vanners have a break as we worked the table. Marley took over for Duston because he kept drinking the Halloween punch, which was punch, ginger ale, frozen berries, and ice cubes shaped like toddler hands. We were making a good chunk of money to go toward the recovery of the victims of the hospital disaster.

I was handing Sheriff Lou a cupcake and saw Manuel buy a rice krispie treat from Trish. I was about to go talk to him when the enormous juggling tree caught my attention.

I had no idea how the person inside the tree costume could see, but I was very impressed. It wasn't a scary tree, but it was enormous and not exactly cuddly. Two branches were juggling four balls, and then a third branch join in. It was pretty amazing. Maybe there were two jugglers inside that costume.

The summer and spring fairy shooed me away for a walkabout, and I forgot about the juggling tree.

Today was perfect. The air was crisp and fresh, and my town was laughing and having a good time. If I could freeze a moment to keep forever, it would be this. I walked around all the booths, buying alfajores and kolache, krakelingen and cannolis. I even managed a few bites before the sweets disappeared into my boyfriend's mouth.

"Penny for your thoughts," Erik said, sipping punch.

"That's about all they're worth," I said, leaning my head onto his shoulder. We walked over to the fountain which crowned our central park. At night, the city made the fountain dance and sing, illuminating it with gorgeous lights. Today it was flowing for the last time before it stopped for the winter.

"Here, make a wish," Erik said, handing me quarter.

"You said a penny." I laughed.

"Like you have only one thought. Take the quarter. I want to hear it all."

"You've got to be kidding," I said as I took the quarter, pretending to look around for anyone who might stop us.

"Not even a little. Come on, you're Irish. You're luckier than I am. If I made a wish, it'd probably go all caddywhompus on me," Erik said. I laughed and made a wish as I flipped the coin into the fountain.

"Funny, she doesn't look Irish," a very familiar voice said. "Maybe it's the Type 4 hair."

This was getting very old. Pun intended. And I had Type 3 hair, but I wasn't about to tell her that.

"Helena?" I said. "What are you doing here?" I was honestly puzzled. I needed to get more serious about shooing her away.

"She's probably here to betray us," Erik said. "Again."

"Not you," Helena said intensely. "I've always done the best for you."

"You lured him to his death," I pointed out acidly.

"I didn't know they were going to kill you," Helena pleaded with Erik, which we all knew was a lie.

"No, Hel," Erik said. "You are not forgiven. You need to go now before you get hurt. I don't want to ever see you again."

Her face collapsed and I almost felt a tiny bit of pity.

"Helena, you should go," I said, not unkindly. "You can't touch us here, and honestly, you're not welcome."

The despair on her face abruptly changed to something more familiar: complete hatred for me.

"I can't touch you, bitch," Helena said, "but I can touch them." She turned and walked away. I frowned. She was heading to the pier, which was barely a five-minute walk from the main street.

"I don't understand what she means," I said slowly, looking around. There was my family. There were all the Main Street business owners. There was the fire crew dishing chili. Agnes and Dani were working the table with Trish.

I didn't see Marley. Where was Marley?

My mind churned, trying to sort the information. There were so many people, and everyone was in costume. My eyes settled on the tree juggler, who had taken a juggling break to pretend to be a tree.

Before my eyes, the branches of the tree eased

back to reveal a gaping darkness inside. No one else noticed the hell tree in their midst, because I had thrown up a glamor without realizing it. No one else should have to see this.

A boot emerged, followed by the figure of a man. The man unfolded himself from the trunk like it was his front door, his face obscured by a wide-brimmed hat.

His head came up. It was Gwydion. He had been in plain sight. His name meant son of trees, I remembered now. Why hadn't I paid attention?

Gwydion put his glasses on and met me eye to eye. The discomfort in my stomach grew into a ball of dread.

"You need to stop blaming me for something I didn't do," I said quietly. Despite the crowd, I knew he heard me.

Gwydion shook his head slowly, the brim of his hat cutting swaths out of the air.

Then he held out a flower crown, a very familiar crown that I had woven earlier for Marley's hair.

Marley. Helena could touch Marley.

CONSTANCE KERSAINT

Chapter Nineteen
Trick or Treat

That's when I heard the scream. It was so faint that I almost didn't hear it, but I was paying attention. When I recognized it, all the blood drained from my face. It was Marley, screaming from the harbor.

Erik was already gone, having understood before me. I chased after him and hoped we were not too late. We dodged kids and perambulating monsters, trying to get to the real monsters.

I never caught up to Erik. He was too fast, but Duston overtook me. It's those long Vanner legs. What was usually a five-minute walk became the longest two-minute run of my life before I finally saw the harbor.

The harbor was frozen over. I looked around wildly. The yacht club was on the far side of this little harbor and the pier was off to the left. Everything in between was a solid sheet of ice that belonged in January, not October.

What held my attention was that Erik and Duston did not stop at the edge of the harbor but ran right on. Helena was standing in the middle of the frozen harbor, her sleeves dripping. Underneath her, the water was solid ice, typically seen in December.

I knew who was under the ice.

I created an icy arrow, sharp and cold, and threw it at Helena. Of course my magic would come easily when I wasn't thinking about it. She made a portal or door behind herself and disappeared into it, my snowy anger flying through where she had been.

I reached Erik and Duston, who were taking turns battering the ice. I saw her.

Marley was under the ice and not moving. Her

eyes were open. The spring fairy costume was floating all around her. She looked beautiful and very still.

"Marley. Marley!" I screamed. I tried to blast the ice, and the frozen lake surface grew more solid. I didn't understand what was going on.

"Callie, back it off. You're making the ice harder," Mom ordered. I didn't even notice her come up. Her witch costume fluttered wildly as she heated the water and weakened the ice.

I fell back, helpless and afraid. We were going to get her out. We were gods. We were going to get Marley out. How long had she been down there?

I heard Grandpa call to Erik, and Grandpa's Halligan tool flew by me, whirring end over end until Erik caught it.

With a roar that assaulted my ear drums, Erik brought the Halligan right down on the ice, cracking the surface. The firefighting tool was perfect for breaking into things. The hooked end of the tool dug deep into the ice, driven by Erik's divine strength.

Erik battered the ice again and the crack deepened, darkened. A third blow and Duston could get his fingers down in the crevice. With my heart in my throat, I hooked my fingers around another edge and heaved the ice away. Erik reached for Marley, his fingers brushing her collar.

I willed the water to rise. A solid block of ice bumped Marley up and into Erik's grip. Erik got his fingers around her collar, yanking her up onto the ice next to him. I got to her and dragged her away from the edge.

Marley was freezing, her damp clothes clinging to her like seaweed. She wasn't breathing and was very blue. I started compressions right away.

"We have to get these clothes off of her, warm her

up," I said, counting the compressions in my head. When I got to thirty, I pushed her auburn hair away from her face and gave her two breaths, then started compressions again.

"Callie," Erik said.

"Why aren't you helping?" I snapped desperately. "Get a blanket or something. Call for help."

"Callie," Mom said.

I stared at her as I did compressions, not wanting to see. I stared at my mom, who could heal almost anything in the world. Then she was blurred because I was crying.

I stopped compressions and gathered Marley into my arms. They let me weep as I held the body of my best friend.

****

I decided. Black is the worst color in the world. I will never wear black by choice again.

I stood in the church basement, where we had held so many wakes, and realized that this was a really shitty first time to be one of the grieving.

I didn't feel as if I was allowed to grieve, though. Marley's parents sat off to the side, giving off prickly vibes. They wanted to be alone, but it was a funeral, so they had to be there.

Earlier, the priest had said some nice words over Marley's coffin. Then the wooden box had been lowered into the earth. I had stayed a long time at the cemetery. I watched every shovel of earth as it filled up the hole.

Erik had been next to me the whole time. He had seen me back to the church for the repast. I was grateful, but I didn't feel grateful. I felt nothing.

I kept moving so I would not lose it. I had rolled the ham and turkey and arranged the cheese slices in graduating shades of orange and yellow next to the fruit salad.

The folding tables were littered with spaghetti bakes, Jell-o pretzel salad, pasta salad, German potato salad, chicken salad, meatball casserole, deli platters to make your own sliders, and so on. The common thing with Midwestern funerals is that there is always too much food. Eating means you don't have to talk. There's nothing we hate more than empty words and useless chatter. So we ate as we mourned.

I had helped set up the dispensers of lemonade and tea myself. Not any pop, though. Carbonated beverages were too vulgar for a funeral.

I ate plate after plate of funeral potatoes just to keep from speaking, crunching through the cornflake crust like it was going to save me. They were delicious, made by the same spinster sisters who made them for every funeral. They tasted like ash in my mouth and sat like stones in my belly.

I had contributed the lemon squares and monster cookies. I thought something elegant and something decidedly pedestrian was in order for the occasion. As I watched Marley's brother's hand sneak up from under the table to steal another monster cookie, I felt a pang. He had been an oops baby, and Marley had been more of a mother than a sister to him. I slid a small plate of food and a cup of milk under the table for him.

The truth of the matter was that this was all my fault. I had killed my best friend. And no one blamed me.

No one would punish me. No one even knew, not from her family. They couldn't understand why their daughter, who had been on the varsity swim team for all of high school, who had gone to State every year, had drowned in the middle of October under a freak frozen lake.

How did they bear it? The grief was palpable; I

could cut it with a knife. It was suffocating and they all stood there, letting it smother them.

I went outside as discreetly as possible, because I felt myself about to break. Again.

Erik was there. I almost resented how supportive he was being.

It was time. Oh, this was going to hurt.

"You know, I've been thinking," I said, like I hadn't already made a decision.

"Yeah?"

"People like us don't have happy endings," I said. He looked at me.

"Sweetheart, there are no people like us," Erik said slowly.

"There's the two of us, and that's too many. How many people have died now, Erik?" I said. The weariness of it all weighed me down, and I know it showed.

"I don't understand where you're getting at."

I needed to do this quick. I didn't deserve this person. I didn't deserve to be happy, and I needed to serve penance.

"I mean that we shouldn't see each other anymore," I said.

There was silence. I stared at all the cars in the parking lot, and I didn't even feel the cold.

"You don't mean that," Erik said. I finally looked at him. He was not happy with what he saw in my face.

"No, I meant every word," I said. "People die when we're together. This is the best solution."

"I don't agree," Erik protested. I had to end this now or I would hold him forever.

"It's not your choice," I cut him off. I wasn't going to argue. "Erik, this is goodbye." And I took off for my condo. He did not follow.

****

The next day, after cleaning the bathroom, I came out to the diner to see Mom sitting at the bar. She was staring at a letter like it offended her. She had a teapot and a pile of mail in front of her.

"What is it?" I asked, taking off my apron. I poured myself some tea from her pot, and she handed me the letter.

Under the letterhead of Osmont & Associates, my mother was duly informed that she was to inherit the estate of one Pritchard F. Poole, who had passed away. His will specifically stated that his common law wife and only issue, that would be me, were to receive the bulk of his sizable estates.

I read the letter twice as my tea grew cold. I set the letter and my teacup down before I threw them both across the room.

I do believe I was being taunted.

Fuckers.

"Please take the money," I said to Mom.

"This is blood money," Mom protested. "This should be yours by rights, not because they're trying to bribe you into sacrificing yourself."

"I am so happy we agree that this is ours, because I would like to pay tuition and buy a car," I said firmly. She looked at me, and I smiled back with more confidence than I felt. "Please, let's get that money into our accounts, and we will deal with what they're going to get out of this later."

"It could be a trick," Mom said, but I could tell she didn't believe that.

"It's overconfidence," I insisted back. "This money is going to be ours. Even if the IRS hunts us down for whatever, we're taking it in good faith. In the normal world, this would be called eighteen years' worth of child support, with substantial interest."

"Now you're rationalizing," Mom pointed out. I knew I almost had her.

"Of course. Think of everything we've been through. This is the least we are owed. I mean, we have to get this checked out by our own lawyers first to see if it's legitimate," I said.

"It is," Mom said. "They don't play games like that. This document is as legal as humanly and divinely possible."

"Okay then, maybe we can actually take a break, a vacation, for the first time in my entire life," I said breezily. "And I'll pay for my entire year of tuition in one go before this all disappears during Grandpa's poker game. It's the one good thing Pritchard ever did for us." I drank my cold tea sadly. That had been a mean thing to say.

"He loved you," Mom said sadly. She said it like it was a fact.

"No, he didn't," I stated. I knew it as surely as I knew my own name.

"Don't say that."

"It's not even an assumption. If he loved me, he would have stayed," I said with absolute certainty. "What did he ever do for us? Everything I am, everything we have, we did on our own."

"People are who they are, no better, no worse. They can't be who you want them to be. You have to accept them for what they are, with all their limitations. Your father loved you as much as he could, but he could never have stayed. The geas wouldn't let him stay," Mom said.

"My curse again," I muttered.

"Some things are more powerful than love and family," Mom said. "I'm going to head out and deal with this. Are you okay handling the diner tonight?"

"Me, Agnes, Dani, Grandpa, Manuel, and Billy the fry. Yes, I believe we can run the diner for one dinner shift as we have numerous times, without you," I said. Mom wagged a finger at me and went to change.

I looked at my cold cup of tea. That's when I made the decision.

I couldn't be like my father. I would not be yoked to someone else's bad decisions any more.

I had to leave. I had to get out of Ottawa County.

****

I'm a fairy goddess who is supposed to be capable of cursing not only my gods but everyone's gods. Despite all that, this train station frightened me.

I had hitched a ride to Holland, and now I was waiting for a train. Next stop: Chicago. I had considered taking the bus, but I could conceivably jump off a bus. I couldn't jump off a train. Now I realized that I had never actually gone anywhere before. Also, this train station was truly terrifying. It was dark and foreboding and someone was asleep in the corner.

I escaped outside to wait. The station was located right by what I thought was the Macatawa river, but I couldn't be sure. This wasn't my town. It was pretty deserted this morning, but maybe it picked up later. I wouldn't be here to find out.

I couldn't stay in Bellhaven. I wasn't safe for anyone anymore. Why should I stay? I was going to get everyone I'd ever loved hurt or murdered. My best friend was dead and buried and for what purpose? It had been a pointless end to a bright life. Marley wanted to counsel kids, for gods' sake. She was going to help so many people and instead, she was the dead kid in her family tree.

"You're going to freeze out here," Duston said. I jerked back on the bench, smacking my elbow hard. I stared at Erik's brother, who stood by my bench with his hands tucked into his jeans.

"What are you doing here?" I gasped. Then Trish came up behind Duston. She went to college in Holland. How did they know I was here?

"Just stretching my legs. Didn't fancy seeing you here," Duston said.

"Don't joke with me. Everything is awful right now, and I don't need your attitude."

"Pretend I'm not here," Duston suggested.

"Not difficult. For the most part, you're like cordwood anyway." I was staring at Trish, who was staring right back at me with that look that said I needed to get my shit together.

"Hey, cordwood's good for burning," Duston pointed out. "Good for something."

"Thanks for the vote of confidence, Duston. I always knew I could count on you."

"Does he work hard to get this pompous?" Trish asked, brushing by Duston.

"He comes by it naturally. How did you find me?" I asked.

"Your mom called me," Trish said, her hands on her hips. The breeze ruffled her hair. She was my beautiful, tenacious, last friend and I loved her. "She said you were at the Holland train station. I couldn't believe it. Why would you be in the town where I'm going to school and not tell me? To top it all off, look at who I ran into on my way to figure out this conundrum."

"Me." Duston gestured at himself. "She ran into me."

"I gathered," I snapped at him. "Now be quiet. Trish, I have so many reasons."

"Yup." Trish sat next to me on the bench and crossed her legs. "I'm all ears."

"We know what they want. They want me dead, and they will kill everyone to get to me. I remove myself from the equation, no dead people," I summarized.

"Didn't Erik try to do that last summer?" Trish pointed out. I was quiet as I stared at my last remaining best friend. She had a point.

"He has never lived past sunrise on All Hallow's Eve in my eighteenth year," I said.

"So he has to still be alive Saturday morning," Trish said.

"Yes."

"Today is Friday," Trish said.

"Yes?"

"Therefore you in fact need to make sure he stays alive tomorrow morning," Trish said patiently.

"Yes," I said, a little more unsure.

"What's to stop the Janssens from killing Erik anyway?" Trish asked. I stared at the Macatawa river.

"They're more focused on killing me," I said.

"What's the priority, your life or his life?" Trish argued. I stared at her.

"Isn't anyone curious why I'm here?" Duston interjected.

"No," Trish and I said in unison.

"I'm here," Duston rolled on as if we had not spoken, "because my woebegone brother sent me. He knew you didn't want to see him because you're in this 'I am the cause of all misery' phase so he ordered me, his older and better-looking brother, to come here and make sure you were okay. Your mom called us, too, just in case he was running away with you to protect us all. Come to realize that you were running away from all of us because you are a coward."

"I am leaving," I ground out, "to keep us all alive, or did you forget the recent funeral we attended? My father was murdered. A hospital was destroyed. And Gwydion will go right through you all until I am dead. I am the reason everyone is dead. If I'm gone, no one else dies."

"If you go at it alone, they will kill you and then murder Erik anyway," Duston said. "You need to be back where it's safe, where your family can keep you safe."

"And how has that been working out?" I jumped up to get in his face. "People are still dying."

"And they're going to kill you much easier if you're out there alone," Duston said.

"When Gwydion and the Janssens come for me, then I will deal with it," I snapped at Duston.

"What are you going to do? Are you going to kill him? You don't have it in you."

"Is that supposed to help?" I said in disbelief.

"I don't know, Calliope. You're moping and my brother may still die. I'm not exactly in the mood to make you feel better."

"Then why are you here?"

"I'm here to make sure you don't abandon us!" Duston said.

"You think that's what I'm doing?" I said.

"If it looks like a duck and quacks like a duck."

"You know what? Fuck you. I don't need judgment from you of all people."

"Oh, am I beneath you, princess?"

"Go jump off a bridge. This is how I break the curse. I don't engage."

"Story of your life," Duston said. "I've known, from the day he put on the torc, that Erik would die before me. Someone would come after him and kill him, and I wouldn't be able to stop it. I wish you had someone, Calliope, a brother or sister, because then you'd understand. After Mom left, Dad was out of it for a while, so it was up to me. This was my first job. It's who I am: I protect my little brother."

"You both need to zip it and get ready," Trish said.

"For what?" I asked, then saw who was sitting next to her.

"No, no, please do continue," Freddy said, playing with a blonde strand of Trish's hair. He had an arm around her shoulders and was watching her face, which was stony and glaring out at the water. "I'm very curious if there is more to young Miss Redmond's grand plan before we commence with what is actually going to happen."

Chapter Twenty
Appointment in Samara

"God, you were quiet," I said before I shut myself up. Trish wasn't looking at me. She met my eyes once and looked away with a grimace. Once again, this was all my fault.

"Now, this is all very simple," Freddy said, all chummy good humor. "The ladies are going to take a ride with me. Duston, you will stay here and watch helplessly unless you want to see lady brains all over your shirt."

"Asshole," Duston said and Freddy suddenly twisted Trish's hair, yanking a pained gasp from her.

"No," I said.

"No what?" Freddy asked. "No, don't hurt Trish, whom we can all agree I can kill before either of you get to me, or no, I won't come with you, in which case Trish dies anyway? Think hard, Callie. You're running out of childhood friends."

"You and your cousins." I shook my head. "Did I cause all of your damage? How could I possibly be at fault for how broken you are?"

Freddy moved so fast I couldn't track him and punched Trish right across the face.

I cried out as Trish tried to recover, pressing a hand against her cheek.

"Anything else you want to say?" Freddy asked. I held my hands up, palms out.

"Where should I go?" I asked quickly. "Tell me where to go. I'll go."

Freddy nodded toward the walkway at the front of the building. I looked back at Duston, who looked angry more than anything, and glanced at Trish. Duston's eyes grew hard and I knew he understood.

I left them and had very little in the way of a plan. Trish had to live. That was all that mattered now. Next in priority was to stay alive to see the sun rise again.

I rounded the corner to see George leaning against a filthy gray van with tinted windows. My heart thundered in my chest, and every fiber of my being urged me to run away. The one time I wanted to feel that magic in my mind, it wasn't there.

"Pretty girl," George hummed. "Come quietly and I won't break you." My brain almost shut down. They were going to hurt me. I reached out desperately, frantically casting about for any scrap of magic or power. Nothing. There was nothing coming to save me.

You never went quietly with a kidnapper. This is what I was taught and what I taught to every kid I ever babysat. You never walked docilely to whatever they had in mind.

I could do this one last thing and prayed to god that Duston was as fast as he always was.

I screamed bloody murder, causing George to jerk back against the van. He stared at me with confusion as I turned and ran.

I made it all of ten feet before George grabbed my shoulder and threw me onto the ground. I slid with the force of his throw and slammed up against the wall of the train station.

I struggled to get up and never saw the kick coming.

****

I jolted awake and wished I hadn't. My head was killing me and I couldn't move. I gave up for a moment. For a long minute, I lay there and despaired. After everything, I deserved to wallow in anguish, just for a little bit.

The last thing I remembered was being beaten

outside of the train station in Holland. Trish, oh god, Trish. Was she okay? I couldn't lose another friend.

I tried to take stock of my situation and felt my arms restrained behind me. I was crumpled on the floor of a moving vehicle, likely the filthy van George was so proud of. I think George went for every pothole just to spite me.

I tried to reach out with my magic but could still grasp nothing. I couldn't understand why I was unable do this whenever I wanted, like every other god currently functioning. What was wrong with me that I was the only one who didn't have powers? Well, currently, I probably had a head injury, but if I was supposed to be such a powerful goddess, where the hell was my magic when I needed it?

I didn't move my head much because it hurt, and I didn't want them to know I was conscious. The shadows of streetlights and buildings flickered across the floor. The sun was setting. It had been morning when I was awake last.

I don't know how long we drove before I felt the van drive down a ramp and into darkness. I presumed we were in a parking garage or a basement.

George parked and shut of the engine. Then we sat. The only sound was George crunching on something from a cellophane bag and Freddy slurping out of a big plastic convenience store cup.

The van door suddenly jerked open and Helena stared down at me in all her blonde glory.

"Get out," Helena ordered, and George jumped to oblige. I was yanked out into what looked like a filthy basement. They had bound my wrists with tape and hobbled me with bungee cords. There was another piece of tape across my mouth.

Helena ripped my triskele from my neck. I started

going for her when Freddy appeared and I almost screamed. He was covered in blood. Trish.

"Both dead, because of you," Freddy said absently. "That's what you're wondering, right? Where is your last remaining friend and your boyfriend's brother. I am here, standing before you, to tell you that your fun little trick caused their untimely demise. Well done."

All for nothing. It had been all for nothing. I had, if possible, made things worse. Honestly, what was the point of me? My knees went and George just held me by my elbow, forcing me to stay upright or risk dislocating my shoulder.

"Shut up," Helena said suddenly. She had wrapped my triskele around her wrist. Did that mean I couldn't do magic anymore? "They're coming."

I finally looked around the cold garage and saw them.

The cold did not seem to affect the three wizened old women at all. At one point in their younger years, they must have been tall sturdy women, but their age had hunched their shoulders and stoutened their middles. They were all three dressed in the dark uniforms of hotel staff.

If I saw them on the street, I would assume they were with housekeeping, with their orthopedic shoes and shapeless dresses. We must be in the loading dock of a hotel. I recognized the hotel name. We were in Muskegon.

When the three old women fixed their dark eyes on me, I felt chilled to the bone. They were older than the jötnar, and several times more horrible. I felt it. And they hated me.

"You're late," Helena said flatly.

"We are the Norn," the least shriveled of them said. "We are not summoned."

"I called you, you appeared. That's a summoning," Helena snapped. I was beginning to see who the brains behind this operation was.

"Have a care, Hidden One," the middle old lady said. "You have not forgotten the days when you served us."

"She's not serving you now," Freddy interjected. He smacked George's hold on me, and in the state I was in, I had no strength to stay standing. "Will you please look at what we brought you?" That was the most respectful tone I had ever heard out of him.

The oldest of the women came forward slowly, since it seemed that walking hurt her feet. I stared up at her wrinkled and warty face. This was not someone who would feel pity for my plight.

The old lady's foot flipped me over with strength that belied her appearance. Then she dug her heel into my chest. I was pinned by a geriatric.

"You brought the raven girl," she cackled as she looked me up and down. "Most interesting."

The other two women crowded above me. It was not a pleasant sight. One of them ripped the tape off my mouth, which took skin with it. My mouth was dry, and I realized I was horribly thirsty.

"Young girl, old soul. Very old soul. Oh, the sins you have committed. How nice it must have been to forget them all," the hag said. She squinted at me. "Something interesting here. Same soul. Different flavor. You came back wrong, Branwen."

"Her magic?" Helena asked intently. "Her manifestation? Will we be able to take enough magic to break the geas if she's not a full goddess?"

"Stupid girl. They are in love. If the girl dies before the boy, the geas will break. She is almost complete, but not in the way you think," the middle-aged hag said. "She is not fully manifested as Branwen. Her magic seems choked. Her soul remains the same." Well, that was a relief.

My voice suddenly turned back on.

"I haven't done anything. I have no magic. I'm not Branwen," I gasped, and the youngest hag stepped on my neck. It was not pleasant.

"I want to eat her eyes," the youngest said. She crouched down and stroked my cheek. "There is still magic in you. Think of how beautiful we'd be again. All that power wasted, locked in her head."

"I brought Branwen here so you would sanction the blót for the sake of us all, not for you to steal it all for yourself," Helena cut in. Then she quickly added, "But I'll make sure to save her eyes and tongue for you after the deed is done."

"Nasty piece of work you are," the middle hag sized Helena up. "Is that how you convinced your inbred family to help you? 'For the sake of us all'? You can't fool us, keeper of the dead."

"We could hang you out to dry, you and your jötnar cousins," the oldest remarked. "Why should we sanction your blood sacrifice?"

"Because you want to be powerful again," Freddy stepped in. The old ladies seem to preen under Freddy's gaze. He showed his teeth with a feral grin. "The bastard girl took your power and wove our lives into a pattern of her choosing. She made you obsolete."

They hissed at him, exactly as a large and pissed off snake would.

"And if you fail, wolf?" the youngest hag said.

"I won't fail. I have the goddess of birds at your feet, the thief of fate. I will kill her tonight, before the break of Samhain, and eat the goddess' soul. Her magic will be ours," Freddy said with the most joyous expression I've ever seen on his face.

He was magnetic. I almost wanted to buy whatever he was selling. He could have been so much more than the thug he was.

The three hotel maids, who were apparently once the Three Norns, weaver of the fates of men and gods, moved around me, shuffling and clucking. They were considering it, because that's the way my luck was running nowadays.

"Was this your idea, young wolf?" the youngest Norn asked.

"Do you care?" he blithely replied.

Then they abruptly turned in toward me and spat. I wanted to flinch, or gag, but I couldn't. I just lay there and let three women spit on me. I felt less. Not just degraded but like something had been shut off or taken from me.

"Let it be done," the oldest intoned. She bared her teeth at me, a nasty, ugly smile. "Her magic is bound outside the limits of her homestead. Kill her there. As her lifeblood spills out outside of her place of power, so the power returns to us, the old gods. And we shall rule again." George picked me up and slung me over his shoulder like a sack of potatoes. The Norns turned to leave.

"But," I said numbly, "I haven't done anything. Erik is alive. He just needs to stay alive until tomorrow morning. Then the geas is broken. You don't need to do this."

"Call it insurance," Helena said carelessly. "Also, we're being paid to. Gwydion really, really has a grudge against you. He doesn't care about our reasons, but you know, we're happy to help."

"But," I started and George punched me in the stomach. It was violent, awful, and sudden, and I almost went down. As I tried to get my wind back, he put tape across my mouth again. Freddy heaved me back into the van and gave me a friendly pat on the shoulder.

"Callie, I know more ways to kill than you have friends," Freddy said. He looked at me for a long minute. "I'm going to do you a favor," he said, then slammed my head against the floor of the van.

****

I wasn't dead. It was a crying shame because my head was killing me. I woke up slowly to the dull beat of my heart in my ears. Casting about groggily, I noted that I was lying on a cold hard ground.

That was the third time I'd been knocked out in a month. Twice in one day was a record. I really should see a doctor about it, if I survived the night.

I didn't try to get up. I felt heavy footsteps all around me and heard deep voices. I cracked my eyes open and tried to get my bearings through my lashes. It was cold, of course, and we were in some kind of large building in which people were in various stages of barbecuing.

"She's awake," I heard Helena say before I was hauled up into a chair. I opened my eyes and instantly regretted it.

I stared at what looked like a frozen warehouse from hell and didn't bother to count the number of frost jötnar who were staring at me with hunger and delight. It was actual hunger, and I did not miss the barbecues and firepits dotting the warehouse.

What's a BBQ without beer? The thought came to me as I noted the great many coolers. I could smell pilsner, bread and butter pickles, and charcoal. Blood sacrifices were apparently pretty festive.

A delighted frost jötnar is kind of horrifying. The teeth alone were the stuff of nightmares. Half of them were dressed like a road crew and shedding dust as they walked. Maybe they had come straight from work.

"It is almost time for this all to be over," Helena said, helping herself to a bottle of IPA, as if I needed more reason to dislike her. She somehow fit right in with this very large crowd of burly people, who all seemed to hate me.

I think we were in a smelting plant. There were ironworks and machinery everywhere. This must be where we were going to wait until it was the perfect time to murder me.

"I'm confused. Are you going to cut off my head or eat my brains?" I said. I was certain I was going to die painfully. Erik was going to live. The curse would be broken one way or another and I had made peace with that.

Right now, though, while I was slowly freezing and amidst a great number of people who wanted to kill and violate me, I wasn't feeling heroic.

"We will do both," Freddy said. "But first, we have some frustration to work off. Several centuries worth, as a matter of fact." I appreciated that he gave me some warning of the torture they had in store before they ritually sacrificed me.

"Why the three of you? I can't figure it out. Why do you three want me dead first and no one else from your family?" I spat.

"They're waiting their turn," Freddy said cheerfully. He jerked a thumb at the tailgate party behind him. "We haven't had a good blót in years."

"We are the oldest heroes of our generation." Helena actually answered the question I asked. "The responsibility of righting your wrongs lies with us." I stared at her.

"You think you're a hero? Murdering someone

weaker than you?" I scoffed at her delusion. Helena glared at me. Oh, she actually believed it.

"You are not weaker than us," Helena said. "You are a fatal accident, a scar, an ugly rip in our story. You are a mistake we are going to erase." Then she started patting my pockets.

"What's this, finally getting your hands dirty?" I mocked her. "Hate to tell you this, but you're not my type." Helena paused long enough to punch me right in the face. I heard my nose crack before I felt it.

"Some things I have to do myself," Helena said pleasantly. "Boys get distracted. Where's my necklace?"

"How the hell should I know?" I sputtered, blood running down my nostrils and throat. If she wanted her necklace, she should have stopped her cousin from murdering the cousin who had the necklace, Duston. I should stop egging her, but I was furious. "You have my necklace. Just kill me now. With your bare hands, right here. It's getting pathetic, how you always have to use someone else to do your dirty work."

"You will die. You always do. And this time you'll die on my terms before you ruin our lives again, you fairy bitch," she hissed.

"If only to get away from your constant blathering, yes please," I said.

"Pretty decent bluster, but it's time for you both to shut up. Watching you two get into a slap fight isn't my idea of a good time," Freddy said, turning my chair around. He seemed to be in a loquacious mood. "You were never meant to be, Callie. Your mother wasof the Tuatha, and your father was destined to be the king of the seven cantrevs of Dyfed. They were never supposed to meet, much less procreate. You're a freak, an anomaly. It's probably why you came out wrong in this life. If your mother hadn't been so soft, she would have done what was right and killed you before you were born." He said it almost kindly.

I felt like my heart was crying. I kept my face stony and cold. My mother raised me strong. I never let anyone see me sweat, much less this bully. *I am better than this.*

I had no idea why they had me facing a blank wall. Then I heard George whooping from above. I looked up at the catwalks above us in the warehouse and saw George let something drop.

Erik. He was beaten and bloody. I think some of his bones were broken, but his torso moved. He was breathing.

"No," I wheezed through my broken nose. It hurt. It all hurt. George jumped down from the catwalk, landing with little effort and a mighty thump.

"We found him not far from here. Mighty convenient, it was," George said. He yanked at the torc, which refused to come off of Erik's wrist. I wish my triskele had given me the same courtesy.

"Well done, brother," Freddy purred. Then he gripped my chin and turned my face up toward his. Again, the teeth were horrific.

"We have a few hours before midnight," Freddy said. "What are we going to do with all that time? Do you like games, raven girl?" I heard chuckles from beneath me.

"You need killing, Fenrir," one of the frost giants called out.

"It won't be by you." Fenrir grinned. He was no longer handsome to my eyes. I knew what a twisted little horror he was, and his face couldn't mask that from me anymore. "The one who is destined to kill me is not yet in this world." He released my chin and I fell to my knees.

"Save some for us, bro." George passed by,

guzzling from a foam cup.

"When your blood spills warm on my body and your soul is in my stomach, I will dance before the fires of the end," Freddy exulted. "At long last, we will have our Ragnarök, and you, White Raven, will hold sway over us no longer."

The thug slammed his fist into the side of my face, whipping me to the left and loosening a few canines.

"This should come as no surprise to you, but you are quite the monster," I gasped, my vision spinning. It was just pain. *Let it pass through you.*

"Gods and monsters go together, little raven," he said, stroking my thigh as he chugged his beer.

I despaired. It was so cold, and I was still tired and kicking myself for being so stupid. I couldn't see any way out of this.

"You bastard." I spat out a tooth.

"No," Freddy said thoughtfully as he stroked my face, "you are the bastard. And before you die, I'm going to make you my bitch."

Chapter Twenty-One
Not a Toy

"Let's see what you're made of, Callie," Freddy said, tossing his beer can to the side. "Sugar and spice and all that is nice." He stroked me, very gently, which horrified me to no end. I reacted and bit into his hand, hard. Then he was slamming his fists into my face, but I managed to take a chunk of his flesh off with my teeth. That had not been my goal, but I wasn't unhappy about it. I even swallowed some of his blood.

When I was on the ground and he was kicking me and kicking me, I tasted his blood on my tongue and felt it. I felt the cold all around me and the earth beneath the cement. It must be his blood. Ingesting his blood must have let me touch magic again.

Ew. Tyrone had mentioned something about theophagy, which meant god eating.

Everything was pain. I was being broken and everything hurt. *What's another sin?* I swallowed the piece of flesh I had bitten from Freddy. I was rewarded with a surge of energy.

I broke my taped bindings and surged up to slam my fist into Freddy's chin. I threw everything into the jab. It hurt like all get out, but I took incredible satisfaction in watching him fly back into a few giants.

"Not a toy, Freddy," I gritted, trying to get a handle on what I could access and what I could not.

It felt dark and heavy behind my eyes, but I could harness magic without having to fight it or beg it. I drew as much of that beautiful power into me as I could and let it hum through my bones. It wasn't enough. It was barely a trickle, but I just needed a fighting chance.

I sparked the smelting machines on and fed off of

the electricity, using it to heal what I could inside me. I hadn't known I could do that. I was probably doing this all wrong, but I was desperate.

Grabbing Erik, I ripped the tape off of his wrists, too, and tried to regroup. One of the giants came at us. I jumped on him and bit into his jugular like a vampire, sucking in a big mouthful of blood.

The giant bellowed in pain, and I ripped part of his neck off with my teeth. He collapsed as I got off of him, and I barely managed to swallow the flesh without vomiting. Blood dripped off my chin as I looked around. There were scared giants, bleeding giants, and giants trying to regroup.

Apparently, I didn't need my triskele to be a Tuatha fairy witch, but the magic I was working with now was different from what Mom had tried to show me before. This magic was colder and wilder and felt so right. Then again, I was different than that girl who had died of a broken heart.

There was no way we could get to the exit. A great many people, all of whom I guessed were Janssens, blocked my getaway.

I was still weak and broken, but I had to get us out no matter what. Gathering all the magic I could, I gripped Erik tight. I pushed us off the ground and jumped high over the jötnar, crashing through a window.

****

I really wished I had passed out, but apparently, I was made of tougher stuff now. I was conscious for every agonizing millisecond of crashing through the window. And the falling, holy geez. The falling through cold, empty air was worse than going through plate glass.

Those few seconds felt like an eternity before we landed on the roof of an ancient truck in the parking lot, making a hefty dent. Erik rolled bonelessly into the truck bed and did not move thereafter.

"Erik," I whispered, because I could not really talk. I moved a leg and burst into tears at the pain. I was not sure if any bones in my body were not broken.

I tried looking around to see how I could get help, but we were in a deserted parking lot. Everywhere was water, which was supremely unhelpful. Michigan is the land of rivers. You can't go more than ten minutes without hitting another river.

Then I noticed the familiar blue girders under the Bellhaven bascule bridge. We were just north of the town, outside of the Tuatha ward that had kept me safe my entire life.

The Norns had instructed that I had to be murdered outside the boundaries of my place of power. This bridge marked the edge of the county. I could feel the magic on the bridge. For some reason, there were no cars, even though it was barely dark. The Janssens must have diverted traffic.

I gave a brief thought that a passerby might be able to help me, then discarded that thought. Any Good Samaritan would be murdered immediately if they tried to help me. We were on our own.

I had to get us to the bridge. Once we hit the ward, my family would come. Perhaps I could use the power from the wards. Something. Anything. Killing me on the bridge would do them no good.

They might kill me out of pure hatred, but one problem at a time.

The door of the warehouse burst open and the frost giants began to pour out. They looked like big, hairy men in jeans and plaid, but I could see the shadow behind them. I could see their true self, the frost jötnar, superimposed on their physical form. Before my eyes, they grew into that other image and started to turn blue, as if the cold were chasing the blood away from their skin.

Several of the jötnar ran forward, roaring. They struck the back of the truck, shoving us halfway across the parking lot. I don't know why. Perhaps they thought it was the thing to do, to show their dominance.

I struggled to move, but everything hurt. The jötnar came at us at a run and struck the back of the truck again, knocking me off the roof into the truck bed next to Erik.

"Hi, sweetheart," Erik whispered, groping for my hand. I gripped his fingers tightly, even though it hurt to do so. It was painful to breathe.

"Hi," I murmured, crying ugly, heaving tears.

"I will love you until the end of the world, even if it's tonight," Erik said quietly. He was dying. His family had beaten him to death, again. It was happening. He was going to die.

"That's not plan A, right?" I asked. Erik smiled faintly.

I had promised that he would not be murdered on a beach. Well, right now we were by the water, and the frost giants of Minnesota were coming after us in full homicide mode.

The Norns had bound me outside of my homestead. I could feel my birthright, right next to us, waiting for me. I just needed to get to it, to get out of this parking lot.

The jötnar were roaring, working themselves into a berserker fury. This was about to get ugly. I could feel it. They wouldn't stop with my death. They would kill everyone, and this would all be for nothing. I could hear Freddy whipping his brethren into a frenzy.

"Erik," I breathed. He looked at me blearily, half-dead already. "I love you." Then, praying I was right, I used the last of my strength to push out of the trunk bed. I hobbled as fast as my broken body could take me and fell into the Bellhaven river.

****

It wasn't cold that shocked the breath out of me. It was the heady, silver riot of power that had been waiting for a way to pour into me. Magic punched into me from all sides. My skin was going to burst.

It was as if chains had fallen off me. The geas the Norns had put on me broke, snapping back at them. Take that, I thought grimly, then focused on not drowning. I felt it all, the river, Lake Michigan, the earth under Bellhaven, the wind, the air, everything. I drew it all in and broke the ward set by the Tuatha before I was born. I freed all that magic and drank it in.

This was different than before. Mom's magic was sweet and summery. I was never comfortable working with her kind of magic. This magic right here, the cold and wild and icy power that enervated me and made me want to sing, this I was quite comfortable with.

I called the water up as I had done with Marley's body and rode a baby glacier to set myself on the Bellhaven bridge. Then I hurled the baby glacier at the frost giants out of spite.

I was angry. I drew recklessly from the earth to heal myself and Erik, knitting back together bones and veins and skin. My nose no longer hurt. Nothing hurt, but I was still pissed as hell.

They had killed my friends and beaten me and degraded me. No more. This was where I would stand up to them. The boy would not die tonight. I would not allow it.

The wind started howling cold and fierce around us, ruffling the beards of the jötnar and nudging the vehicles parked on the road.

Erik sat up, strong and amazed. I drew together a swirling ball of ice the size of a soccer ball between my hands, pouring all my hate and rage into it. It wasn't a big ice ball, but it was potent.

When I let it loose, it was as if I had fired it from a cannon because it shot at the smelting plant and blew it up with a spectacular explosion of fire and brick and glass. The noise was deafening. The spray of debris showered us liberally.

The jötnar roared in fear and excitement. Spears come out of nowhere and the noise was horrendous. This was what they lived for, chaos and the promise of a good killing. Freddy emerged from the crowd and marched toward us, George behind him.

Freddy sauntered toward the bridge, ripping off his clothes and working himself up into a berserker rage. Erik was long forgotten. He wanted me dead now.

"The time is well-nigh, little bitch!" Freddy shouted, spittle flying from his mouth. "The one who will take my life is not yet in this world. You cannot kill me!" I squared up to him. I was done being bullied.

A fire ax whipped past me, ruffling my hair, and slammed butt-first into Freddy's head. Normally, that would have killed a person. This strike only dazed Freddy, driving him back in a stumble.

"Once again, moron, you're wrong," Duston said grimly, striding up next to me. "I am very much in this world."

"You're alive," I gasped, gripping his arm. The big, beautiful oaf was alive.

"Of course I'm alive," Duston said. He saw my face. "Trish is fine. I got her away from Freddy, but couldn't get to you and save her, too."

Behind Duston, we saw more people, enormous people on fire. The leader was enormous, as tall as the second story of the now-destroyed warehouse. Behind them all, I thought I could make out Grandpa.

My mind shut down temporarily. There's only so much I can take.

"Uncle Sutherland," Duston said, indicating the burning king in front. He turned to me. "Surtr, he's the king of the fire jötnar."

"Fire giants?" I said faintly. "How many different jötnar are there?"

"Just the three types of giants. Listen, I'm going to go get my brother," Duston said and abruptly left.

"Oh, yeah sure," I said, then almost fell over when an enormous black bison-thing galloped past me to join the fray. I stared after it, squinting. It was Garth, if the dog had been supersized with a cosmic ray gun.

Then I heard my name being called and turned to run south to Grandpa, through the fire jötnar as they rushed past me to clash with the frost jötnar. Norm ran by with a broadsword, his face grim, and he methodically slashed though the ice giants to get to Erik. I was certain those ice giants were his cousins.

I didn't care right then. I rushed right into Grandpa Doug's arms.

"Mom?" I gasped.

"Your mother is fine. She went to get someone important," Grandpa Doug said, folding his hands over my face and setting his palms on either side of my nose. "Stay still." Before I knew it, my nose wasn't crooked anymore, and I felt as if I had been punched again. Ow.

"Where's Gwydion?" I gasped, processing the pain.

"Beats me," Grandpa said, eyeing the berserker battle between giants dispassionately.

"What do we do?" I asked desperately.

"This is your holy war," Grandpa Doug said, his

hands in the pockets of his overalls. He looked comfortable. "What do you want to do?"

"I want to keep Erik alive until sunrise to break the curse," I said quickly. This was the same wish I had made at the fountain during the Fall Festival. This was the answer to all my prayers.

"Okay then," Grandpa said, watching the jötnar battle each other. I blinked, waiting for the almighty Dagda to fix things.

"Okay?" I echoed.

"If you want to keep the boy alive until sunrise to break your geas, keep him alive," Grandpa said. "Tell me what you need help with." Well, all right then.

I turned back to the fight. Norman Vanner clotheslined a frost giant, plowing his arm right into the giant's neck and then drop-kicking the giant across the road. That was a little shocking to me because it was Norman, but this man was a god. Duston had linked up with Erik, and they were not hiding. The Vanner brothers were going berserker, slashing through their brethren in swaths of blood.

Helena was on the other side. Somewhere, Marley was telling me to let it go.

Unfortunately, Marley wasn't here anymore. I marched into the battle, and the giants parted for me.

My vision went red. I was afraid and I was angry. Then and there, I made a decision. I wasn't going to be afraid anymore. I took a hold of my anger and channeled it into something unfriendly and powerful, pulling the cold around me like a thick blanket of magic.

Something inside me started building, growing. It felt right. This felt like shoes that fit perfectly or a sweater knitted for me.

Then George's arms were locked around me like a blue vise. The icy winter of him on my skin was like a stain. He looked faintly ridiculous as a blue boy, but I didn't tell him that.

"I will kill you with cold, little raven," George promised. Well, that made me angrier, and I slammed my head back against his nose. It hurt me, but it hurt him more. His arms loosened enough for me to drop out of his grip and stumble away. I lashed out a leg and caught him in the stomach.

"Hey, asshole," I gritted out. "I'm from Michigan." And kicked him again, square in the blue face.

George staggered back a bit, then swung a haymaker at me.

I caught his arm and held him in place as I stared him down. Oh yeah, I had super-strength now.

"You keep telling me I'm a story, that I'm Branwen, the princess of birds. Well, stories change. I don't talk to birds. I'm not that girl who turned to stone on a cliff. I'm not a victim. I'm not a fairy princess anymore," I stated, angrier than I had ever been my whole life.

I remembered something Erik showed me. I grounded myself, taking hold of one of the guard rails. The power crackled through me. It owned me tonight. And I let it flow, because it was yearning to break free of its confines.

We are the elements. That's what Mom said. We are the moon and the sun and the wind and the water. I took a deep breath and closed my eyes, searching the roiling clouds above for what I needed. George thrashed at me with his free arm. My eyes snapped open, and even though I felt like I was going to have an aneurysm, I urged two clouds to rub together. A sizzling bolt of lightning struck the bridge tower, lighting it up like a Christmas tree.

I was electricity. Every person who was touching the railing got fried to a crisp.

I let the electricity flow through my body into George. And then I blew the air out of my lungs, and the electricity flowed out like a blue, crackling snake. George jerked back, not fast enough, and my electric current enveloped him like a disease, suffusing his body and singeing his hair.

I let the currents bounce around his body, just a little, because I was furious that I had let him torture me.

Then I blasted George's body through the middle of the battle raging on the bridge. Jötnar were plowed down or bowled over. I cleared a path between the Vanner brothers and Freddy, and singed the concrete bridge to an oxidized crisp for good measure.

Erik smiled at me, a welcome flash of teeth among the blood and death raging around us. Then he turned to face Freddy, twirling a metal pole in his hands like a quarterstaff.

"My damage branch will rend you!" Freddy roared.

"You get creepier every year, Freddy," Erik said before he feinted left. Freddy fell for it and went to counter. Erik immediately followed and slammed the pommel of his sword up into Freddy's chin.

"Loki isn't awake, cousin. He remembers nothing of who he was before. I will fulfill his destiny and take your life, Vindler." Freddy smiled. "And I'll enjoy every minute of it."

They crashed together, taking out friend and foe as they fought.

Duston was holding his fire ax and facing George, who was staggering up after I had used him as a bowling ball. He was smoking, just a touch singed.

"Hey, Duston," George said with discernable fear.

His face wrinkled as he screwed up his courage. "Go Wolverines." Then he yelped when the enormity that was Garth knocked him over. "Garmr! Get off!"

"This is the line," Duston said, coming forward as he shook Helena's silver chain out. "You're on the wrong side of it." George charged Duston, who whipped the chain from his wrist and lassoed it around George's neck.

"Oh, that necklace," I said to myself as I tested out a compact wind gust on an ice giant. It worked and with a clap, the giant was blown off the bridge.

"Víðarr," George whispered, staring at Duston. "I'm sorry. We didn't know. Please, Gleipnir hurts."

"You're almost useless, George," Duston said grimly, yanking the silver chain Gleipnir to the ground, taking George with it. Gleipnir was the only chain in the world that could hold a jötnar. "You don't usually know anything. This situation is not exceptional."

I left them and kept moving to find Helena. I walked through the battle, and no one dared to come close to me. Helena was standing across from me. She wasn't watching the fight. She was watching me.

"I warned you," I whispered to myself, not noticing the sky rumble above us. "I warned you to keep this between you and me, to keep my friends out of it."

The crackle of electricity jolted through my limbs, and I soothed it like it was a puppy.

"My friends," I said, my head pounding and my heart racing. "My family. My lover. You keep hurting me, asshole gods, and I am done!"

I leapt above the fray and felt the wind in my hair and the lightness of being carry me to where Helena was. I landed and got a good grip on the back of her neck before she recovered from the shock of seeing me airborne. Then I jumped again, a mighty leap on the center of the bridge and away from her allies.

I loved being strong.

I crashed into the concrete and threw Helena down. The sound of her head bouncing off the ground was very pleasing.

"Let me ask you something," I said conversationally, but I made sure everyone, every jötnar, fire and ice, and Vanir, could hear us. I tapped her with my foot and Helena bounced a few feet away. "In that past thousand years, have you ever apologized for bringing Erik to that beach? For lighting the fire that called the jötnar to murder him? Do you feel any remorse?"

The look on Helena's bloody face said it all.

"Then I won't say sorry either," I said. "I will never apologize again."

"I loved him," Helena said helplessly.

"No, you didn't," I told her. "When you love someone, you protect them. You wanted to possess him and threw a tantrum when you were denied."

I looked over at Erik just as two frost giants shove him back against one of the bridge pylons. Freddy punched Erik across the face; Erik spat out blood.

I glared at Helena, and something in my face terrified her. Then I cut loose. All the power, the anger, that had been building. It welled up like a tsunami gathering up for a surge. The magic that I could command terrified me.

I didn't understand why I had a maelstrom in my heart, but it was right, and it was all mine. I had conjured a tumult of snow and ice, swirling in the atmosphere, and it answered to only me.

This wasn't Branwen's magic. Her gifts had been sweet and gentle and lovely. She could make bird sing and trees bloom in the winter.

This magic dancing at my fingertips, eagerly

waiting my order, was violent and merciless.

Oh, there it was now. I knew my name, my real name. I had been going about this wrong the whole time.

I looked at all of them as icicles started forming in concentric rings around me. My storm winds swirled around me, picking up speed.

These folks should know who they were dealing with.

"I am Cailleach, the god of all winters. I rule the storm winds, and you will not hurt me again," I swore, then called down a blizzard storm of hell on their heads.

CONSTANCE KERSAINT

Chapter Twenty-Two
Summoned to Tourney

My icy tornado slammed into them like a Buick taking out a deer. Every jötnar stopped fighting because they were knocked to the ground by my rage. There would have been screams if my winter winds had let them breathe.

I heard Freddy roar and felt the ground shake violently. His eyes were wide and wild, but there was something else. I think he was scared.

I had a vague sense of Grandpa and Norman watching me. If they wanted to let this play out, I'd give them something to see.

Freddy yanked himself over to an SUV and threw it at Duston, but Erik had seen it coming. My favorite person on earth lifted a truck and batted the SUV away with a force that hurt my ears.

Duston reached out to Erik. Then the brothers charged Freddy. Duston never made it because he was attacked and fended the giants off Erik's flank.

Erik had the silver chain in his hands in a loop. He whipped Gleipnir around Freddy's neck like it was a lasso and pulled him sideways. Freddy fell to the ground and slid, hollering bloody murder. With a running leap, Erik pinned his cousin to the ground.

I let up my blast of icy wind. The jötnar stayed on the ground, stunned.

Erik looped Gleipnir around Freddy's throat and yanked up, but Freddy somehow elbowed Erik in the face. They rolled around with the force of a hurricane, the ground shaking. Freddy got his teeth on Erik's arm at one point.

I was done with this. I was going to end it. I took

Helena's wrist and bit into it, sucking blood viciously.

Her blood opened a pathway for me, clear as day, to her magic, her very soul.

I could touch it. I could weave it. I could destroy worlds with her blood on my tongue.

Also, *ew*. This would not become a habit.

I pulled Helena's head back by her hair and slapped a palm against her chest. She screamed as I pulled something out of her, and I took immense satisfaction in her pain.

Duston had done this with me long ago, when he had set the wards on the school. He had used my magic, but now I saw that he had been infinitely gentle and careful with me.

I showed Helena no such courtesy as I sucked the essence of her person, her soul, into me. I took her magic as she would have taken mine and I felt no remorse.

Helena was the ruler of Hel. I could feel it inside of her, the essence of her divinity, her connection to the realm of the dead.

I could absolutely cook with that.

I drank every bit of life and power out of her, the very essence of her being became mine as I lobotomized her. Then I ripped my triskele from her wrist and dropped her. She fell like an empty shopping bag. I had all of what she was inside of me, and I drove that power down through the bascule bridge into the Bellhaven river. It swirled and darkened beneath us.

I held the triskele above my head, driving Hel's magic around it. I had seen something like this once, a pattern on a loom. Somewhere in my past lives, I had seen someone else weave magic to open a door. I used that as a blueprint and did the same.

I threw my charged triskele down into the Bellhaven river. The triskele spun bigger and impossibly bigger. The raven heads blurred and glowed. Then we were all looking at a swirling gate to Hel.

I motioned for the three raven heads to part and they spun away from each other, making a black depthless hole. We saw endless fire and smoke and screams billow out from the whirling vortex beneath the bridge. It was a never-ending nightmare, and I held open the door.

Erik heaved Freddy's bound body off the bridge and Freddy fell. He screamed for a very long time. Duston dragged George forward and threw him down into the Hel gate.

I gripped the back of Helena's shirt and dragged her to the guardrail. It took very little effort to throw her over the guardrail and into the maelstrom underneath. She made no sound as she fell.

When I couldn't see or hear them anymore, I closed the gate and fell to my knees. There was a shift beneath me, and I clinically noted that the bascule bridge was likely not stable anymore.

I breathed. Was it over? I looked at Erik and he jerked me to my feet, his eyes still wild.

"Is it over?" I asked.

"I don't know." Erik pushed my hair back from my face, cataloguing my injuries. I had a few.

"I'm Cailleach," I told him. "Same soul. I came out different. Don't know what's going on."

"Same build, different badging. Like a Valiant and a Dart. Or a Camaro and Firebird."

"Sure," I agreed, with no clue what he was talking about. I started to relax as I looked around.

"You dare!" a horrible voice thundered, hurting my ears. The bridge shook underneath us.

Nurse Angie stood on the north side of the bridge, crying as she watched the water where the gateway to Hel had been. I didn't understand what she was doing there. I moved to get her away.

Then she howled, her jaw expanding to a nightmarish angle. Okay, definitely a god.

"Who?" I couldn't even finish the question. Gwydion appeared, finally. He stood behind Nurse Angie, his hands in his pockets. She must be an accomplice of Gwydion's.

I turned and the Vanner men were behind me. In the flickering halogen bridge lights, they looked as tired and beaten as I felt.

"Angrboda," Norm supplied. "Mother of Fenrir, Hel, and Jörmungandr. All of whom you recently banished to the underworld."

"They're alive. They tried to kill me, but we let them live," I argued.

"You should have tried to kill them instead of being nice. Eternal torture in the underworld is a fate worse than death, and now you owe a debt," Norm explained. Somehow, I just did not believe that his argument would hold up in court. Many, many strange and shadowy people were gathering around us, so maybe he knew what he was talking about.

"I am owed!" Angrboda roared, advancing toward us. "I invoke the old laws and my three insults shall be avenged."

"Avenged how? Where is this heading?" I hissed at Grandpa Doug. He said nothing and put his arms around my shoulders. Then Grandpa looked up. There was nothing in the sky.

Right then, the air sizzled and from the clouds, my mother and an older woman with wild red hair descended. I didn't even see where they had come from, they appeared so suddenly. Tyrone suddenly popped into existence between us and Angrboda. He waited for my mother and the other woman to be on firm ground.

"My lady Morrigan." Tyrone bowed to the older woman. "Lady Brigid. The old laws have been invoked."

"Name the charge," the Morrigan ordered in a voice that made you stand up straight. She was so regal that I would have been intimidated if I was paying more attention. I was having trouble focusing, because this had been quite a trying day.

"Three insults avenged in blood." Gwydion filled in the blank this time. "Branwen has banished three of Angrboda's children. My deepest apologies, you are Cailleach now."

He had no expression on his face, but I knew, I just knew that he had planned this all from the start. No, it must have been one of several plans.

"You planned this," I accused Gwydion.

"Always have a backup, little raven," Gwydion advised. "Never trust an ice giant to get the job done." Every ice giant still standing turned toward Gwydion. They may not have been able to eat my soul, but I hoped they would finish Gwydion off if I failed.

"They tried to kill me! I defended myself," I protested.

"Then you should have killed them, as was your right, but you banished them instead. That is an insult, not justice," Gwydion said. I shook my head.

"I don't want to kill anyone."

"Your intentions are noted, but by our laws, you have wronged them," the Morrigan said.

"What about their intent to eat my soul and steal my magic?" I asked. I got a good look at the Morrigan's face and had another shock. Oh dear, I thought I knew who this woman was.

"Three banishments are greater offenses than a curse. Your actions are being judged, and in banishing

Fenris, Jörmungandr, and Hel, you have injured their mother, Angrboda. The charge stands," the Morrigan judged.

"The settlement," Tyr intoned grandly, "is yours, Angrboda."

The person who I used to know as Nurse Angie seemed to expand and turn blue. She stared at me with breathtaking hatred.

"We settle this by tourney," Angrboda gritted out through tears. A roar erupted from the jötnar, frost and fire alike.

"A what?" I hissed, gripping Grandpa's arm.

"A tourney is a duel, two champions fighting each other. It's essentially a battle by proxy," Grandpa said, patting my hand, his sharp eyes on the proceedings.

"We could have used that earlier," I snapped, looking around. I couldn't keep up.

"If I may," Norm cut in. "We have a chance here to break the geas. The caster of the curse can break the curse."

Oh. That was news to me.

"The goddess stands here manifested, on the eve of Samhain, when her winter begins. In a few hours, the curse will be broken. I humbly request the tourney be postponed until after sunrise," Norm said formally.

"I must say, I too am very interested in being done with this curse," Tyr said. "The decision, though, falls to the damaged party. Angrboda?"

"That bitch dies now!" Nurse Angie screamed. I could feel her anguish. I could also feel the concrete bridge sway underneath our feet. I think I wanted off this bridge.

"The damaged party has spoken." Tyr shrugged. "Name your champion, should you choose not to battle yourself."

"My champion is Vindler," Angrboda, mother of monsters, spat spitefully. Erik stumbled forward in confusion, pushed by invisible hands. He and I stared at each other.

Every god gaped in shock, which quickly turned to terror. A whole battle had just been fought for Erik's survival, and now one of their own was endangering his life again.

It was hours yet until dawn. He had to live a few more hours or this was all for nothing. If he died before sunrise, we were all doomed to repeat this tragedy.

I couldn't do this again. I knew this was all my fault, but it had to stop.

"Do something," I pleaded with Norm.

"I can't," Norm said, his face anguished. "I can't interfere in a tourney. This isn't my story."

"I'm really starting to hate that sentiment," I muttered, folding my hands to my face.

Norm went to help his son. Duston was there, too, putting a hand on Erik's shoulder.

Erik looked up at me. He was trying to not show it, but he was scared. I could see it. Everyone could see it.

Work the problem, work the problem, I chanted in my head. There was always a solution. I may not have been the fastest or the strongest person out there, but I could think my way out of anything.

"Tuatha!" Angrboda screamed. "Choose your champion."

I had to do it. The caster can break the curse. No one had a better chance than me.

"Our champion is," Grandpa Doug started.

"Me," I said quickly, stepping forward. I had no idea who he was going to call, but I was almost sure that I was the most powerful Tuatha present. Maybe. I was totally guessing.

Mom was not happy. She knew that I had absolutely no idea what was going on but damned if I wasn't going to try. She took my hand and squeezed.

"Ten minutes until tourney commences," Tyr announced.

Mom put her hands around my shoulders and squeezed. I didn't cry. I wanted to.

"Listen to me, you have to last until the sun comes up. You don't have to beat him, just last. Be standing at sunrise," Mom said. "Cailleach rules the winter. When the sun rises, it will be Samhain, the first day of winter. You can break the geas at sunrise."

"Last at what? Standing? What are the rules?" I asked.

"Gwydion and I will keep the music going. When we stop at sunrise, one of you kids has to be standing, like your mother said," Grandpa said.

"That didn't make any sense. Is this a dance fight? I don't dance."

"You have to fight Erik," Grandpa said, looking at me weirdly. Like I could have known that. I was still bleeding from the last fight.

"*Fight* him? I can't fight Erik," I protested. Who made these rules?

"You are our champion for the tourney, Callie, freely offered. Now, I've got Uaithne," Grandpa hefted his electric guitar that had somehow magicked from his living room, "and Gwydion can sing. No matter what happens, when the music stops, you better be alive."

Such a small thing to ask.

I was afraid. I had just defeated three gods and I was terrified.

"Alive," I repeated. I had doubts. I shoved them deep down into a box I never open, but I had doubts.

I just had to do it. I didn't have room for doubts.

"Is she ready?" the Morrigan said. I jumped. She had come up out of nowhere. I was distracted from my upcoming trial by her face, though, and the way she held herself. The Morrigan looked intensely familiar. I looked at her and found myself looking at my own eyes in the Morrigan's face.

The Morrigan looked like an older version of my mother.

"Later," the Morrigan said. "Now you must pace yourself." She sounded as officious as a judge. She stared into my eyes hard, reinforcing my resolve. "But you're very strong. Don't let the circumstances defeat you. Hold on to what's important."

My heart was gripped with a fear that could not be imagined, that I never dreamed of or wanted. What if I couldn't save him? What if he killed me?

I shook away most of my fears and strode forward with my chin up and my shoulders back. I'd be damned if I let them see me afraid.

I stopped by Gwydion. He had the decency to not seem smug, but here was the architect of all my pain.

"Let me be crystal clear," I said to Gwydion, "I will kill you." He smiled approvingly.

"Ever your father's daughter."

"Shove it," I said.

"You haven't been able to hold on to your lover for thousands of years. You won't be able to tonight." Gwydion grinned. "Just like your mother, always making the wrong choice."

I opened my mouth to reply in kind when a memory flashed across my mind, an image clear as day.

"You made me a daisy chain once," I said suddenly. Gwydion stood, still as a stone pillar. "Summer was almost over, and you took me for a walk over the hills by the loch so that Mom and Gran could finish preparing for the harvest festival. You told me stories to make me laugh."

We stared at each other. Then I was knocked to the ground. I gasped for breath and scrambled away. I didn't hear any start bell. All around, music started, something old and grim.

Erik stood over me, his eyes crazed. He was beyond berserker. He kicked at me, and I managed to push myself away with some goddess-strength.

Erik would never willingly hurt me. What was this?

"Begin!" Tyr called belatedly. Grandpa and Gwydion sat on opposite sides of us, Grandpa with a guitar and Gwydion with a small lap harp.

I thought this was all very unfair as the music swelled in earnest. I could have used some warning.

"Erik?" I asked, trying to look everywhere at once. "What?" I couldn't finish the question because he lunged at me. I barely dodged him and scrambled to the middle of the bridge. I just didn't want to be cornered. To be honest, I had no idea what I was doing.

"Erik?" I asked, a plea in my voice. He had always been steady, dependable. I felt as if half of my heart had been ripped from my chest. I didn't want to do this without him. I didn't want to be without him.

Something had taken hold of Erik, controlling him. There was no intelligence behind his eyes. He went at me again and I fell to the ground, catching a glimpse of Gwydion as I fell.

The look on his face. He had done it. He had driven Erik berserk.

I scrambled to my feet before my destined love stomped me to death. I commenced with an ungraceful and embarrassing game of keep away. I couldn't hit him. I think I could have actually fought well, but I couldn't bring myself to do it.

Then it came to me, the answer appearing out of the jumble of my thoughts.

Hold on to what's important, Mom said. *Hold on to your lover*, Gwydion had taunted. I knew this story. I knew what to do.

Gwydion's voice was beautiful, a clear melodious tenor. I recognized the song, "The Unquiet Grave". Jerkface was taunting me with a ghost story. Now I was angry.

Erik's body twisted and jerked, like someone possessed going through an exorcism.

Grandpa Doug was shredding a hard G major riff on the guitar he called Uaithne, something that certainly belonged to the 1970's.

I jumped forward and threw my arms around Erik's neck. It was in no way decorous, but I wrapped my legs around his waist and held on tight, my head next to his.

I held on. I would not let go. He shivered violently and transformed.

I held a wolf, which snapped and growled at me. Oh yes, I knew this story well. All I had to do was hold on.

A paw caught my shoulder and claws ripped a path down my back. It hurt like hell and I screamed. All I had to do was hold on. Right. This was going to be harder than I thought. I wasn't going to waste effort maintaining my dignity. The goal here was survival.

I screamed as the boy I loved turned into a red-hot column of steel and I could smell my own flesh burning. For the first time, I had a sense of my godhood because any normal human would have failed by now. My body was stronger and more resilient than it had been before. I must not falter. I could not fail.

Bridget Redmond appeared in a flash of light and smoke by Gwydion. He closed his eyes, refusing to look at her, and kept singing.

"Tourney, Brigid," the Morrigan said to her. "You cannot interfere." Mom glanced at the woman who was either her mother or aunt, and stayed by Gwydion, who was singing a sad, sad song in a lilting language I didn't understand.

"Stop this now, Gwydion," Mom whispered to him. I was screaming my lungs out as I was burned, my skin bubbling and blistering, but I could still hear her words. "Leave them alone and I'll come with you."

Back in the part of my mind that could still form rational thought, I rebelled against the very idea. She was doing it for me.

I was mostly occupied by trying to stay conscious as my boyfriend writhed in my arms, but I was still aware of wanting to save my mother also. I couldn't do both, though, and I was committed to Erik's salvation. For right now, my mother was in control of her own destiny.

Mom stared at him with those big sea-green eyes. I saw the look on Gwydion's face, as Erik's current form of a spiky steel column scraped my flesh from my bones. Gwydion loved my mom and was still hurt she hadn't chosen him. He showed no remorse, though, and even I could tell he was determined to see things through. I was a dead girl.

Gwydion stared at her sadly, still singing, but he started singing to her. It was an old ballad I recognized, a man singing about promises unfulfilled and a dead lover moving through the fair. I understood then—he was telling my mom that the course could not be altered now. The time for her to choose him was long gone.

However, my mom was here now. I needed that. All my life, the strongest support I'd ever gotten, sometimes the only support, was from my mother. She was strong and smart and resourceful and she never quit. I was her daughter. I was the same.

I stared at her now and took strength from that. My mother loved me and believed I could overcome all obstacles, just as she had.

Then I heard a fiddle. It was a wonder I could hear anything since I was certain one of my eardrums had been pierced by a spike and burned. No, it was a fiddle. I wasn't hallucinating that.

The fossegrim was playing with Grandpa Doug, something I could make out in the early light. You know, I would ponder the fall-out of a Scandinavian river spirit helping out a Celtic trickster god later. Right now I was being flung about by a big white bull.

I would not fail. The white hide of the bull turned pink as my blood soaked through the hair. I was a princess of the Tuatha de Danaan. Surely I had an endless supply of fairy blood to bleed.

My arms were wrapped around the neck of a rough-scaled dragon which lifted me high into the air and shook its reptilian head violently. My grip was precarious because everything was streaked with my blood and I was scratched up further from the sharp scales, but I held on. Mom always said my stubbornness was an asset, I thought to comfort myself.

I heard another fiddle accompany Gwydion's harp. A giant with a horse's head and backward hooves for feet nimbly playing the fiddle with Gwydion. A glashtyn. *Great, the gang's all here.*

I let the pain pass through me. *It's not real. It's electricity along my nerves, a trick of the mind.* I knew my brain wanted to shut itself off from the pain, but I would stay conscious. I would hold.

Then my boyfriend transformed into column of

ice so cold and dry that the surface stuck to my body and twisted, ripping off swaths of my skin with it. I could see the steam come off the ice where I bled on it because it was no longer dark.

I heard Gwydion's voice. I heard it surge. Then I heard it stop. The music stopped. No more guitar, no more song, no fiddle, nothing but dead silence.

I cracked my blood-crusted eyes open. I could see the ground. I lifted my head and saw the bridge illuminated. The sun had peaked over the horizon. It was daybreak on Samhain, the day after Halloween.

I felt the curse break, because the anger, grief, and pain that I had used all those years ago to create the geas snapped back at me. I could almost see the magic, grown old and frayed with centuries, as it sped at me and reentered this new body my soul resided in.

That shit hurt. I tried to scream and it came out as a strangled croak from my ruined throat. The bridge shook underneath us and every god fell to their knees.

I was so tired, but I needed to finish the job. All the magic was flowing back to me and I reached out through them, weaving. Some long-forgotten lesson came back to me, at my grandmother's loom, as she showed me how to see the pattern before I wove and set the pattern permanently.

I held the magic of all gods in my power, and I saw how I had warped the threads of their destinies into my curse. I also saw what they should have been, and with a mighty jerk that hurt just about everyone, I yanked our destinies back to where they belonged. Mostly. I was really tired and getting more so. I couldn't repair everything, but I got really damned close.

Then I remembered a lesson from my mother, a way to gracefully return or end a flow of magic. With the last of my resources, I knotted off my connections and returned control of magic to hundreds, maybe more than a thousand.

I gave them back their magic and their destinies, the way they were meant to be.

We had done it. We were free.

CONSTANCE KERSAINT

Chapter Twenty-Three
All Hallowed

I was a living thing of pain.

The moment I finished repairing the damage the curse had done, I regained feeling and it was bad. This hurt more than when the hospital collapsed on me or when Freddy beat me until I thought I was going to die. This made me almost wish I was dead.

I heard Angrboda scream in despair, and for a moment I thought it was me screaming. Sutherland roared something deafening that I didn't understand, and the frost giants converged on Angrboda. Then they vanished.

The angry screaming giant woman who wanted me dead, the block party of frost giants who were preparing to cook me, everyone vanished into thin air. I didn't care. They were one less problem I had to deal with. More importantly, I needed painkillers very, very badly.

Then his arms came around me. Erik's arms. Erik was himself again. He was alive. The blood all over him was mostly my own. In fact, my blood was everywhere. I should be dead.

I was burnt, cut, bleeding, ripped to shreds, but I somehow found the reserve to search out my nemesis.

Gwydion had fallen to his knees. He was staring off at nothing, his eyes glassy, his mouth slack. A shadow fell across my vision. Oh, it was the Morrigan. I was afraid I was passing out.

"You are owed. You have been damaged," the Morrigan judged. "The kill is yours."

I stared at her, then at Gwydion.

Besides the fact that I could not stand under my

own power, I couldn't do it. I couldn't kill the man who had killed my father, who wanted to kill me.

"He betrayed the Tuatha and caused the murder of many, including my father. Mete out the punishment that fits that crime. I will not carry out the sentence," I said. The Morrigan looked at me with no emotion and nodded.

"It was a crown I made you. A crown of daisies," Gwydion said suddenly. I remembered the flowered headband I had loved as a child. It had been festooned with daisies. The old story had seeped through time into my life.

I turned away and he spoke again, stopping me.

"You could have been mine. You should have been mine." Gwydion's face twisted. And then his face took on a serene cast as he gazed on me with something I couldn't define. I was strangely comforted. "I would have been so proud to be your father, Callie."

My vision blurred. I had waited my entire life to hear those words, but I didn't want them from him. My vision grew fuzzier. Then I realized that I was looking at an enormous wave, not passing out. At first I couldn't comprehend what I was seeing, but Lake Michigan had somehow surged up the Bellhaven river and was now heading straight toward us.

A wall of water came up over the edge of the bascule bridge. The wave roiled and rolled in on itself. Then two horses, one black and one white, surged forth from the water and fell on Gwydion.

The white horse clamped its teeth on Gwydion's neck and the black horse got a hold of his torse—then they pulled. The white horse lashed out with its front hooves, which were turned backward, and we heard Gwydion's spine break. With a dull rip, they jerked Gwydion apart.

Before his blood could really hit the pavement,

the bäckahästen and the kelpie had returned to the water, and the water retreated to the normal Lake Michigan shorelines.

They took what was left of Gwydion's body with them.

And I wept for my father's killer.

****

I was looking at the ground because it was too hard to list up my head. I watched my blood drip on the ground. Then someone was supporting me. Several someones.

"Come on, sweet pea, the Morrigan will take care of that," Grandpa said.

Erik and Duston carried me over to the Morrigan, who was standing next to Mom.

"Got your bell rung good, didn't you?" the Morrigan said. I assumed she was speaking rhetorically because my throat was burned and bleeding. "We will talk about your theophagy later."

The Morrigan put her hand on my torn shoulders, and I whimpered like a kicked dog. Then it was as if a cool breeze was enveloping me after a hot day. I tasted some mint and breathed in a grassy scent before I was able to stand up under my own strength.

I had scars, shiny newly healed scars. The inside of my arms where I had held on to a red-hot metal pillar were smooth, as if long-healed from a horrible burn. I knew my back would be marked by long claw marks. It was too much to hope that I would come out of this unscathed, but I wasn't bleeding out on the pavement anymore. That counted for something.

"Cailleach," Mom said gently. I looked up, tired beyond all imagining.

"What a lovely surprise," the Morrigan said, not sounding surprised at all. "My granddaughter is changing

279

things again. Here, this belongs to you." The Morrigan held up my triskele. I went to take it, but my fingers didn't work well since I was exhausted.

I squinted. There were only two ravens on the pendant now instead of three. The raven that usually flew at the top of the pattern was now an owl. The Morrigan fastened the necklace on me. It felt lighter now. I guess breaking a curse and opening a hell portal took something out of it.

"There's an owl on it now?" I said, not quite able to do questions. God, I needed a nap.

"Cailleach's symbol is the owl. She can turn into one," Mom explained.

"Oh, that's nice," I said numbly. "I don't plan on doing that anytime soon."

"Yes, we all agree that you deserve to rest. But in all seriousness, no more eating gods," the Morrigan said sternly.

"It was only a little bit and completely by accident," I protested.

"She's so much like you," Grandpa Doug said to the Morrigan. I looked around, hoping someone would confirm things.

"Callie, this is your grandmother," Grandpa explained. The glare my gran leveled at my grandpa should have turned him to stone, but he merely smirked at her roguishly.

I've seen pictures of Gran, but I've never met her. She was one of those things we never talked about. When I could focus again, Mom was chatting with Gran.

"She's dating a barbarian thug," I heard Gran say.

"Callie's smart, and Erik's a good kid. Something new is happening, Mom. This could work out."

"How do you know?"

"I'm not sure, but I have hope, faith."

"That's practical," the Morrigan scoffed.

"Mom," Bridget said warningly. I blinked. She sounded exactly like me. Actually, I realized, I sounded just like her.

Gran turned toward me and Mom looked, too. Two pairs of identical almond-shaped green eyes caught me. I was being summoned. This time, it wasn't a tourney. It was family.

I came up and found myself edging toward Mom, facing Gran, the Morrigan. Gran took my hands in hers and I was at ease.

"Hi, Gran," I said. I had never said that word before, but it came naturally, calling this woman Gran. In my mind's eye, in another girl's memory, this same woman rocked me to sleep after a nightmare. This was the woman who had taught me to see patterns before I wove them.

"Hi, Callie. I'm sorry I haven't been around," the Morrigan said.

"I thought it was because of Grandpa Doug," I said in a daze, and she chuckled.

"That's part of it. I am so sorry I haven't been here for you before this, but I want that to change, if you're willing," Gran said.

"Where?" I started, and then words failed me. I was worn out, and it was too much work to try to string words together into a coherent sentence.

"She's a circuit court judge in Rochester, New York," Mom said. "Let's get you into the car and you can rest. You've done a lot today, honey. I'm so proud of you."

Car. Rest. Please. I started moving when the burly king of the fire giants charged over. I didn't even brace myself or turn. Someone else could fight this battle.

"Now what?" Sutherland asked Norman bluntly.

He did a good job pretending I didn't exist.

"Now we live our lives as we choose, free from a curse," Norman said blandly. Sutherland grimaced.

"We are gods now, Njordr," Sutherland said. "The storm hag has cast our god-killer from this world." While I understood that Sutherland was using one of my titles, I still wrinkled my nose at being called a hag.

"Call me Norm, and we're only gods if we want to be. Do you want to go to war because it's what we've always done? I want to run my shop and live in peace," Norm said.

"And if you really want your god-killer back, we can discuss it later," I added, flexing my healed fingers. Sutherland looked at me with immense distaste. I was too exhausted to be afraid of the giant king. "We can probably bring Fenrir back if he's that necessary."

"Or maybe you could do it," Tyrone suggested.

"Do what?" I asked, and saw his sly smile. "Kill your god? Why would you even suggest that? No, I would never."

"You just killed Gwydion," Sutherland said grimly. He looked at me more warily. "She is outside our story. She could possibly kill us all."

"You're right. I am outside your story. And you don't get to tell me who to kill, I already told you I won't. We are all currently outside of our stories. I will choose my own fate, and you should do the same. Are you going to blame me for everything that goes wrong?" I asked.

"Old habits die hard." Tyrone shrugged.

"As my daughter has suggested, all gods will keep the peace with each other. No more fighting. No more killing," my mother said. Now I could see something else, the queen she had been. The jötnar king and the Vanir nodded in agreement.

"And who will enforce that peace?" the Morrigan

asked. We all jumped a little.

"We all will," I said, really quite done with all of this. Sutherland looked like he wanted to protest. "Tyr, write it up. The Æsir, the Vanir, and the jötnar will police yourselves, and all Tuatha present will police the Tuatha, just as we always have. I just opened a portal to Hel, and I will do it again if someone tries to kill."

"I agree with the mistress of the winter storms," Norm said.

"And I," Mom said firmly. Sutherland grumbled, but nodded gruffly. They trundled off to sort their family. I hoped they left the state soon.

"Is it over then?" I asked, looking at Mom. "Are we done? Please say we're done."

"We don't know. The story may go back to what it was before you changed it. Or someone in Erik's family may still try to kill him before Ragnarök. However, we are all still alive, and I am rather certain that the Vanners and the Janssens are going to refrain from murdering a teenager for now. This is farther than we've ever gotten before."

"Others will likely be waking soon," Norman said. He stared pensively out over the water.

"I, for one, am very glad that I'm still alive," Erik said. I smiled, even though it hurt my face, and leaned in. I've had a crap day. I'm allowed.

"For the record, I am also glad, little bro," Duston said. "Doesn't change the fact that we all have no idea what happens next."

"This could lead to a bad fight," Erik said. I felt his chest vibrate as he spoke and it comforted me. He was alive. He was with me and he was alive.

"Then I'll have to rescue you again. S'all good, I'm used to it by now."

"Don't taunt him. That's just tacky," I

admonished Duston, more out of habit than anything else. I had never been this exhausted in my life.

"Enough, all of you," Mom said. "Let's go home."

Norman put his hands on Erik's and my shoulder. His gaze was on my mother.

"A truce between our families, Brigid," Norman said. "We have never had a future before. We need to consider how to keep them safe."

"They've always been safer apart," Mom said. I jerked, but Erik held me steady.

"This isn't just your decision," the three that were six or perhaps just one said. "The truce will continue as it did before. She who was Branwen, and is now Cailleach, broke her curse. He who was Vindler has avenged his murder. They are entitled to this peace, their recompense."

Mom looked resistant but then nodded assent, followed by a round of ayes.

As Mom went to offer Grandma our spare room, I realized I was starving.

"Grandpa, are you eating pork rinds?" I asked in disbelief.

"Don't judge me," he said, crunching away. He always had snacks in his truck. "We just triumphed in glorious battle. I need sustenance."

"You know what the doctor said."

"Life is for living."

"Give me one." I dug into the bag. Mom and Grandma Morgan, the Morrigan, maybe just Morrigan, something, came up with mirrored exasperation at Grandpa.

"Okay, let's get the kids home. You, daughter, stay here while I get the car." Mom pointed.

"Not moving, Mom." I showed her my palms.

"The last time you said that, you ran away from home, picked a fight with frost giants, and broke an ancient curse," Mom said drily, then went to get the car.

I sat at the edge of the sidewalk. I snuggled in close to Erik for warmth and because, to be honest, I felt better when I was with him. Complete. Also, confused as all get-out, but one thing at a time. We watched the sky brighten over Lake Michigan.

"I have no idea what to do now," I told him honestly.

"Sorry we missed Halloween," Erik said.

"Just as well. I'm in college now," I said grandly. Erik snorted. I generously did not take offense, despite having recently saved everyone from a malevolent curse.

"I think we should celebrate. We changed lives," Erik said. "If it makes you feel any worse, there's a pretty decent chance your family will try to kill me next."

"Thanks for that, exactly what I wanted to hear. As I have demonstrated tonight, they'll have to go through me first," I said, staring at him intently. I wanted to get my first relationship right, which meant I had to keep my boyfriend alive.

Erik dropped his forehead against mine.

"I will love you until the end of the world, even if it's tonight," Erik said, then looked surprised. I don't think he meant to say that. They might have been his words, but more likely they were the sentiment of a boy long dead.

"That's not plan A, right?" I asked. Erik shook his head.

"Want to catch a movie tomorrow?" Erik asked. I burst out laughing. It sounded a little hysterical, but it was an honest-to-goodness laugh. That was most definitely Erik talking and not a Viking youth from thousands of years ago.

"What day is today?"

"It's Saturday morning, the day after Halloween."

"Pretty sure I'm grounded," I reminded him.

"Maybe your mom could give me a pass," Erik suggested. "I did save your life."

"With my help!" Duston interceded from somewhere not in sight.

"Movie sounds good. Something with an explosion and a car chase," I suggested and he laughed. I stared deep into his hazel eyes and felt safe, like I was home.

"You have the cinematic tastes of a ten-year-old boy," Erik whispered into my hair, tickling my ear. I turned my face to him and looked him straight in the eyes. With a smile on his lips, Erik kissed me.

Our first kiss in this lifetime happened as the sun rose on a beautiful, crisp Saturday morning, next to a sparkling Bellhaven river. Our first kiss sealed it for me. I love this boy, the one who cared for me, protected me, made me laugh, and understood me. I loved this boy, in this time and this place. This was my choice.

These lips touching mine were heaven's gift to mankind, and I was a very lucky recipient. *I have earned this. Wow.*

I heard Mom clear her throat and broke out of my trance. Mom and Norman were staring us down from the cars. Mom had her warning eyebrow raised and Norman looked amused. They had just witnessed me being asked out by the boy of my dreams. They could at least have the decency to pretend they weren't watching.

Erik laughed and put his arm around me as we went to the cars.

I am Calliope Redmond, born and raised in Bellhaven, and I have a family who loves me. I am the echo of a goddess long-gone. I just got accepted into a rehabilitative therapy college program. I have a date tomorrow with a guy who makes me feel warm when we kiss and likes my jokes. I will forge my own destiny.

First, though, I really needed ice cream. Possibly a nap.

The End

CONSTANCE KERSAINT

Evernight Teen ®

www.evernightteen.com

www.ingramcontent.com/pod-product-compliance
Lightning Source LLC
Chambersburg PA
CBHW050713180626
46814CB00002B/416